AUGUST SUNRISE

MERRY FARMER

AUGUST SUNRISE

Cover design by Erin Dameron-Hill (the miracle-worker)

ASIN: B0796X14PB

Paperback ISBN: 9781980674177

If you'd like to be the first to learn about when the next books in the series come out and more, please sign up for my newsletter here:
http://eepurl.com/RQ-KX

 Created with Vellum

CHAPTER 1

LONDON – MAY, 1879

*M*iss Marigold Bellowes turned heads wherever she went. It was a fact of life she'd lived with since emerging from the schoolroom into society. She was well aware that she possessed a figure men stared at and coloring that women envied. Her blonde hair had just a touch of copper to it, proving that her parents had named her well, and her green eyes were the sort that unnerved those she stared at for too long. But Marigold wasn't foolish enough to believe her looks were what enthralled people. That honor went to her father's money.

"Is Lord Kendrick staring again?" she whispered to her best friend, Lady Lavinia Prior, as the two crossed St. Stephen's Hall, heading toward the stairs that would take them to the Strangers' Gallery overlooking the House of Commons Chamber.

Lavinia—who was younger than Marigold by five years and quite pretty herself, with thick, chestnut hair and dark eyes—glanced over her shoulder, then sniggered. "He is, poor thing."

Marigold's answering sigh quickly turned to a giggle. "I've refused his proposal three times. You'd think the man would go and sniff up another tree."

Lavinia laughed out loud, then raised a hand to cover her mouth, her cheeks going pink. "I don't know whether it's cruel of you to say that or if you're doing the man a favor by snubbing him."

"I'm doing him a favor," Marigold answered as they joined the queue to the gallery stairs. "Clearly, Lord Kendrick is only interested in marrying a woman who can bolster the sagging fortunes of his estate, if rumors are to be believed."

Lavinia hummed sagely. "They are to be believed, according to Mama. That's why she hasn't tried to thrust me at him."

Marigold winced for her friend and rested a gloved hand on her arm before they started up the narrow stairs to the gallery. "Is she still trying to snag a titled husband for you?"

Lavinia let out an ironic laugh. "She's trying to match me with anyone prominent and influential enough to meet her exacting standards, no matter what I think of things. Lord Kendrick doesn't come close to meeting her mark. Not when his chances of bankruptcy are so high."

"And I suppose that's why he hasn't given up on me," Marigold sighed, feeling far guiltier than she should. But as more than a few men needed to understand, financial difficulty on their part did not necessitate feelings of love and a desire to wed on the part of whatever female they set their hearts, or rather, their billfolds, on.

They reached the top of the crowded stairs and stepped

out into the Strangers' Gallery, a stretch of tiered seats in the balconies above the House of Commons chamber floor. The gallery was open to any members of the public who cared to observe the proceedings of government, but women rarely attended. At least, they rarely attended when it was business as usual. But change was afoot. A group of men, both in the House of Commons and in the House of Lords, had been making noise about passing a bill that would increase the rights of women. It was a long way from granting them equal standing with men or the vote, as Marigold wanted, but anything that would secure a woman's right to her own property and her life was a step in the right direction.

The bill was due to be debated that day, so more than a few women had taken up seats at the very front of the gallery. Marigold tapped Lavinia's arm and pointed to a section of seats at the front, then made her way toward them.

"To be honest," she said, continuing their conversation, "I've reached the end of my tether when it comes to men hoping to win my hand, as though it's some sort of prize. The fact that my father has made a smashing success of his business should not preclude me from having a real marriage based on love."

They reached the front row amidst the hubbub of dozens of conversations, but Marigold had been loud enough to catch the attention of Lady Stanhope, who glanced up at her with shrewd, calculating eyes.

"Well, that's quite an introduction," Lady Stanhope said, her lips twitching into a smile. She scooted to one side, patting the bench beside her. "Do sit next to me."

"Lady Stanhope." Marigold greeted the woman with a fond grin.

Everyone who had spent any time observing Parliament or getting involved in political circles knew Katya Marlowe, the Countess of Stanhope. She was regarded by many as the most powerful widow in England. Her husband, the Earl of Stanhope, had died fifteen years before, leaving her with three children, a title, vast estates, and, reportedly, a huge sum of money. Her son, Rupert, the current earl, was not yet eighteen and was still at university, so Lady Stanhope continued to manage the Stanhope legacy. At a year shy of forty, she was a strikingly handsome woman, with sharp, bold features, dark hair, and piercing blue eyes. She was rumored to have had a string of lovers after her husband's death, and was considered to be friends with several prominent politicians.

"Still batting fortune hunters away with a stick?" she asked as Marigold settled onto the bench beside her.

Marigold laughed. "I can't fault them for trying. I just wish they would try somewhere else."

Lady Stanhope smiled. "Good for you for not giving in and marrying one just to make the others go away."

"Believe me, there have been times when I've been tempted," Marigold said with an ironic twist of her lips. "If I could find just one man who I thought I could be happy with, who would appreciate me for myself and not what I can do for him, then I'd fasten the leg-shackles tomorrow."

Lady Stanhope arched one severe eyebrow. "Why not seek out a man who can do something for you?"

Marigold paused in the process of settling her reticule and parasol by her side. "How would I do that?"

Lady Stanhope raised her shoulders slightly in a shrug and glanced out over the chamber. "Simple. Think about matrimony the way a man does. Consider what your aims and goals in life are and set your sights on a man who can fulfill those goals."

"That's rather mercenary, isn't it?" Lavinia asked, glancing around Marigold to study Lady Stanhope.

"Men do it all the time," Lady Stanhope said with a wave. "Robert only married me because my mother was a Romanov, and he wanted his children to have royal blood. Why shouldn't we marry for similar reasons?"

"Why is it that you never remarried, Lady Stanhope?" Lavinia asked.

Marigold felt a flush of embarrassment for her friend's impertinent question, but Lady Stanhope merely chuckled.

"There are a great many reasons I haven't remarried, my dear," she told Lavinia, then leaned closer to Marigold, as if sharing a secret. "I have too much power, too much influence, on my own. And besides." She inched closer still and lowered her voice to whisper to both women, "I am not the sort to be unfaithful, which would vastly limit my ability to sample the many delicacies that the men of the world have to offer."

"Oh, my!" Lavinia pressed a hand to her mouth and snapped straight, her face turning bright puce.

Marigold, on the other hand, laughed so loud that several sets of eyes—both male and female—turned to them. Only then did she cover her mouth, blushing with merriment as much as embarrassment. "I like the way you think, Lady Stanhope," she whispered.

Lady Stanhope sat a little straighter, beaming with pride and mischief. She tilted her head and studied Marigold. "So what are your goals, my dear? Who do you want to be?"

Marigold blinked rapidly under the assault of such an

important question. "I'm not sure. I don't think I've ever thought about it."

"Yes you have," Lady Stanhope countered immediately. "A woman like you, who has turned down half a dozen offers of marriage, who continues to receive those offers even as she approaches thirty, and who attends sessions of Parliament when the rights of women are being discussed, has most definitely considered what she wants from life."

Marigold's startled expression melted into a cunning grin. "I suppose you're right." She darted a glance around to gauge if anyone was eavesdropping. Since ministers were flooding into the gallery below and taking their seats, as if the session were about to start, their conversation went unnoticed. "I want to be the wife of a powerful man," she confided, mischief bubbling up inside of her.

"I thought so." Lady Stanhope nodded in approval.

"I want to have a say in the world," Marigold went on. "At the moment, the only way to do that is as the wife of a powerful man and the mother of his children, but I want to align myself with those who are fighting to give women power of their own."

"Would you enter politics yourself if you could?" Lady Stanhope pressed her.

Marigold hesitated. She glanced to the gallery as the Sargent at Arms called the room to order. The men crowding the benches on either side of the room seemed worn and full of cares to her. They were a stern, grey mass of seriousness.

"Perhaps it would be more enjoyable to be the power behind the throne," she said in a circumspect voice, tilting her head to one side.

"A wise observation," Lady Stanhope said.

A different swirl of emotion filled Marigold's heart.

"And I have always wanted to be a mother." She took a breath after her statement, caught by the seeming paradox that wanting to give birth and hold public power seemed to present.

"You can be a mother and a powerful woman," Lady Stanhope told her, in a hushed voice as the men below began to speak. "In fact, I'm certain my children would argue that I'm frightfully powerful, in spite of and because of them." There was a mischievous glint in her eyes as she glanced to Marigold.

"Does your son think so?" Lavinia whispered.

"More than my daughters," Lady Stanhope answered.

Marigold wanted to laugh again, but the gallery had settled in to watch proceedings below. She smiled to herself all the same, her heart beating with excitement and promise that had nothing to do with the drone of parliamentary business below. She'd always considered motherhood and ambition to be two separate beasts, and believed she could only feed one of them. But if Lady Stanhope could wield influence and raise children as well, then so could she.

However, Lady Stanhope was right about something else, though she had hinted at it more than stating it outright. If she wanted to be the woman she'd dreamed of being, she would have to choose a husband for what he could do for her, the same way men tried to pitch woo to her because of what her father's money could do for them.

In the true way of men, Marigold had to sit through a lot of unnecessary business and debate about topics that made about as much sense as corsets for puppies before the bill to advance the rights of women was brought up. As soon as the issue of extending the budget for rail lines in Surrey was finished and voted on, the MP from Bury St. Edmunds introduced the bill for women's rights. A flurry of activity ensued as both the men on the floor and the observers in the gallery prepared for the fight.

Marigold watched the Liberal side of the aisle with interest. The bill was supported by several Liberal MPs and fiercely opposed by the Conservatives, as was just about every other bill that extended the rights of women, the working class, or anyone not currently enfranchised. Lord Hartington, the Leader of the Opposition, stood in a huddle with a handful of other MPs, looking ready to stand up and debate. But he wasn't the one who broke away from the group to approach the box.

A shiver of something warm and exciting swirled in Marigold's gut. "Who is that?" she whispered to Lady Stanhope.

A fond smile spread across Lady Stanhope's lips. "That, my dear, is Mr. Alexander Croydon."

"Who is he when he's at home?" Marigold went on, her eyes trained on him. She couldn't account for the way her heart suddenly beat faster and harder, other than the man's obvious good looks. He was tall, with broad shoulders and a fit physique. His hair was graying at the temples, but he didn't seem particularly old, all things considered. His confident grin as he took the podium and cleared his throat made Marigold want to lean in to listen.

"My lord Speaker, members of the House, and especially my distinguished colleagues on the other side of the aisle," he began. "What would any of us be without the women in our lives?"

His question was met by various grunts and guffaws.

"We would be nowhere," he went on. "And nowhere is precisely where these brave and valiant women who form and shape us are in the eyes of the government of this kingdom. They are the very backbone of our society, and yet, in the eyes of the law, they are reduced to the status of servants or children. They are not even entitled to the property that they bring into a marriage. If they should choose to break free from a union that is abusive or degrading, they are left with nothing. We propose to change all of that. Therefore, we are introducing this bill to extend the rights and legal protection of women, their persons, and their property."

Both sides of the chamber erupted into shouts of encouragement or derision. Mr. Croydon allowed it to continue for a moment, as if building up for his next assault. He glanced straight up into the gallery as he waited, directly at Lady Stanhope. Out of the corner of her eye, Marigold watched Lady Stanhope raise an eyebrow and nod in approval. A thousand questions about what the relationship between the wily widow and Mr. Croydon could be popped to Marigold's mind.

Then Mr. Croydon's gaze shifted to her.

Their eyes met. Marigold's breath caught in her throat. Mr. Croydon's eyes were almond-shaped and blue. They burned with cleverness and confidence...and something new. The clamor in the room faded to the background, and for a moment, all she saw was his handsome, self-assured expression, his poised smile. She smiled back before she could stop herself, pressing a hand to her heart.

A moment later, he turned back to the men around him and continued. "The bill we propose encompasses the three major legally sanctioned offenses against women: property rights, legal recourse in cases of divorce, and the right to maintain custody of children in case of abandonment or neglect."

Marigold's breath came rushing out. Whatever connection she and Mr. Croydon had had in that split-second of wonder, it was gone. The electric energy that had coursed through her ebbed as he dove into a long, complicated speech spelling out the laws and changes that needed to come. As desperately as Marigold wanted to hang on his every word, she was buzzing with the need to know so much more than he was saying. How had she never noticed the man before? Why hadn't he attended any number of social events that made up the season? Had he been in attendance and she just hadn't noticed him? That seemed impossible.

Beside her, Lady Stanhope made a curious, humming noise. It was intriguing enough to drag Marigold's eyes away from Mr. Croydon. She blinked when she found Lady Stanhope watching her instead of the proceedings on the floor.

"They say that he could succeed Lord Hartington as leader of the Liberal Party," she said, the mischief in her eyes making her angular face appear downright wicked.

"Oh?" Marigold asked, the single syllable coming out high and breathy.

"They also say that, in the event of an election, which is quite likely next year, he could be tapped for Prime Minister."

"Prime Minister." Marigold nodded, heat rising up her neck to her cheeks.

Lady Stanhope's impish grin widened. "He's unmarried, you know."

Unaccountable joy burst in Marigold's chest. She wasn't so naïve that she couldn't see what Lady Stanhope was getting at. Set your goals and pursue them with focus. Seek out a man to marry who could assist you in achieving those goals. Her gaze snapped back to Mr. Croydon. He stood tall and proud, speaking into a sea of grunts and objections from the other side without so much as a flutter.

Marigold had the impression that the man could withstand a storm and come out singing.

"He's a friend," Lady Stanhope nodded, her eyes flashing with cunning. "And not one of my *special friends* either." She paused to let that sink in, then added with feigned casualness. "I could introduce you once the debate is done."

Tingles broke out along Marigold's skin, and in some peculiar places that she only ever thought about when she was alone. "I think I'd enjoy that," she said, pretending as much nonchalance as Lady Stanhope was.

"Really," Lavinia laughed quietly by her side, shaking her head. "You're as bad as mother."

"And why shouldn't I have Lady Stanhope introduce me to Mr. Croydon?" Marigold asked, as giddy as if she and Lavinia were in a schoolroom, mooning over the boys. "We should go after what we want."

"If you say so." Lavinia continued to giggle.

The remainder of the session passed as if being carried along by a snail moving through treacle. Marigold couldn't pay attention to anything else that was said once the vote to table the bill for further discussion came up. After that, it was a war of attrition to keep still until the session was ended and both the ministers and observers rose to leave.

It was all Marigold could do not to sprint for the stairs, using her parasol to bat aside anyone who got in her way.

"Steady on, dear," Lady Stanhope whispered in her ear as they shuffled slowly into the queue departing the gallery. "You're an intelligent, well-placed heiress, not a bitch in heat."

Lavinia gasped, bursting into nervous giggles. "Lady Stanhope, you say the most shocking things."

"Of course I do, dear," she said with a smile. "One

doesn't suffer widowhood without being able to say shocking things."

At last, as Marigold's heart pounded against her ribs, they made it to the stairs and down to St. Stephen's Hall. The tall, echoing space was packed with men rushing about their business or standing in clusters to discuss the day's business. Lady Stanhope took the lead as they started across the floor, gesturing for Marigold and Lavinia to follow her.

Marigold searched ahead for any sign of Mr. Croydon, and when she spotted him speaking to two other men at the far end of the hall, under a painting of King John agreeing to sign the Magna Carta, she went dizzy with expectation.

"Alex, there you are," Lady Stanhope greeted him in the most casual way possible as they approached. "I've someone I'd like you to meet."

The two men with Mr. Croydon said a final word and nodded before stepping away and going about their business. That left Mr. Croydon alone, like a lead actor on the stage, with no one to share the spotlight. He was even more handsome up close than he had been from the gallery. His eyes were blue, with enticing lines around them that indicated good humor. But there was also a feeling of gravitas about him, and, if Marigold wasn't mistaken, a hint of wariness. Clearly, he was a man of experience, and not all of it good.

"Lady Stanhope." He greeted Lady Stanhope as informally as she had him, taking her hand and drawing her close, then kissing her cheek when she raised it to him. Marigold was both shocked and fascinated by the intimate greeting, and more than a little envious. "How good it was to see you in the gallery today. And your charming friends." He glanced to Marigold.

Their eyes met, and once again, Marigold had that fluttering feeling that the two of them were the only people in the world. It was a ridiculous, sentimental notion, one she would have laughed at if other ladies had described it to her, but she couldn't deny how good it felt.

"Alex, I'd like to introduce you to Miss Marigold Bellowes," Lady Stanhope said.

Mr. Croydon blinked, his brow lifting, and turned to Lady Stanhope. "Percy Bellowes's daughter?"

A painful twist of disappointment hit Marigold's heart. He knew who her father was. Which meant he knew her worth. Which made her feel suddenly worthless.

"The very same," Lady Stanhope went on, still smiling. "But who gives a fig about her father? Miss Bellowes here was particularly interested in your debate. She has a brilliant mind and inquisitiveness to boot."

"Does she?" Mr. Croydon glanced to Marigold again, and for once, for once in her entire life, Marigold knew a man was looking at her not for the contents of her father's bank account, but for her own merits.

"How do you do, Mr. Croydon?" She offered her hand, doing her best to imitate Lady Stanhope's cool, superior demeanor as she did.

"I'm quite well," he answered, taking her hand and bowing over it.

A zip of electricity shot up Marigold's arm. It was so delicious that remaining calm and letting go of his hand to turn to Lavinia took every ounce of her effort. "May I introduce my dearest friend, Lady Lavinia Prior?"

"Lady Lavinia." Mr. Croydon repeated the motions of taking Lavinia's hand and bowing over it. "I hope you enjoyed today's debate."

"It was fascinating," Lavinia said, her smile broad and as

teasing as Lavinia was capable of. "But Marigold is the one who knows more about these things."

Mr. Croydon glanced back to her. It was so ridiculously obvious that both Lady Stanhope and Lavinia were pushing her in front of him that they might as well have carried signs. Strangely, though, Marigold couldn't bring herself to mind.

"I was particularly impressed with—"

"Croydon!"

An angry, male voice cut Marigold off, and all four of them turned to see a glowering man in a disheveled suit with enormous muttonchops framing his face marching toward them. Lady Stanhope made a noise somewhere between frustration and disgust, and Mr. Croydon's expressions snapped closed, his eyes narrowing.

Marigold held her breath, the feeling that she'd walked into the middle of a drama shivering down her spine.

CHAPTER 2

"*T*urpin." Alex clenched his jaw, irritated beyond measure at the man barging into what was turning out to be the most pleasant introduction he'd had in a long time. He pulled himself to his full height and glared down at his rival. "What can I do for you?"

Stocky, red-faced, and irritable, Daniel Turpin marched up to him, giving the ladies only a cursory frown before ignoring them. "You're a damn fool, Croydon," he growled.

Lady Lavinia squeaked, her eyes going round with shock. Lady Stanhope had the opposite reaction. She smirked and rested one hand on her hip, staring at Turpin. Miss Bellowes merely arched an eyebrow, glancing to him in question.

Alex glowered at his rival, highly aware of Miss Bellowes's scrutiny. "I beg your pardon, sir. There are ladies present."

"Bugger all ladies," Turpin snorted. Lady Lavinia looked as though she might faint, but Turpin pressed on. "They shouldn't be here in the first place. Politics is a man's game. Women should keep to their place in the home. Which is exactly why you're a damn fool."

If they had been at a club, or even in the street, Alex would have throttled Turpin for his appalling manners. As it was, he had to restrain his impulse to punch the man's bulbous nose. "We no longer live in the Dark Ages," he said, narrowing his eyes in distaste. "Our entire culture has made great strides, both in technology and society. Women attend university now, hold professional positions."

"They shouldn't," Turpin interjected.

"Our own queen is a woman."

"She is not a woman, she is a monarch. And as for the rest of them, the whole lot are good for just one thing. Two if they know how to cook."

Lady Stanhope made a disgusted noise and shook her head. Turpin turned on her.

"You, madam, are the worst of the lot," Turpin sneered.

"Why, thank you, Mr. Turpin," Lady Stanhope smiled. "I don't believe I've ever received such a glowing compliment."

Miss Bellowes made a strangled sound and pressed her hand to her mouth, but her eyes sparkled with mirth. The sight sent a jolt of need through Alex that was as inconvenient as it was surprising.

But Turpin wasn't done yet.

"If you and your cronies have your way, all hell will break loose, and the natural order of things will be upended," he went on. "Your proposals are a disgrace to mankind and a complete abdication of your God-given duty to master the fairer sex. You will be stopped."

Alex clenched his jaw as rage welled up in him. He knew too well what men like Turpin meant by man's duty to master women. He'd watched his father "master" his mother with a balled fist on too many occasions. And he'd rescued Violetta from a sadistic manager who ruled her life with the same iron force. It cut him to the core to know that both women had met miserable and untimely ends, and that Violetta's death had been his fault.

The sudden, painful memory set him off-balance, and he felt his edge in the argument slipping away. "More and more men believe as I do every day, Turpin. I may be the representative for this bill, but I am not its only champion. The rights of women will advance, whether your backward-thinking lot want them to or not."

Turpin laughed, his lip curled in a sneer. "You think so? Do you forget that you and your friends are not in power?"

"Perhaps not at this time, but we all know that this government is coming to an end. Change is in the air."

"Even if there is an election," Turpin went on, his eyes narrowing, "the Conservatives still hold the majority. And we will continue to do so."

"But for how long?" Alex swayed toward him, growing hot with anger. "Disraeli can barely clap together a vote about the most basic things. The balance is shifting, and as it does, women and the working class will rise. Mark my words."

"I mark nothing," Turpin spat. "If it's the last thing I do, I will move heaven and earth to ensure that your foolish and destructive bill never receives a vote, let alone a favorable one. Women are weak and must be kept in the home, subject to their husbands."

"And what if we don't have husbands, Mr. Turpin?" Lady Stanhope asked. Alex had nearly forgotten the ladies were there, and was pleased to see Lady Stanhope with her arms crossed, one eyebrow raised. Better still, Miss Bellowes had adopted a similar posture, gazing at Turpin with such disdain that Alex was surprised the man didn't incinerate on the spot.

Turpin turned to Lady Stanhope and barked, "You should rot in hell," then turned sharply and stormed off.

A gaping silence followed in his wake. Alex was sure he should have apologized, but he didn't want Turpin's foul behavior to be forgiven. Instead, he said, "That man is a thorn in the side of progress and modernity."

Lady Stanhope hummed in bitter agreement. "Pity there are so many others just like him."

"Not for long," Miss Bellowes said. Alex glanced to her with a surprised lift of his brow. She met his eyes with a clever glint in hers. "It is as you said, Mr. Croydon. Times are changing. We live in an exceptionally modern world. Women are capable of so many things nowadays, and the laws of the land and society must evolve to catch up with them."

Alex didn't know which to admire more, Miss Bellowes's words or the manner in which she delivered them. She was clearly intelligent and well-spoken, and he would have to be blind not to see that she was a first-rate beauty as well. Her hair was the color of the first kiss of a summer sunset, and her complexion was as clear and soft as rose-petals. And he wasn't usually inclined toward such frivolous descriptions of feminine beauty. Violetta had been a beauty, before age and illness dulled her spark, but Miss Bellowes was a natural. That, combined with her father's business empire, made him wonder how on earth she remained unmarried.

"I'm terribly sorry that our introduction went awry," he said, shifting to face her fully and returning to the important business at hand. "I was about to say that any friend of Lady Stanhope is a friend of mine." He made certain to nod to the startled and pale Lady Lavinia so that it wasn't blatantly obvious where his interests lay. Although it was likely obvious anyhow.

"And I was about to compliment you on your speech," Miss Bellowes said with a growing smile that did wonderful things for her eyes. "But now I feel as though I should complement you for the way you handled that dreadful man."

Alex frowned, blowing out an impatient breath. "Turpin is our chief opposition in Commons," he said, clasping his hands behind his back and glaring down the hall to where the man had joined some of his more odious cronies. "We've been dealing with the complications and blocks he's thrown in our way where the advancement of women's rights is concerned for years."

"I'm impressed that you've been seeking our advancement that long," Miss Bellowes said.

He turned back to her. "But of course. There have been men who are dedicated to supporting the rights of all people for ages."

"Really?" Lady Lavinia blinked. "I've never heard of any."

Alex sent her a kind smile. "Our voices are often not heard over the clamor of what some see as more pressing issues."

"You can say that again," Lady Stanhope drawled.

"On behalf of womankind, Mr. Croydon, I thank you," Miss Bellowes said, her smile as fetching as it was mischievous.

Alex was caught up in the charm of it and made an overelaborate, good-humored bow. "You are quite welcome, Miss Bellowes. My sincerest hope is that we can continue to fight for the cause until backward-thinkers like Mr.

Turpin are eliminated." A pinch of frustration hit him as he spoke. "I only wish it were easier to root men like him out."

"Is there no way to sway his like to your side?" Miss Bellowes asked.

Alex winced. "I'm afraid it would be easier to carve a tunnel through Mt. Aetna with a hairpin. Men like Turpin are so deeply set in their ways." He glanced down the hall again, disheartened at how many men he could pick out who were opposed to everything he and his friends were working for. Turpin was the worst of them, but not the only one. "If there was only some way to remove Turpin from the picture," he sighed, thinking aloud. "He's the lynchpin in Commons."

"Just as Shayles in in Lords," Lady Stanhope added.

Alex glanced back to her with a grim look. "Indeed. Each of them is as bad as the other."

"I won't argue with you there."

"Is there a way to take men like that out of the parliamentary picture?" Miss Bellowes asked.

Alex shrugged slightly, wishing he had a better answer for her. "The only certain way would be if men like Turpin were defeated in a general election."

"But you said an election is just around the corner," Miss Bellowes said.

Alex nodded. "It's very likely. But even so, men like Turpin have their seats virtually guaranteed, due to, well, not precisely rotten boroughs, like the old days, but close enough."

"So it would take something extraordinary to prevent people from voting for him, should there be an election."

"Precisely."

"Well, then," Lady Stanhope said, cunning and calculation in her eyes. "It looks as though I have my work cut out for me."

"You, Lady Stanhope?" Lady Lavinia asked, blinking at Lady Stanhope in awe.

Lady Stanhope's grin grew to diabolical proportions. "I have my ways," she said. "I'll see what I can do."

Alex met her steely gaze with a smile of his own. He was damned lucky to count Katya Marlowe as a friend. Not for the first time, he felt as though he needed to send Lord Malcolm Campbell a bottle of the finest scotch as thanks for introducing them all those years ago. How Malcolm could have let the woman go was beyond his comprehension.

The conversation hit a slight lull, but before any of them could find a way to continue it the rumble of male conversation was split by a piercing cry of, "Lavinia?"

Alex turned to find a matronly woman storming up the length of the hall, a wide-brimmed hat decorated with too many feathers on her head. Lady Lavinia blushed scarlet and buried her face in her hands.

"Lavinia, there you are." The woman marched right up to them, stopping with the precision of a general as she reached their group. She sent Lady Stanhope a sharp glare, then tilted her chin up and turned away from her. Alex glanced anxiously around to find several of his peers looking on with amused expressions, but the matron seemed oblivious. "Young lady, I told you that I would only allow you to attend this ridiculous event if you promised to return home immediately after it was finished."

"But mother, it only just finished a few moments ago," Lady Lavinia sighed, her shoulders wilting.

"Moments ago is not immediately," her mother informed her. "I never should have let you come in the first place. Men do not care for women who are too politically informed," she glanced sideways at Lady Stanhope, "and there are certainly no eligible bachelors in the Palace of Westminster."

Miss Bellowes cleared her throat, although Alex suspected the sound was intended to hide a laugh. "Lady Prior," she said. "May I introduce you to Mr. Alexander Croydon, who has just given a powerful speech to Commons about the rights of women?"

Lady Prior tilted up her nose and raked Alex with a glance. He felt in an instant that he came up wanting, but could only muster amusement for the woman's censure.

"A pleasure, sir," she said, entirely unconvincingly, then turned back to her daughter. "Come along now. Your painting lesson is in half an hour."

Lady Lavinia sighed. "Mama, you know I'm hopeless at painting."

"Refined young women should know how to paint," Lady Prior snapped back.

"Fifty years ago, perhaps," Lady Lavinia mumbled. She straightened her gloves and turned to go, glancing to Miss Bellowes for help.

"I should go as well," Miss Bellowes said dutifully. "But it was an absolute pleasure to meet you, Mr. Croydon." The warmth in her eyes echoed her words.

"Likewise, Miss Bellowes." Alex bowed to her, wanting desperately to take her hand and kiss it, which was as silly as it was appealing. "I do hope we meet again soon."

"As do I."

Miss Bellowes smiled, then turned as though being dragged reluctantly and started after her friend, who had been shuffled off double-time by her mother. Alex watched her go, laughing at himself for the burst of warmth that filled his gut...and lower.

"Thank you," he said, turning to Lady Stanhope. "I owe you for that. Now, if you'll excuse me, I've got an engagement to keep. I hope we'll see you at Armand's house later." He nodded and turned to go.

"Not so fast." Lady Stanhope caught his arm, tugging him back to face her. "You and I have a few things to discuss before you scurry off to whatever it is you men do when left to your own devices."

"Do we?" Alex grinned. He liked spending time with Katya, for whatever reason. They all did. She was undeniably good fun.

"It's time, Alex," she said, her expression filling with seriousness.

Alex felt the same quiver of nerves he had felt as a child when his nanny caught him misbehaving. Katya had that effect on men. Which was probably why so many of them were clamoring to get into her bed. "Time for what?"

Her mouth twitched to the side and she planted her hands on her slender hips. "I just introduced you to the woman you're going to marry."

An electric chill shot down Alex's spine, bristling out to his skin as if he'd been struck by lightning. "I beg your pardon?"

"You heard me." Katya's grin turned triumphant. "The two of you were born for each other."

Heat flooded Alex's face. "Forgive me if I don't share your romantic notion of people being born for each other."

"You can believe it or not, but it's true," she went on. "Marigold Bellowes is bright, quick, and rich. She's turned down scores of marriage proposals, proving that she has enough of a backbone not to let herself be backed into a situation that goes against her best interests."

"Then why would she entertain any sort of proposal from me?"

Katya chuckled, shaking her head. "You share goals. She wants to be a woman of power and influence, which any woman who marries you is destined to be, and you need a fiery beauty to keep you on your toes."

Alex crossed his arms, studying Katya in an attempt to determine how best to disappoint her ambitions. "My toes are just fine," he said.

"I don't think they are," she fired back.

"I've gone almost fifty years without a wife—"

"And the time has come to correct that."

He pressed his lips together and breathed out through his nose. "Miss Bellowes is too young to be wasted on a man of my age."

"She's mature beyond her years, and you need a woman still in her child-bearing years." Katya arched a brow, daring him to come up with another argument.

The trouble was, she'd skated too close to the heart of why he'd shelved the idea of marrying at all.

"I have James to consider," he said, lowering his eyes as guilt and regret wrapped around his heart. "Violetta has only been gone for—"

"Almost three years," Katya finished for him, a note of compassion in her voice. She stepped closer, resting a hand on his cheek. "I know you loved her, Alex, though heaven only knows why. She was never your equal."

Alex's eyes flashed to hers with a sting of anger. "Violetta was a sweet, beautiful woman. She didn't deserve...." He swallowed suddenly, jerking away from Katya's hand, sick with the memory of their last, wasted years together. "She deserves more than your pity."

"She does," Katya agreed solemnly. "I'm sorry if it

sounded as though I was disparaging her. But she went straight from the stage to your bed. Miss Bellowes has had the finest education money can buy for a woman. She would complement your ambitions perfectly. And don't pretend you didn't find her attractive."

Alex sighed, scrubbing a hand over his face. "There's no point denying that I found Miss Bellowes to be charming and engaging."

"Engaging being the operative word in this situation," Katya said with a grin.

"Why would she want me?" he asked, far more serious than he wanted to be. "I'm not some dashing young buck with a heart just waiting to be filled."

"No." Katya folded her arms in front of her, studying him with her sharp eyes. "You're a lonely man with a heart crushed by guilt who needs to shake off the dust of the past to embrace the possibility of happiness before it's too late."

Alex huffed a laugh in spite of himself. "Now there's a frightening assessment."

"Frightening, but true." Katya shifted her weight and studied him more deeply, which was as terrifying as everything she said. "You're ready, Alex. It's time."

He wasn't brave enough or dense enough to ask what she thought he was ready for. Katya wasn't the only one of his friends to pester him about marrying lately. "I have work to do here," he argued.

"And Marigold could help you with that."

"Is she planning to stand for office?" he asked with a wry twist to his mouth.

"She doesn't need to. Every powerful man needs a woman standing behind him, cheering him on."

"And you think Miss Bellowes is that woman for me."

He crossed his arms, but behind his cool façade, his resistance was crumbling.

"I know she is."

"Well, if you know it, it must be true." Sarcasm was heavy in his tone, but they both knew his statement was genuine.

"It's time, Alex," she repeated. "You've been ready to move on for months now. I hereby give you permission."

He considered arguing that he didn't need anyone's permission, but something soft whispered through him, easing the tension he'd held close for three years now. That something felt distinctly like relief.

"I'll arrange for the two of you to casually bump into each other at a few social events in the next week," Katya went on, her eyes bright with cheer. "It shouldn't be too difficult to arrange. I can think of half a dozen hostesses planning events within the next few weeks who would be overjoyed to have both of you attend."

"By Jove, Katya, you have a wider, stickier web than even Malcolm has."

At the mention of Malcolm Campbell's name, heat and challenge flashed in Katya's eyes. "Malcolm doesn't know half of what I do, or with whom I do it."

Alex bit his tongue over the comments he wanted to make. Perhaps it was a good thing that whatever had been between Malcolm and Katya had fallen apart years ago. The two of them would likely burn London to the ground if they were ever under the same roof for too long.

"Very well," he sighed, knowing not a thing could change Katya's mind once she grabbed hold of an idea. "I'll extend my social acquaintance with Miss Bellowes, but I can't promise marriage."

"That's what you think," she murmured, reaching up to

pat his cheek. "I predict it will be a month before you see that I'm right and take steps to prove it."

"A month?" Alex arched one brow. "You think I'll propose to the woman in a month?"

"I don't think it, I know it."

CHAPTER 3

*A*s it turned out, Katya was wrong. Three weeks was all it took.

Alex had never been one to gad about London, attending every social event imaginable, when Parliament was in session. But the day after his conversation in St. Stephen's Hall, no fewer than six invitations arrived on his doorstep. He attended a private concert which featured a renowned soprano at the home of Lady Millicent St. George, and Miss Bellowes happened to be there as well. She was also at the lecture hosted by the Philosophical Society of London. It was no surprise to find her at both the ball hosted by the Duchess of Devon and Mrs. Conrad Firestone, and after the fortnight he'd experienced, he couldn't bring himself to be shocked that she was seated next to him at supper at Lord Farnsworth's house.

So by the time he discovered Miss Bellowes and Lady Lavinia seated in the box immediately next to his at the theater three weeks after Katya made her matrimonial prediction, Alex was ready to give in.

"Mr. Croydon, we simply must stop meeting like this,"

Miss Bellowes laughed as she took her seat on the other side of the boxes' partition from him.

She wore an emerald green dress cut in the latest style that showed off the creamy flesh of her shoulders. The fact that Alex could imagine himself stroking, and even kissing, that flesh only furthered his suspicion that Katya was right in every way.

"Come now, Miss Bellowes," he answered her, not bothering to hide the fondness, or the mischief, in his gaze. "I think we both know that the two of us are being thrust together deliberately by a mutual friend."

Miss Bellowes blushed a tantalizing shade of pink, her expressive eyes bright with interest. She must have been an innocent where relations between men and women were concerned, otherwise he would have heard gossip about her from the indiscreet members of his club. But the way she tilted her head just so and wet her lips ever so subtly hinted that she was a peach ripe for the picking. His trousers were suddenly too tight, but the pressure was tantalizing instead of embarrassing. Which was probably helped by the house lights dimming.

"I've been looking forward to this for weeks," Miss Bellowes confided in him as the orchestra struck the opening chords of the overture.

"Are you a fan of Gilbert and Sullivan, then?" Alex asked.

"Absolutely," she answered, turning to him with a smile. "H.M.S. Pinafore has been sold out for weeks. I was shocked when these seats became available for us at the last minute."

"Were you really?" he asked, his mouth twitching into a knowing grin.

She laughed. "No, not really."

There wasn't time for more conversation. The overture

reached a jaunty pitch, and the curtains were raised on a chorus of sailors singing about sailing the ocean blue. Alex couldn't have cared less about them, though. In the glowing darkness, Miss Bellowes's features were outlined with what seemed like threads of gold. She leaned forward enough to show that she was genuinely interested in the show, as opposed to merely in attendance to see and be seen. Her lips were open in a soft smile of enjoyment.

Alex wondered what it would be like to kiss her. Surely, she would fit perfectly in his arms. Her mouth was such a pleasant shape, and her lips full and plump. He leaned back in his chair, imagining how they would feel pressed to his skin. And vice versa. He was certain she would taste sweet and sigh wantonly as he introduced her to the beauties of passion.

Only when the first female chorus burst onto the stage in a flurry of color and ridiculousness did Alex blink himself out of his increasingly heated fantasies to realize what was going on. He hadn't indulged in imaginings about a woman for years. There'd been no need to fantasize with Violetta. She'd left nothing to his imagination, and had given him whatever he wanted in bed. He'd remained steadfastly faithful to her, even when the fire of their romance had dulled to a sense of responsibility. He'd been tempted into a handful of intimate situations in the nearly three years since Violetta's death, but none had blossomed into anything more than a temporary release from natural urges.

Watching Miss Bellowes as she laughed and sighed her way through the first act of the play, however, awoke something in him that he'd thought was long gone. He wanted to do more than relieve his tension with her. He wanted to test the extent of her cleverness with conversation. He wanted to learn her deepest desires and wheedle out her darkest secrets. She was simply too intriguing to pass by.

Damn Katya for being one step ahead of him.

When the lights rose for intermission, Alex had made his decision. He stood, turning to Miss Bellowes.

"Would you care for a breath of fresh air?" he asked, hoping that his expression conveyed his true question, whether she'd consent to a private word with him.

She rose slowly, almost as if inviting him to contemplate her shapely and appealing form. "That sounds delightful," she said, snapping open her fan and fanning herself. The slight sheen of perspiration on her face and shoulders from the heat of the gaslights brought to mind other ways Alex could make her sweat.

"We'll rendezvous in the hall." He paused, glancing to Lady Lavinia. "If your friend doesn't mind."

"Oh, not at all," Lady Lavinia said, her smile a little too excited.

Alex nodded to the ladies, then made his way through the other patrons sharing his box to the hallway. The hall was crowded with those who could afford box seats chatting and cooling themselves between acts. Alex pushed through them so that he was waiting by the door when Miss Bellowes emerged. He immediately offered his arm.

"I believe there are several locations just off the lobby or in upper hallways where we might catch the breeze from outside," he said, leaning closer to her.

She slid her arm into his. "I think you're right. Lady Stanhope was just telling me yesterday how marvelously modern this new theater is."

"Was she?" Alex grinned, once again feeling as though he owed Katya a gift of gratitude. Perhaps a castle.

"Although it isn't half as impressive as the theater Mr.

D'Oyly Carte has promised to build for his company soon," Miss Bellowes went on. "They say that theater will be entirely lit by electricity. Can you imagine?"

"We live in exciting times, without a doubt." A fact which inspired an idea Alex couldn't pass up. He glanced farther down the hall, past the grand staircase dozens of patrons were descending. "Have you ever ridden an elevator, Miss Bellowes?"

Her face lit up. "Only once before. Does this theater have one?" She glanced around expectantly.

"It most certainly does." Alex nodded to the far end of the curving hall, to a lonely grate that stood in front of a narrow door. He picked up his pace, leading Miss Bellowes straight to it.

"There doesn't seem to be an attendant," Miss Bellowes said as Alex pulled open the door and gestured for her to step inside. "Should we leave it for another day?"

"Certainly not," he replied, mischief and other, far more intriguing emotions thrumming through his veins. "As it happens, I know how to operate an elevator."

"Do you?" She stepped into the tiny elevator car, then turned to face him as he entered. "You're a man of many talents, Mr. Croydon. Rising parliamentary star and elevator operator."

He chuckled, shutting the grate and the door behind him, then pivoted toward the hydraulic controls. "And a few other skills besides those."

"I wonder what they could be."

He left her implied question unanswered as he flipped the elevator switch to up and pulled the lever to send it into motion.

Marigold gasped and pressed a hand to her stomach as the elevator swooped up. "Are we not going to the ground floor to get a bit of fresh air?" she asked, sounding more breathless than she wanted to.

She wanted to seem as cool and casual as Lady Stanhope was, but in truth, her stomach was a jumble of butterflies and her heart thundered against her ribs. It was arguably scandalous for her to allow Mr. Croydon to sweep her off on her own. Sensible young women did not step into elevators with older, single men. But she was well past the age of being a fainting debutante, and being found out in an intimate situation with Mr. Croydon might actually help her ambitions rather than thwarting them.

And yet, the elevator was so close, he was such an imposing presence, and the wickedness in his eyes as he brought the elevator to an abrupt halt between floors, where only the faintest reflection of light reached them, and where the scent of machinery and his cologne filled her nose, had her trembling ever so slightly.

Anything could happen in an elevator. She could be ravished at any moment. The thought left her skin tingling with expectation and inner parts of her throbbing.

"I think you and I need to have a bit of a talk, Miss Bellowes," he began in a low, almost wolfish voice, swaying closer to her.

This was it. He was going to tear open her bodice, lift up her skirts, and do all of the unspeakable things that she wished beyond wishing that people actually would speak about so that she *would* know. Her breath came in shallow gasps as she anticipated the feel of his hands on her.

"What would you like to talk about, Mr. Croydon?" she asked, attempting to channel every bit of Lady Stanhope's mannerisms.

To her surprise, instead of capturing her in his arms and ravishing her with his lips, he crossed his arms and leaned against the side of the elevator, studying her with a smile as beautiful as it was devilish.

"My friends have been pushing me to marry," he said.

Marigold blinked, her stomach feeling as though the elevator had burst into motion again. "They have?"

"Yes. Evidently, I've long since exceeded the proper amount of mourning for...."

His words faded and he lowered his eyes with a sudden switch in mood.

Marigold's heart began to twist and pulse along with the lower parts of her. "I didn't know you had a...love," she said softly, not knowing how else she could both express sympathy and coax information out of him.

He raised his eyes to her, his smile wry, but also sad. "I should pretend I've been a saint," he said. "But I suspect you're far too clever to believe that."

"Well," she shrugged, wringing her closed fan in her hands. "You're a man of a certain age. It would be unlikely for you to have remained unattached for so long, even if you weren't married."

"She was unsuitable, you see," he said, faster, his words clipped, as though he had to tell her instead of wanting to tell her. "She was an actress, so of course marriage was out of the question. But all that is in the past. My friends are growing impatient, and here we are."

Marigold opened her mouth to ask more, what had happened to his actress, what her name had been, whether he'd loved her. But before she could make more than a squeak, he swayed closer to her.

"I've finally come to the conclusion that my friends are

right." He stared intently into her eyes, undisguised desire shining from him.

All thoughts of his past lover flew from Marigold's mind. Her heart kicked inside of her, and her throat went dry. "Mr. Croydon, are you proposing to me?" she managed to ask.

"I believe I am."

"Well." She laughed breathlessly, pressing a hand to the low neckline of her dress. "I never would have dreamed I'd receive such an intriguing proposal in such a curious place." She glanced around at the cramped quarters of the elevator, feeling as though the walls were closing in even more, urging her toward him.

"As I understand it, Miss Bellowes, you have been proposed to in every conventional sort of place already." He shrugged, seemingly casual, though his smile grew by the second. "I figured you would appreciate a...different sort of setting."

"For a different sort of proposal?"

"If you like."

As simple as his words were, they sent a shiver down her spine, straight to the part of her she should most definitely be ignoring, but absolutely couldn't. She wasn't about to let herself be so quickly overpowered by a man, though. Even if her bones were turning to jelly and the urge to do outstandingly naughty things pulsed through her. Instead, she crossed her arms in a mirror image of him.

"What benefit is there for me in this proposed marriage?" she asked, holding her head high.

Mr. Croydon's smile grew so wide that she was certain he would burst into laughter...or kiss her. "Are the benefits not obvious?"

In an instant, Marigold felt the power shift in her favor.

She narrowed her eyes and faced him boldly. "Come now, Mr. Croydon. For a man who argues so eloquently for the rights of women, that was a boorish question."

He did laugh then. "You are quite correct, and I beg your pardon." He nodded to her. "I should have remembered that I am not speaking to some flighty girl in her first season. I am speaking to a woman of intelligence and strength who knows her own mind."

He could have whispered love poetry into her ear while nibbling on her neck and she wouldn't have felt the same rush of desire. Every warning she'd ever been given about the dangers of seduction came rushing back to her at once, instantly to be cast aside. Being seduced was brilliant fun.

"My father didn't earn his fortune by entering into unfavorable business partnerships," she said, determined to keep the upper hand. "I learned well from him. Never give anything away for nothing. Choose your allies and your partners with utmost scrutiny."

"This is why you haven't accepted the dozens of other proposals you are rumored to have received," he said. It wasn't a question. He studied her with a look of heated admiration, leaving her feel both like a coveted prize and a mouse about to be pounced on by a hungry cat.

"Precisely, Mr. Croydon." She nodded, praying her trembling wasn't noticeable.

"So what are your terms, Miss Bellowes?" he asked. "What could entice you into marriage to a man of advanced years who is shameless enough to corner a woman in an elevator that is part of a crowded theater, where no one would hear her cry out if there were trouble."

His words should have frightened her, but instead they made her oddly aware of how heavy her breasts had become, how tight her nipples were as they brushed against her chemise with each shallow breath, and how warm and liquid the secret places between her legs felt.

"I want to be the mother of the Prime Minister's son," she burst out before she could think of a cleverer response. She blinked in surprise at her own answer, but the truth of it was undeniable. Her smile widened.

Mr. Croydon's answering smile managed to convey delight without a hint of mocking. "I shall endeavor to help you achieve that goal, Miss Bellowes," he said.

His voice was so rich and deep, and his expression so ravenous, that Marigold was left in no doubt that he was referring to the part about creating a son far more than that part about being Prime Minister. The mysterious parts of her that had been awakened as she'd watched him deliver his speech to Commons, and that had grown and warmed over the past few weeks of constant encounters that were anything but random, burst into full-blooded feelings that were as new as they were overwhelming. If any of the men who had begged for her hand in the past decade had made her feel half as ready to surrender her virtue as Mr. Croydon did with a few simple words, she would have been married with half a dozen children already. The urge to thoroughly ruin herself with this man was almost ludicrous.

And yet, she didn't have to ruin herself at all. She could have everything she'd ever wanted—position, influence, children—and indulge in the flurry of new sensations that begged her to explore them, all with one simple word.

"Well then." She shrugged one shoulder, tilting her chin up to him, but the quiver in her voice was a dead giveaway that no matter how bold she appeared, he had the upper hand. "How could I refuse an offer like that?"

"Is that a yes, then?" For a moment, he seemed genuinely surprised, but also incredibly pleased.

Marigold let some of her haughty demeanor drop. "Provided my father agrees, yes, it is."

"Wonderful," he said, letting out a breath of relief. Could he have had any doubt? In an instant, the sly, teasing look was back in his eyes. "Of course, with all sound business deals, you should have a chance to sample the merchandise before making up your mind."

A shiver shot down Marigold's spine. She barely had time to breathe the words, "Should I?" before his arms were around her, pulling her flush against him.

He slanted his mouth over hers, their lips meeting with whisper softness at first. When she let out a scandalously pleased sigh, he increased the pressure. His one hand dropped as low as it could down her back with the ridiculous bustle that she suddenly wished she wasn't wearing, but the other cradled her side so close to her breast that she was tempted to twist until he cupped her completely. His tongue teased along the crease of her mouth, and when instinct pushed her to part her lips for him, it slipped in beside hers.

The sensation was breathtaking. The taste of him was new and alluring. She had no idea what she was doing, but he seemed to sense that, nibbling at her lips and thrusting his tongue along hers as if tutoring her in an art she was eager to learn. Her whole body felt like liquid in his arms, and she was certain beyond a shadow of a doubt that he could have done anything to her, anything at all, and she would have gladly let him. That knowledge was both frightening and exhilarating.

"We'd better stop," he said at last, straightening, but keeping his arms around her. It was a good thing too. If he had let her go, she would have spilled to the floor in a puddle of desire. He seemed to be having a hard time catching his breath as well, and his face was flushed. Seeing that only fired Marigold's blood more. She'd had that effect on him.

"I truly worry what would happen if we didn't," she answered, meeting his eyes as every nerve in her body sang.

His reddened lips curved into a devilish grin. "Something neither of us are ready for," he answered, "but that I believe we will both enjoy tremendously after the vows are spoken."

Damn his hide, he was making her want to anticipate those vows and explore all of the hints and whispers her married friends had shared with her about sexual relations right then and there. She never would have dreamed she'd be so wanton, or that she'd feel that way about a man that, admittedly, she barely knew. But Mr. Croydon—Alex, she supposed she should start calling him—was so delicious, and his touch did such forbidden things to her. Lady Stanhope would have been proud.

"The second act has probably started by now," she said, breathless.

"You're right, of course." His grin sent swirls of giddiness through her. He cleared his throat. "Perhaps you should return to your box alone and allow me to—" He paused, making a strangely silly face, then finished with, "relax a bit before being seen in public."

She wasn't sure what exactly he meant, although she had an idea that it had to do with the fit of his trousers. "But of course."

He pivoted to work the elevator controls, and they descended to the hall with the boxes. It was quieter now, and strains of the music from act two wafted up from the theater itself.

"One last thing," Marigold whispered as he reached for the door.

"Yes?"

"Could we have a short engagement?" she squeaked, suddenly wanting to laugh at herself.

"I'll speak to your father tomorrow," he answered.

"I'll make certain he clears his calendar to receive you."

Instead of a simple "Thank you", he stole another kiss. The feel of his mouth over hers was so good that she closed her eyes, leaned into him, and prayed that it would go on forever. If this was what it was like to be a foolish, strumpet of a woman, then she was ready to embrace a harlot's life.

No, she was ready to become a man's wife at last.

CHAPTER 4

*A*nyone in London who wasn't a complete fool knew to tread lightly around Percy Bellowes. The man had taken his father's small manufacturing operation and, within the course of twenty years, turned it into a vast industrial empire that spanned the textile, machinery, and shipping businesses. He was rumored to have more money than Croesus, and to have reduced the men who had applied for his daughters' hands to quivering piles of jelly when they stood before him.

Alex had argued law before a crowded House of Commons, and had had audiences with Queen Victoria herself. He was certain that asking Percy Bellowes for Marigold's hand in marriage would be child's play compared to that.

He was wrong.

"And what makes you think a bounder like you would be a good match for my eldest daughter?" Bellowes accosted him, pointing the stem of his pipe at Alex as he leaned against an enormous, mahogany desk in the office of his grand and spacious London home. "You have a reputation, you know," he went on before Alex could open his mouth to reply. "A reputation for taking up with actresses and other trollops."

Twin spikes of anger and embarrassment snaked up Alex's spine. Under any other circumstance, he would have defended Violetta with every breath he had, informed the man she was a lovely, sweet woman who'd had a hard time of life and didn't deserve the reputation or the end she'd had. But sense told him that defending his deceased lover to the man whose daughter he was hoping to marry wouldn't be a strategic move.

"All of my wild oats have been sewn," he said instead, his jaw tight. "The time has come for me to take a wife worthy of the Croydon name and ready to step into the limelight of the position I plan to hold someday."

He hoped the hint of his political ambitions would work in his favor, but Bellowes just narrowed his eyes to suspicious slits and said, "You mean your friends have bullied you into doing the respectable thing at last. I'm friends with Lord Dunsford and Edmund Travers, you know. I'm well aware of what they say about you in regards to matrimony."

"Yes, well, um...." Alex fumbled for the right response. Peter and Edmund had needled him about marriage as much as Katya over the last few years.

"Why should I let my dearest daughter go to a man who is marrying because of the pressure of his peers?" Bellowes asked, jabbing the air with the stem of his pipe once more. "Why should I hand her over to you when half a dozen other men have wanted her?"

Alex swallowed. The interview had to go better than this if he were to have a chance of securing Marigold. And after the tension and the kiss they'd shared in the elevator the night before, he had to have her. Reason had nothing to do with it, but reason was exactly what he needed on his side now. And yet, he couldn't possibly come out with the truth and tell Bellowes that if he didn't get his daughter in bed as soon as possible, he'd likely go blind with need.

"The fact that my friends have been urging me to marry in no way detracts from the admiration I have for Marigold," he said, using the same voice and posture he used to deliver biting arguments in Commons. He could feel the heat rising up his face, though, and figured he probably looked like a damn fool. "Almost from the moment I met her, I was charmed by her intellect and wit."

"So you think you can use her to make a good impression on the wives of ministers you need to sway to your cause?" Bellowes pressed him, arching a brow.

Alex wanted to curse and scrub his face in frustration. The man was going to turn every argument he had on its head. No wonder he had more money than the Queen.

"It is my understanding that Marigold wants to take a more active role in political society," he said, feeling the sweat dripping down his back. "I would simply be giving her the outlet for those ambitions."

"Oh!" Bellowes's brow flew up. "So you think you're doing my daughter a favor, do you?"

"I would hope that—"

"And I suppose you think you'd be doing her a favor by venting your lusts on her, now that your actress has died and you need someone else to—"

"Violetta was a kind and beautiful woman who does not deserve your scorn," Alex snapped before he could stop himself. He winced at his combative tone, but so help him, he was through with the meanness of the world when it came to women who had fallen through no fault of their own. "I loved her the best I could, and I took care of her when many others would have cast her aside. So for you to imply that she was just another replaceable fixture in my bed, one I am seeking to fill with Marigold, is an insult of the highest degree, sir. To me, to Violetta, and to your daughter."

The air crackled in the silence that followed. Alex braced himself for another tongue-lashing, but to his surprise, Bellowes raised his pipe to his mouth and smiled. A fragrant puff of smoke followed before he said, "Good man."

Alex blinked. "I beg your pardon?"

Bellowes puffed a few more times. "I like a man who cares for the women in his life, no matter who they are. My own mother was a seamstress in Oxford Street. I don't care if my Marigold marries for love or not, but I want to be damn sure that the man who takes her from me will care for her as she deserves."

Alex let out a breath, resisting the urge to wipe the sweat from his brow as though he'd finished a grueling race. "I can assure you, sir, I will take great care with your daughter." Whether the infatuation he felt for her blossomed into love or not. After all, Violetta never had anything to complain about, even after the first ardor of their relationship cooled. Perhaps if she had complained, she wouldn't have met her sad end. Although if she had left him, he wouldn't have James.

"To be honest, sir," he said, pushing forward to banish those thoughts. "When we discussed it, your daughter made clear to me that she is in favor of this union because it will further her personal aims."

Bellowes laughed and shook his head. "That's Mari for you. She bossed you into proposing, didn't she?"

Alex's mouth twitched into a sideways grin. "In a

manner of speaking. Though I can assure you, the feelings are mutual."

"And orchestrated by the indomitable Lady Stanhope, no doubt."

"No doubt," Alex repeated with a wry expression. His shoulders began to loosen, and his heart rate eased away from panic levels.

"Well then." Bellowes pushed away from his desk and circled around to take a seat at the large, leather chair. "Have a seat and we'll battle out the details of the union."

"Thank you, sir." Alex moved to take a seat in front of the desk. "I promise to do my best by your daughter."

MARIGOLD PRESSED HER EAR TO THE DOOR OF HER father's office, like a girl half her age peeking to see what Father Christmas was up to. She cursed the thickness of the door and the quality of the wood that kept her from hearing more than a drone of voices. Of course, her father had arranged for a sound-blocking door on purpose, since he conducted his most sensitive business at home instead of at his office along the waterfront, and the number of times his children had been caught with their ears to the door in years past was legendary. The only thing Marigold had been able to hear clearly was Alex defending someone named Violetta for the space of about ten words before he lowered his voice again.

"Oh, this will never do." She sighed and straightened, wanting to kick the door.

"What will never do?"

With a gasp, Marigold turned to find Lavinia approaching from the front hall. She'd completely forgotten that Lavinia was due to join her for tea that afternoon when

Alex arrived, but the idea of having her friend with her for the momentous occasion upon her was a brilliant one. She motioned for Lavinia to hurry and join her at the door.

"Mr. Croydon is here speaking to Papa," she whispered, leaning toward the door again.

"Oh!" Lavinia picked up her skirts and rushed to the door. "Oh, oh, is this what I think it is?"

Marigold smiled from ear to ear and nodded. She pressed her ear to the door, hearing nothing but the mumble of men's voices again, and Lavinia did the same.

No sooner had Lavinia's ear touched the door, though, then she jumped away. "I can't do it," she said breathlessly, pressing her hand to her chest. "Aside from the fact that Mama would never approve, I couldn't possibly listen to such an intimate conversation that has nothing to do with me."

"It has everything to do with you," Lavinia whispered. "Who do you think I'll be asking to be my maid of honor?"

"Oh!" Lavinia brightened, then burst into a giggle and hunched forward, ear to the door again. After a few seconds, however, she whispered, "I can't hear anything."

Marigold sighed and straightened. "Neither can I. And really, I'm far too old to be listening at doors."

Lavinia stood as well. "I don't suppose there's anything we can do but wait."

"More's the pity." Marigold grinned. Her heart was so light that she wanted to jump up and down or twirl in circles. She settled for clapping her hands to her mouth for a moment, then squealing, "I'm going to be married."

"I'm so happy for you." Lavinia rushed forward to hug her.

The two of them embraced, then Marigold gestured for Lavinia to follow her down the hall and across to the parlor.

"Levins, could you have tea sent up, please?" she asked the butler as they passed through the entryway.

"Certainly, miss." Levins bowed and headed for the kitchen stairs.

"Does it bother you to marry a man so much older than you?" Lavinia asked once they'd seated themselves in the formal parlor.

Sunlight streamed through the windows, adding to the joy in Marigold's heart. "Not at all," she sighed happily. "Mr. Croydon is distinguished and experienced, not at all like those drooling, hideous caricatures of old men who heroines in novels are constantly being sold off to."

"Yes, but aren't you worried about his *experience*?" Lavinia asked with a hint of dread, her cheeks flushing bright pink.

Marigold was instantly taken back to their moment in the elevator the night before, the way his eyes had bored into her, full of carnal knowledge, the way she'd wanted to give in to him in every way possible. Just thinking about it sent flutters through her.

"Not at all," she whispered, leaning toward Lavinia conspiratorially. "I think his *experience* could be one of his greatest assets."

"But aren't you the least bit frightened by it all?"

"Why should I be?" Marigold straightened, tilting her head up with a faux haughty look. Her insides quivered all the same. "Those things are a natural part of a sophisticated woman's life. I'm sure it's nothing at all to be frightened by."

Lavinia's eyes went as wide as saucers. "I'm not so sure. You remember the things Irene Danville used to say when we were at school."

Marigold fought not to laugh. She and Lavinia had attended Mrs. Collingswood's Finishing School together

47

years ago. Marigold had been a year away from graduating when Lavinia had enrolled, and in spite of their age difference, they'd become fast friends. The other girls had teased Lavinia with stories expressly designed to give her nightmares. Irene in particular had enjoyed spinning tales of her older sister's depraved husband who ravished her in hundreds of dastardly ways, none of which Marigold believed for a moment.

"Irene Danville is now a happily married woman with three children and another on the way," Marigold laughed. "I'm sure she's eating her own words now."

"Still," Lavinia said, folding her hands soberly in her lap. "If what Mama tells me is true, a husband can be a difficult burden to bear."

Marigold's lips twitched as she fought not to laugh at her friend outright. "Mothers everywhere attempt to frighten their daughters into chastity because they know that if the truth got out, we'd all be like...like Lady Stanhope."

Lavinia gasped and her eyes went wide, then she dissolved into laughter. "Don't let Lady Stanhope hear you say that. Or Mama, for that matter."

"Lady Stanhope would hold her head high and tell me I am absolutely right," Marigold said, nodding for emphasis. "I intend to follow her example instead of the one put forth by the fainting Mamas of the world."

"By taking a string of lovers?" Lavinia teased.

Gretta, the Bellowes's maid, chose just that moment to enter the room with the tea tray. Her brow shot up and she nearly missed a step.

Marigold raised a hand, laughing. "We're just being silly, Gretta. Don't worry. I have no plans to take a string of lovers."

"Yes, miss," Gretta said, resting the tea tray on the table between the chairs where Marigold and Lavinia sat.

"Although," Marigold added in a whisper, "I may end up with a husband very soon, depending on how Papa's meeting goes."

Gretta's face lit up. "Congratulations, miss. I'm happy for you. Would you like me to pour?"

"I can do it," Marigold said, letting Gretta know she was free to go with a nod. She turned to Lavinia and whispered, "Soon I'll be able to do a great many things."

Lavinia giggled so hard she snorted, which only made both of them giggle more.

"I would still be terrified out of my mind on my wedding night," Lavinia said once her tea was poured and in hand. "The whole thing involves removing your clothes in front of *a man*," she whispered, her face going red.

"What's the trouble with that?" Marigold asked with false calm, even as the idea of undressing in front of Alex filled her with nervous tremors. She really would have to do a better job of training her emotions to be as bold and casual as her outward demeanor.

Lavinia blinked at her as though she'd lost her mind. "That means naked," she whispered. "With someone else looking at you. Someone else *male*."

"So?" Marigold shrugged, raising her teacup, and trying hard to keep it from shaking. "Turnabout is fair play. You get to see the man naked as well."

Lavinia had just sipped her tea, and spit it out in shock. She laughed to the point of tears, and Marigold joined her.

The two of them were giggling madly, blinking back tears and incapable of rational speech, when Alex and her father appeared in the doorway. The shock nearly made Marigold drop her teacup, and if Lavinia hadn't already set hers aside and leaned back into the chair as she laughed uproariously, Marigold was certain her friend would have tumbled to the floor. As it was, the two of them struggled to compose themselves and stand.

"Why is it that my otherwise steady daughter is always reduced to silliness when you are in her presence, young lady?" Marigold's father demanded.

Marigold knew her father well enough to see that his frown was teasing and his eyes were filled with fondness and approval, but Lavinia began to choke as her laughter turned to horror. Marigold leapt to her side, throwing a supportive arm around her friend's back and thumping it to make the coughing stop.

"I'm sorry, my dear," her father said with a chuckle. "Just having a bit of fun. You know me. It's a glorious day, after all. I've just palmed off Marigold on this irascible rake."

Marigold sucked in a breath and glanced from her father to Alex. Indeed, Alex stood with his hands behind his back, an incredibly pleased smile on his face. His blue eyes sparkled as though he'd won a parliamentary debate and a prize at a county fair all in one.

"You said yes?" Marigold asked her father, her voice an octave higher than it should have been.

"I did." Her father nodded, then gestured to Alex. "Behold, my dear. Your future husband."

"Oh, Papa, thank you." Marigold checked on Lavinia, and when she was sure her friend was all right, she skipped across to kiss her father's cheek. When that was done, she turned to Alex, wanting to kiss far more than just his cheek.

"I trust you are pleased?" he asked, a thousand times more formal than she wanted him to be. He certainly contained himself far better than he had in the elevator.

"Very pleased," Marigold answered with a cool nod, taking her cue from him.

"Your father and I discussed it," he glanced to her father, "and he has consented to having the banns published as soon as possible so that we can be married in three weeks' time."

A ripple of excitement shot through Marigold. They'd discussed the night before that they should have a short engagement because of the fire between them, and it hadn't been a joke. She should be thinking about her imminent rise in social status, should have focused on the good she could do once she had his power and influence behind her. But the only thoughts that flooded her mind were all of Irene Danville's stories of debauchery, and how she was but three short weeks away from learning the truth.

"I have so much to do, then," she said all the same, drawing herself up to her full, regal height. "Preparations will need to be made. A church will need to be reserved, and a venue for the wedding breakfast and reception." She glanced to Lavinia. "Dresses, flowers, food. There's so much to do."

"I will gladly help you in whatever way I can," Alex said with a nod.

"I may need your influence to pull this off," Marigold said, her heart beating up a storm.

"Have a seat, then, and we'll get started," her father said, gesturing toward the sofa. He turned and called over his shoulder, "We need more tea in here."

They fluttered into motion, taking their seats and beginning discussions about what would, out of necessity, be a smaller event than a man in Alex's position should have had. Not more than three minutes had passed, however, when, instead of Gretta with more tea things, a handsome man in this thirties with bright auburn hair and a simple but finely-tailored suit, who Marigold had never seen before, stepped into the room.

Alex rose instantly. "Phillips, what brings you here?"

"Urgent business, sir," Phillips said. His look was grave, and he darted an anxious glance to Marigold and Lavinia.

Alex frowned and stepped over to him. "Mr. Phillips is my valet and man of business," Alex explained briefly, then focused on the man. "What news?"

"It's Turpin," Phillips said. "He's brought the restriction bill up for a vote."

Alex's expression flooded with alarm. "But it's not on the docket for today. It hasn't even been approved."

"I know, sir. I believe that when he saw you were not present this morning, he figured he could throw a spanner in the works."

Alex cursed under his breath, causing Marigold's brow to shoot up. He rubbed a hand over his face, then turned to her with an anxious, apologetic look. "I'm sorry, my dear. I have to address this immediately."

The fact that he'd referred to her as his dear was quickly eclipsed by the way he marched for the door. Marigold stood, following him. "Go," she said. "I understand completely. Some things are far more important than planning a wedding."

They paused in the doorway, and he turned to her with a smile. "I thank you for your understanding." He hesitated, then reached for her hand, bringing it to his lips for a quick kiss. "I promise, I'll make it up to you."

"I'm sure you will." Marigold smiled, squeezing his hand when he lowered it.

A moment later, he was gone. Marigold watched as he and Mr. Phillips strode down the hall. Levins stepped forward with Alex's coat and hat, then escorted them to the door.

In the silence that followed, Marigold let out a sigh. One instant she'd been filled with joy, and the next it was almost as if nothing had happened. Everything had changed so fast, and with one snap of the door closing, it was life as usual.

"I can see you actually want to marry the man," her father spoke behind her. Marigold turned to him, catching his slightly-pitying expression. "But Alexander Croydon will not be an easy man to be married to."

A prick of anger followed her father's words. "What are you talking about, Papa?" She feigned casualness once again as she walked back to her chair and took a seat, reaching for her cold tea. "Alex is a marvelous man. He is important and influential."

Her father smiled sadly at her. "You may find that important and influential men are married to their work as much as to their wives."

"Then I will be married to his work as well," Marigold declared, tilting her chin up in defiance.

Her father chuckled and shook his head. "Your mother, God rest her soul, loved me dearly. But even before her illness, she came to see my work as her bitterest rival. It threw a wedge between us that I deeply regret."

Marigold's heart squeezed at her father's sad declaration. She had been only seven when her mother had died and had only limited memories of her. In the over twenty years since then, she'd liked to think that her father had never remarried because he'd loved her mother dearly, even though he'd always insisted it was because the demands of his work wouldn't have been fair to any woman married to him. A chill slithered through Marigold as those words took on new meaning.

"I'm sure everything will be fine between Alex and I," she said with a shrug. "I'm as interested in politics as he is, and Parliament only sits for a few months out of the year. Our life together will be happy." Her smile returned, warming her.

"There are other things that could ruin—" Her father stopped mid-sentence and pressed his lips together. He let out a breath and shook his head. "I'm being too hard on him," he said, smiling and sitting forward to help himself to a biscuit from the glass bowl on the tea tray. "I'm quite certain that you and Mr. Croydon are a fine match, and that you will never want for anything, my dear. Don't you agree, Lady Lavinia?"

"Oh yes. I agree entirely," Lavinia smiled.

"This is a perfect match," Marigold added, trying to feel pleased for herself.

One thing stuck out in what her father had said, though. Or rather, one thing didn't stick out. He hadn't mentioned anything about love.

CHAPTER 5

Three weeks wasn't enough time to plan a wedding, but somehow, Marigold pulled it off. Alex had no idea how, not so much because he was mystified by Marigold's organizational skills—although he was—but because in the time since he'd spoken to her father, he'd barely had time to have tea with her, let alone sit down and plan a wedding.

"Are you certain she's going to show up and go through with it?" his younger brother, Edward, asked as the two waited at the front of the modest church in Kensington, close to the Bellowes house.

Alex wasn't certain at all. Their whirlwind courtship seemed like a dream he'd awoken from to find parliamentary business tearing along as usual. Turpin had pulled his strings and made his deals with the devil to push back the vote on the women's rights bill while vexing the Liberals with his own suggestions for a repressive bill. The whole thing had caused a fierce debate that needed Alex's complete attention on a daily basis. And although he still very much wanted to marry Marigold, doubt had been creeping up on him since speaking to Percy Bellowes. Had they flown into the whole thing half-cocked? Was his proposal fueled by needs he could have satisfied at any of the higher-quality brothels in town? Would Marigold regret shackling herself to a man as committed to government as he was to her?

And those questions didn't begin to scratch the surface of larger, more personal doubts. Did he have anything left to give a woman after Violetta? What would Marigold make of James?

James. Bloody hell, in the whirlwind of their speedy courtship and parliamentary business, he'd forgotten to tell Marigold about his son.

"That's the face of a man about to embark on a voyage of marital bliss." The wry comment came with a hard slap on the back from Malcolm Campbell.

Alex flinched, face heating over the fact that he'd been caught staring, horrified, into space by one of his oldest friends. "It's no more serious than the way you looked the night you married Tessa," he fired back.

Malcolm's teasing grin turned into a sad smile of regret. "There were extenuating circumstances for Tessa and I, God rest her soul. You, on the other hand," His mischievous look returned, "have no such worries. You're marrying a beautiful heiress who, reportedly, has a good head on her shoulders. So why the frightened bunny look?"

Alex rolled his eyes and stared flatly at his friend. "So help me, Malcolm if you ever refer to me as a 'bunny' again...." He let his threat hang for a moment before adjusting his stance and steering the conversation away from him and his worries. "I heard about the business with Peter's nephew."

A bitter look entered Malcolm's eyes. "William was murdered by Shayles, pure and simple."

"Can you prove it?" Edward asked.

Malcolm clenched his jaw and rubbed a hand over his face. "Not yet. But there's no doubt in my mind."

"Is that why Peter isn't here?" Edward asked.

Malcolm's expression lightened. "No, Peter isn't here because he's too busy consoling his bride and beginning preparations for the new heir."

Alex laughed at the surprise revelation. "I hope for his sake that there are no problems this time." They all knew the heartbreak and misery Peter had gone through with his first wife's barrenness. What surprised Alex was how quickly Peter had managed to bring about the potential joy of an heir with his new wife. His friend would be a much better father than he'd ever been to James. "I wish them all the best," he added.

"And I wish you the best." Malcolm thumped his back once more. "It's about time."

Alex crossed his arms. "Have you been talking to Katya?"

A look that was halfway between hunger and defiance flashed in his eyes. "Not if I can avoid it."

Edward snorted and shook his head. "Only a fool runs from the one person wiser and more cunning than them."

Malcolm glared at Edward for a moment before clearing his throat and saying, "Speaking of people who run, no word from Basil, eh?"

Alex blew out a breath at the change in conversation. "I would have sent him an invitation if I had the slightest clue where the fool has run off to."

None of their group of friends had the slightest idea where Basil Waltham had disappeared to. He'd been missing for more than two years now, ever since embarrassing himself pitifully over a certain Miss Elizabeth Gray, now Lady Royston, and even though they were all constantly on the look-out for him, it was as if the man had dropped off the face of the earth.

"At least Armand made it," Malcolm went on, turning and waving to their tall, serious-looking friend, seated beside Katya in a pew several rows back, engaged in deep conversation with her.

Armand was perhaps the most unique of Alex's friends, having studied medicine and gone into practice before suddenly inheriting a title and estate, and the peerage that went with it all. He was as adept at arguing in the House of Lords as he was treating complicated illnesses, specifically in the fledgling field of gynecology. But it wasn't Armand who caught and held Malcolm's attention.

"That bloody woman," he muttered, color rising on his face as Katya bit her lower lip and winked at him.

It was Alex's turn to thump him on the back. "Why don't you just put all of us out of our misery, and yourself to boot, by admitting you were wrong and begging her to marry you."

Malcolm snapped to him with a look of fury in his eyes like only Katya could inspire and grumbled an oath that would have made sailors blush, following that with, "Mind your own business," before stomping off to the other side of the church to take a seat.

Edward laughed as he and Alex resumed their proper places. "I'm beginning to think that Basil isn't the only one running from his problems."

Alex didn't have time to answer that. The organ burst into the loud strains of a wedding march, and the doors at the back of the church flew open. A dazzling ray of light filled the vestibule, and out of that walked Marigold on the arm of her father. All else was forgotten. She was resplendent in a white dress, cut in the latest fashion. Her masses of golden hair were caught up in an elaborate style, and topped with a sheer, white veil. As her father escorted her up the aisle, the curious wedding guests watching her in approval and adoration, all Alex could think was that yes, he'd made the right decision after all.

Percy Bellowes paused at the front of the pews to kiss his daughter's cheek, his eyes waterier and more full of sentiment than most Englishmen would be willing to show. He whispered something in her ear, then walked her the last few steps to Alex.

"Keep her happy, or I'll tear your balls off and stuff them down your throat," Bellowes growled under his breath with a fierce glare.

A genuine twist of fear hit Alex's gut. He didn't have the best history of keeping women happy. This time would be different, he swore to himself. His balls depended on it.

Marigold's long-suffering sigh of, "Papa, really," turned Bellowes's comment into a cause for humor.

Alex nodded to Bellowes, then took Marigold's hand, beaming at her. "You look perfectly lovely," he said.

She blushed, making the picture even prettier. "Thank you."

They stood there staring at each other for a few too many moments before the priest cleared his throat. Alex arched a brow, as though he and Marigold had been caught misbehaving, and escorted her the last few steps to stand in front of the priest.

"Dearly beloved, we are gathered here today in the sight of God to join this man and this woman in holy matrimony."

Alex drew in a breath, standing straight and doing his best to pay attention. It struck him that he'd managed to avoid standing in exactly that spot for almost fifty years, but now here he was. He glanced up at the painted cherubs and image of God above the altar, praying that he was doing the right thing. He thought of Violetta, how madly they'd loved each other...until they hadn't, and about how lonely she'd been at the end. For her sake, he'd have to do a better job of being a man where Marigold was concerned.

FOR ALL THE IMPORTANCE THAT WAS PLACED ON THE transformation in a woman's world, Marigold was astounded by how quickly she went from being a maiden to a wife.

"And do you, Marigold Louise Bellowes, take this man, Alexander Nathaniel Croydon, to be your lawfully wedded husband, to love, honor, and obey, in sickness and in health, until death do you part?"

She took a deep breath, her heart singing with joy and excitement, and glanced to Alex. "I do."

He smiled, almost as though he were relieved she'd gone through with it. The lines around his eyes were filled with happiness, and even though he was a powerful and imposing figure in his expensive suit, the grey at his temples lending him an air of distinction, Marigold felt a rush of possessiveness. He was hers now, and she was his.

"Then by the power invested in me by God and Her Majesty, Queen Victoria, I now pronounce you husband and wife."

Marigold held her breath as Alex turned to face her fully, lifting the veil so that he could kiss her. Was that all it took? A few words, and her life had been altered forever.

He slid one arm around her waist, bringing her close to slant his lips over hers in a kiss. It couldn't hold a candle to the kisses they'd shared in the elevator, but even so, a hundred people watching them sighed with happiness and romantic sentiment instead of gasping in shock and scandal. All because of a few words.

The world was a strange place indeed.

The ceremony was over, but as soon as Alex whisked her down the aisle and out to the carriage that waited to take them home, to the wedding breakfast and an afternoon of celebration, a carnival of festivities began. Everyone who had attended the wedding and then some piled into the Bellowes house, and even though the residence was large for a townhouse, it felt as though there were people up to the rafters, talking, laughing, and wishing her and Alex well.

"Have you ever seen anything like this?" Lavinia asked, nearly needing to shout, as the two of them wove their way through the crowd to find a bit of refreshment.

"It's worse than the most popular balls of the season," Marigold agreed with a laugh.

"That's what you get for marrying a star of Parliament," Lavinia told her.

Marigold glanced over her shoulder, seeking out her husband in the crowd. He stood near the middle of the room, a flute of champagne in one hand, surrounded by stuffy-looking men who she'd seen on the floor of Commons, all congratulating him roundly. He looked up and met her eyes for a moment, joy and a mock look of panic on his face. Marigold laughed and shook her head, then continued on with Lavinia.

They only made it a few more feet before Lady Stanhope stepped away from the conversation she'd been having to intercept them.

"Mrs. Croydon, you're positively glowing," she said.

Marigold laughed, her spirits too high to mind that a bite to eat would have to wait. "I suppose I have you to thank for that."

Lady Stanhope gave a modest shrug, but the spark in her wicked, blue eyes said she knew full well what she'd accomplished. "I expect we'll begin to see great things from you as well as your husband soon."

Marigold pressed a hand to her heart. "I wouldn't know where to start."

"Oh, my dear, I think you do," she shot back, arching a brow. "I saw the way you were charming Mr. Gladstone earlier. He seems quite taken with you."

"I couldn't breathe when he was standing there talking to us," Lavinia agreed. "But you just went on as though he were the butler when he used to be Prime Minister, for heaven's sake."

"Mr. Gladstone is a pleasant man," Marigold said with an off-hand gesture.

Lady Stanhope laughed. "You may be the only one who's ever said that." Her grin turned sly. "But if you can charm the man who ruled this country—no offense to our dear queen—and may one day rule it again, if your husband doesn't take that honor from him, then you can set your sights as high as you'd like."

Marigold laughed, but a quiver of fear tickled her gut. How much power did she really want? Marrying Alex had happened so fast that she hadn't stopped to consider what her new position would mean. Evidently, Lady Stanhope had, which left Marigold with a whisper of doubt as to whether she'd been manipulated into the whole thing.

"All I care about right now is enjoying this wonderful party that my father put together for me," she said.

"You put it together," Lavinia added. "Your father simply paid for it."

Lady Stanhope studied Marigold with a smile of admiration. "You arranged this event?"

"She did," Lavinia answered.

Lady Stanhope scanned the room, giving Marigold the impression that she was marking each guest and assigning points to notable and significant members of society. "Well done, indeed."

"I simply invited my friends and Alex's," Marigold said. "And perhaps a few people I knew would be interested in the sudden wedding of an MP."

Lady Stanhope focused on Marigold again. She was about to make a further comment when their group was interrupted by an exasperated sigh from Lady Prior.

"Lavinia," she said in her most scolding tone, grasping her daughter's arm. "What have I told you about engaging in public conversation with undesirable sorts?"

"Mama!" Lavinia squeaked, turning pink with embarrassment.

Lady Stanhope merely laughed, completely nonplussed. "You'd better whisk her away, Matilde. I can feel my influence corrupting her more by the moment."

Lady Prior made a distinctly unladylike sound and tugged on Lavinia's arm. "Come away, Lavinia. You can rendezvous with Mrs. Croydon later. I've spotted several eligible men I would like for us to be introduced to."

"Oh, Mama." Lavinia shook her head, sending Marigold a wary look and Lady Stanhope an apologetic one, before letting herself be marched off into the throng of guests.

"What do you suppose Matilde Prior would say if she knew I could introduce her daughter to half a dozen highly prized gentlemen?" Lady Stanhope said, standing by

Marigold's side and tapping her chin as they watched Lavinia stumble off.

"She would suddenly change her opinion of whether the men in question were truly the right sort, due to their association with you, I think," Marigold said, then touched her fingers to her lips. "I'm sorry. That may have been too harsh."

"Not at all," Lady Stanhope laughed, turning to face her again. "Especially since you're right."

They shared a mischievous look. Marigold was filled with the satisfying feeling that the older woman could be her friend as much as her mentor. That feeling grew when Lady Stanhope took her arm and led her slowly to an alcove at the side of the room, guarded by two potted trees.

"I wonder if anyone has had a word with you about tonight," she said, looking as wicked as ever.

Heat and expectation that felt embarrassingly out of place in a room packed with a hundred people filled Marigold. "If you mean what I think you mean," she said, glancing around to make sure no one could overhear them, "sadly, my mother died when I was quite young, and I suppose Papa didn't feel up to the task."

"Then I will give you the only words of advice you'll need," Lady Stanhope declared, stopping between the potted trees and turning to Marigold with a triumphant smile.

Marigold let out a panicked laugh, glancing every which way, certain everyone in the room was now listening in. "Right here? Now?"

Lady Stanhope shrugged. "When several dozen people are conversing all at once, it's as good as being secluded on an island in the middle of the North Sea." She paused. "I suppose that's a bit of advice you might do well to remember in the coming years as well. I've had some of the most intimate conversations of my life in crowded ballrooms."

"Is this destined to be an intimate conversation then?" Try as she did to appear as sophisticated and calm as Lady Stanhope, Marigold's insides filled with butterflies.

Lady Stanhope rested a hand on her arm and leaned in to say, "Sexual relations are one of the finest joys in life, my dear. And if my guess is correct, you've married a master of the art. Trust him and enjoy it."

Marigold was certain she'd gone beet-red in a heartbeat. She was suddenly so hot that she was sure the trees on either side of her would catch fire. "I don't know what to say to that," she managed to stammer in reply.

"There's nothing to say, my dear. All you need to do is listen to me. There are any number of ninnies out there who will try to tell you that a woman, even a married woman, should be chaste and horrified at mankind's carnal instincts."

Marigold thought instantly of Lady Prior. "I believe that."

"But they couldn't be more wrong," Lady Stanhope went on. "Passion is a woman's prerogative, my dear. And pleasure is our recompense for the pain of surrendering our freedom to a man. Grab hold of that pleasure with both hands and revel in it. Don't ever let any of these frigid mamas or milksop misses tell you sex is dirty or disgraceful. It is power, my dear. It is divine."

Marigold pressed a hand to her stomach, finding it suddenly difficult to breathe. Her skin tingled as though Lady Stanhope had shared with her one of the secrets of the universe. In fact, she might have. The benediction that the priest had spoken over her and Alex didn't feel as world-changing as the simple speech Lady Stanhope had just made.

"Ah, so this is where my lovely wife has gotten off to."

The tingling that spread across Marigold's skin, and deeper, doubled as Alex strode up to them. The heat that was making her giddy seemed to coalesce in secret places, as much as it had when the two of them had been alone in the elevator. She glanced to Alex, meeting his eyes and finding the hunger she remembered and had dreamed about beneath his jovial, public smile.

"Ah, Alex." Lady Stanhope shifted to stand between the two of them. "I was just having a word with your lovely wife."

Marigold's breath caught in her throat. Aside from the woman's audacity for calling Alex by his given name in public, she wouldn't put it past Lady Stanhope to tell Alex exactly what they'd been talking about, and she wasn't sure she could endure the full intensity of those emotions in her father's ballroom.

"Good words I hope." Alex smiled at her, his brow lifting with a hint of a question.

"I'll leave her to explain to you later," Lady Stanhope said. Marigold breathed a sigh of relief. "But before I leave the two of you alone to continue dazzling your cadre of important guests, I have a wedding present for you."

"A wedding present?" Marigold asked, wondering why she hadn't mentioned anything before.

Lady Stanhope gave them both one of her most mischievous grins, then opened the reticule that had been dangling from her wrist throughout the party. She took from it a small but fat envelope, handing it to Alex.

"You said you wanted a way to get rid of the man," she said, arching one brow cryptically. "There you have it."

Alex's brow knit in confusion as he looked at the envelope. It wasn't sealed, but when he opened the flap to peer at the papers inside, his frown deepened. "I don't understand."

Lady Stanhope grinned. "You will when you've had a chance to look it over in detail." Before Marigold could ask what the envelope's contents were, Lady Stanhope went on. "And now, if you will excuse me, I see that Malcolm is here and I haven't had a chance to ruffle his feathers in months. I wish the two of you every joy in the world."

She squeezed Alex's arm and kissed Marigold's cheek, then sailed off into the sea of party guests, which parted easily for her. Marigold stared after her, mystified, then nearly laughed out loud when Lord Malcolm flinched at Lady Stanhope's approach, hard enough to almost upset one of the footmen carrying a tray of champagne. The way he and Lady Stanhope stared at each other was as explosive as dynamite.

"I take it they know each other," Marigold said, sliding her arm through Alex's.

He smirked. "They used to be lovers."

"Really?"

"More than a decade ago." He shrugged. "Nothing ever came of it, though."

"Why not?"

"None of us really know." He frowned, turning the envelope over in his hands.

"What is that all about?" she asked.

He handed the envelope to her. "I'm not sure. Sometimes it takes a while to decipher Katya's clues."

Marigold peeked into the envelope, reading what she could of the writing that was visible to her. It was a constable's report about a woman named Ruby Murdoch, but that was as much as she could read. "She seems to think this will stop someone? Stop whom? And from what?"

Alex turned to her with a feigned scolding look. "Do you really want to spend your wedding party pondering the mysteries of Katya Marlowe?"

"No," Marigold answered, closing the envelope and handing it back to him. "We have much better things to do."

"We do indeed," he said, lowering his voice to a timbre too scandalous for public use.

The butterflies in Marigold's stomach launched into action once more as Lady Stanhope's words came back to her. The divine mysteries of passion seemed just a heartbeat away.

CHAPTER 6

The butterflies didn't disperse as the party carried on through the afternoon and well into the evening. None of the people who had been invited seemed to be in any hurry to leave. Not when the infamous Percy Bellowes was providing enough food and drink for an army, or when there were so many influential people on hand to wheel and deal with.

"We should make our escape while we can," Alex whispered to Marigold after a lavish, formal supper, when yet another round of drinks was being poured.

Marigold glanced over her shoulder to him, and the butterflies raged. "Can we really leave so many guests to their own devices?"

His hand rested lightly on her waist, and his smile hinted at everything that was to come. "I believe your father and sisters have things under control."

A flush painted Marigold's cheeks as she quickly scanned the room. Her father looked to be haranguing Mr. Disraeli. Only her father would take it upon himself to lecture the Prime Minister at a wedding reception. Her sisters, Flora and Catherine, who had made last-minute journeys from their husband's country homes, were doing a fine job of entertaining the other guests and ensuring they had as much ice cream as they could stomach.

"So they do," Marigold answered Alex.

"Then hurry." He took her hand, making a bee-line for the door. "Before anyone notices our flight."

A few people did notice their escape, but no one tried to stop them. Marigold couldn't make up her mind whether she would have wanted them to or not. As soon as they reached the grand staircase in the front hall, she picked up speed, leading Alex up to the second floor and down the family's private corridor.

They'd made arrangements to stay at the Bellowes house for the wedding night, since it was easier to stay under the same roof as the party than to fuss with traveling several blocks through busy London streets after dark.

"Mrs. German had the maids prepare the French room for us," she said, wincing over the tremor in her voice as she reached for the handle of the door at the end of the hall.

"That sounds promising," Alex said.

Everything seemed entirely too quiet as Marigold pushed open the door and stepped into the remote bedroom. The din of the party still rang in her ears, even though she could only barely hear the rumble of the guests downstairs. There she was, suddenly alone with a man who now held complete sway over her.

The French room was the second largest bedroom in the house, after her Papa's. The enormous bed was piled with pillows and bolsters and a thick, down coverlet encased in pale blue silk. The maids had decorated the room with bouquets of pink roses and lavender that filled the space with the most delicious scent. The pale blue, velvet curtains were already closed, and her nightgown and robe were laid out across one of a pair of wing-backed, stuffed chairs that stood on either side of a white marble fireplace. A robe and pajamas that must have been Alex's were draped across the other chair.

"What a delightful room," Alex said, shutting the door behind them and turning the key in the lock.

A deep quiver shot through Marigold's gut at the click. She pressed a hand to her chest to still her racing heart. It didn't matter that she'd known this moment was coming for weeks, now that it was here, she fluttered like a bird in a cage.

But no, she refused to let herself be intimidated by something that nearly every woman experienced at some point in her life. Lady Stanhope's words came back to her. This was her right.

She turned to face Alex, sending him the most coquettish smile she could manage. *Lady Stanhope, Lady Stanhope, Lady Stanhope*, she told herself. All she had to do was behave as though she were Lady Stanhope.

"The room isn't the only thing that's delightful," she said, swaying carefully closer to him. She could have done without the breathless hitch in her voice, but as long as she could convince Alex she was a woman of the world, she would be all right.

And then he stepped forward, closing his arms around her and bringing his mouth down over hers in a fiery kiss. She tilted her head back, and he moved a hand to cradle her neck as his mouth explored hers even more boldly than he had in the elevator. Her senses were overwhelmed in a heartbeat as he slipped his tongue alongside hers. But it was the intensity of the need that rippled off of him more than

71

the physical invasion that blossomed into something that was both desire and fear in her gut.

"I've wanted you from the moment I first saw you," he confessed.

His hands shifted to her sides as he kissed her again, and for the first time, Marigold realized how large they were, how large he was. He could crush her if he had half a mind to. When he reached up, cupping her breasts through the silk and cotton of her clothes, her legs felt as though they would betray her if she needed to run. But she held on, gripping his arms as his hands and mouth explored her, reminding herself that this was what she wanted.

"Now," Alex said, breaking away from her at last and leaving her feeling like a quivering rabbit. "How does this dress come off?"

"I...there are buttons up the back." She tried her best to send him a flirtatious grin before turning her back to him. As soon as she was faced away, her smile dropped, and she gulped for breath, pressing a hand to her stomach for courage.

"I see." Alex stepped closer to her, his hands brushing her back as he began to undo the row of tiny buttons holding her bodice together.

For a moment, Marigold squeezed her eyes shut, embarrassed that they were suddenly stinging with tears. A man was undressing her. A man who, in all honesty, she barely knew. He would take her clothes off, look at her naked body with lust, then take her to the bed and have his way with her. Lady Stanhope be damned, the little she knew of carnal relations didn't feel particularly divine in that moment. It felt terrifying.

"There," Alex said as the last button popped and her bodice sagged.

He went to work on the intricate fastenings of her bustle and skirt, giving Marigold just enough time to take several deep breaths to compose herself. This was good, she reminded herself. This was what married couples did. She forced herself to shrug out of her bodice, denying the fact that she was shaking, as Alex tugged the ties of her petticoat free.

"Perfect," he hummed, pushing the pile of fabric and cage that was her bustle, skirt, and petticoat down her legs. He circled his arms around her waist, pulling her back flush against his chest. With practice and precision, he unhooked her corset, letting it fall to the pile of wedding dress that they stood in when it came free. Then he splayed one hand across her stomach and stroked the other across her breast, only the thinnest layer of cotton between them. "What a beautiful view," he murmured.

She couldn't shake her thoughts away from the fact that she was now nearly naked while he was still fully clothed. Without the layers of her wedding costume, she felt tiny and helpless in his powerful arms. Divine indeed! She felt as though she were inches away from disaster.

"Let's get rid of the rest of this," Alex murmured, kissing her neck before reaching for the hem of her chemise.

"Wait." She clamped a hand over his to stop him, panic seeping around her edges. She scrambled for an explanation for her hesitation that wouldn't make her look like a ninny. "It's not fair." She twisted to glance up at him. "You haven't taken anything off."

"So I haven't," he said, grinning down at her like a wolf about to devour his prey.

He stepped back and unbuttoned his jacket, shrugging it off and tossing it aside. His eyes never left hers, even when she stepped out of the cloud of silk at her feet and inched backward to the bed. His waistcoat came next, then he shrugged out of his suspenders and tugged his shirt from his trousers. He managed to coordinate toeing off his shoes with undoing the buttons of his shirt, then peeled his shirt off over his head.

The sight of the broad expanse of his chest, muscles well-defined, nipples tight, just a dusting of hair, sent twinges of pleasure and panic through Marigold. Why had she thought making him undress would put them on more equal footing? He was even more overwhelming stripped bare than he was clothed. And when he unfastened his trousers, pushing them down and kicking them aside, her fear reached a fevered pitch.

He was huge and imposing. Nothing in all of the art she'd observed depicting the male form prepared her for the raw sight of his erect manhood. She hadn't had any idea that men could be so solid or so...purple. A wreath of dark curls surrounded his staff and what hung beneath, but all she could focus on was his thickness and the flared tip that stood straight up, bold and aggressive. How was she possibly supposed to fit that inside of her?

"Is that fear or hunger I see in your eyes?" he asked as he approached her slowly, a devilish grin reaching his hooded eyes.

Marigold backed all the way against the bed, until she had nowhere to go, and gripped the coverlet in desperation. He would think she was a silly goose not worthy of his time if she admitted her fear.

"Which do you think?" she answered. Her voice shook horribly, and to hide it, she ran the tip of her tongue over her lips the way she'd seen an actress do once.

It must have been the right move. Alex's grin widened, and his eyes blazed as he closed the distance between them.

She did her best not to gasp when he reached her and pulled her into an embrace. His mouth slanted over hers once more, taking hers with deep passion, but it was the rest of his body pressed to hers that made it impossible for her to catch her breath. His spear was hot and solid between them, and he moved his hips in such a way as to rub it between the two of them. Her body reacted exactly opposite of her mind. A tingling ache pulsed through the very center of her even as what breath she managed between his fevered kisses grew fast and shallow.

When he swept her chemise up over her head, tossing it aside, she froze with fear. His hands explored her breasts, his thumbs brushing over her nipples, as he kissed her lips, her cheek, and her neck, but she felt it all as if her body were at the opposite end of a tunnel from her mind. She couldn't move a muscle as he eased her back onto the bed, kissing her shoulder and collarbone as his hands tugged at the drawstring of her drawers.

He rocked back, quickly pulling off her drawers, stockings, and shoes, leaving her completely exposed to him. Then he was on top of her completely, shifting both of them farther across the coverlet. She was beyond the point of trembling, so terrified as he kissed her, fondled her breast, and wedged himself between her legs that tears stung at her eyes that were impossible to hold back, even when she squeezed them tightly shut.

"Marigold?" Alex's voice sounded as though it were a million miles away. His mild, sensual tone quickly turned serious. "Oh, God. I'm sorry. Darling, I'm so, so sorry."

With a sharp intake of breath, Marigold snapped back into the moment. Her body had gone as rigid as a statue. Alex lay beside her instead of on top of her. His wolfish expression had been replaced by kindhearted concern. He stroked her hair—still pinned in its elaborate style—and the side of her head. She blinked a few times to focus on his face.

"I'm so sorry," he repeated. "I should have noticed sooner."

"N-noticed?" she stammered, her voice high enough to be a girl's.

"That you were...nervous." She could tell he was choosing his words carefully so as not to hurt her more. "I shouldn't have been so eager. This is your first time."

"You...no, I...it's...." She could barely form thoughts, let alone voice them. Her mouth had gone dry, and she bit her lip to moisten them, afraid she might cry in earnest. "I don't want to be a ninny."

"You're not a ninny," he laughed. It was an oddly reassuring sound. "You're just inexperienced. And I'm a randy old fool, dazzled by your beauty." He cradled her face, smiling at her, and stroked his thumb over her cheek. "Here. Let's get a little more comfortable."

He let go of her, rolling to the side, and began tossing the mountain of pillows and bolsters off the side of the bed. Feeling started to return to Marigold's limbs, and as he peeled back the coverlet and sheets, she was loose enough to crawl under them with him. He carefully tucked everything over them, then settled onto his side, facing her.

"Better?"

Marigold nodded, still feeling ashamed down to her toes.

He nodded to her hair. "Do you need help taking all the pins out?"

"Oh." She reached up to touch her hairstyle. "I suppose that would be more comfortable."

"Let me."

They both sat, Marigold shyly turning her back to him, and Alex began pulling the flowers and pins from her hair. Whether it was deliberate on his part of not, his actions gave her the time she needed to breathe, wipe the last of her tears from her face, and settle her nerves. It certainly wasn't the way she imagined her momentous wedding night progressing. Tears definitely weren't supposed to be part of the picture. As Alex finished with her hair, setting the pins on the table beside the bed and running his fingers through to get her locks to relax, she felt like crying because she'd been crying. The whole thing was laughable.

"There," he said at last, circling his arms around her. He settled her between his legs, her back to his chest, but instead of the fear that the same gesture had raised in her before, she only felt shame. He kissed her slumping shoulders. "It's all right," he said softly, brushing her hair back and stroking her arm. "There's nothing to be embarrassed about."

"Oh, I think there is," she murmured.

"Why?" he laughed gently.

She twisted slowly, dragging her eyes up to meet his. "Men like you want a woman who can match their passions."

He let out a breath, smiling tenderly, and shook his head. "Men like me—" He pressed a kiss to the side of her head, his arms holding her. "—want a woman who cares for them but knows her own mind too."

Marigold blinked. "Do you want to be loved?"

A flash of something old and painful filled his eyes before he answered, "Of course I do. Don't we all?"

Marigold nodded, but guilt constricted her throat. She hadn't married him for love. She didn't love him now. But every moment that he sat there, holding her when he could have ravaged her, built the case for loving him in her heart.

She shifted her body a little more toward, him, draping her legs over his under the sheets. "I want to be the right kind of wife for you."

He laughed, brushing the side of her face and kissing her lips lightly. "You already are."

She shook her head, cheeks burning. "No, I mean, I know this part of marriage is important to you. I want to rise to the challenge."

He kissed her again, his lips stretched in a smile. "You mean you think I'm some sort of ravening beast with a gargantuan sexual appetite, and you want to keep me satisfied."

He was joking just enough to put Marigold a little more at ease. "Well, yes, of course," she tried her hand at joking right back. "I wouldn't want that sort of depravity running loose in the halls of Parliament. It's my duty to slake that kind of hunger."

The heat of desire was suddenly back in his eyes, but with a slower sort of smolder. "Do you truly wish to be a slayer of carnal desires?"

Marigold's lips twitched into a grin. He was teasing her, and yet, at the same time, he was making her a serious offer. "Yes," she said, resting a hand on his chest. She could feel his heart pounding beneath his skin. "I'm so ashamed that I panicked, because what I really want is exactly the opposite."

He studied her, the heat and fondness in his eyes telling her that he understood. "There's nothing to be ashamed of," he said, then kissed her with just a hair more passion than his last half-dozen kisses. "If you want to be a sensual lover, then we can work on that together." He kissed her again, parting her lips and teasing his tongue against hers. "It takes practice to learn how to be together this way. It was my fault that I tried to leap straight to step twelve instead of starting at the beginning."

He kissed her with more passion still, his hand slowly rising from her waist to the underside of her breast. This time, his touch felt magical, and the heat of his body stirred deep emotions within her.

"There are steps?" she asked, still breathless, but no longer ashamed of it.

"No," he laughed, momentarily light-hearted. "I made that up. But we should start with the most basic of pleasures before seeking out the more ambitious ones."

"Oh?"

One syllable was all Marigold had time for. He closed his mouth over hers, but instead of just kissing her, he pivoted around her, laying her on her back, her head against the pillow. Gently, he rested his weight over her, nudging between her thighs and into the same position he'd been in when she froze. Only this time, freezing was the furthest thing from her mind. This time she felt as though a fire were building inside of her that could consume her.

"Tell me," he said, serious again. "At any point, if anything I do makes you uncomfortable or frightens you again, tell me and I'll stop immediately."

"You will?" Her heart lifted with a joy far more potent than any caused by his kisses.

"Absolutely." His expression was as solemn as the grave.

"Isn't there a point after which a man can't stop?"

"Balderdash," he said. "That's nothing more than a boorish excuse to push a woman further than she wants, which I will not do with you."

Mad as it was, his offer to stop at any time filled

Marigold with the desire to go on as fast as possible. "If that's the case," she said, stroking a hand up his arm to thread her fingers through his hair, "then please resume step one."

He smiled. "I believe we've already advanced to at least step three." His voice lowered to a sensual growl.

"Then what's step four?"

"This, I believe."

He drew his hand up her side, his fingertips leaving what felt like trails of fire, and closed a hand around her breast. At the same time, he kissed his way down her neck and chest, adjusting the rest of his body as he went, to kiss her breast. When he closed his mouth over her nipple and brushed it with his tongue, Marigold gasped with pleasure. Suddenly, everything felt right. Lady Stanhope was right after all. The sensations his mouth evoked in her were heavenly. Her body, which had felt so normal for most of her life, was suddenly an instrument for him to play, and the music was sweet.

"Do you like that?" he asked after teasing her nipple to a throbbing point.

"I do, actually," she replied, feigning casualness while writhing impatiently under him.

Alex grinned with wicked understanding and shifted so that he could hold and tease her other breast. "I thought you might. I could tell from the way you kissed me in the elevator that you have a passionate nature."

"Barring a few unforeseen hiccups," she whispered, proud that she could joke about what had been painful just minutes before.

Alex nodded gravely. "Already forgotten."

He bent to kiss her other breast, teasing her with his lips

and teeth and taking forever to repeat the delicious things he'd done with her first nipple.

"You have exquisite breasts, you know," he said instead of giving her the pleasure she now craved. "I must inform you that I foresee myself wanting to fondle and suck them quite a bit in the years to come."

His combination of ridiculous formality and semi-crude language sent spirals of need straight to the secret place so intimately nestled against his thigh. "I do wish you'd get on with it in the present, thank you very much," she replied with an equal amount of formality.

He answered with a low laugh, bending to suck her nipple into his mouth. The warm, wet sensation left her panting, and the most scandalous noise escaped from her throat. That only seemed to encourage him as he continued to lick and suck and squeeze one breast then the other.

That in itself left Marigold overheated and hungry for more, but when his mouth left her breast and traveled farther down her stomach, the sensations more and more wicked the lower he went, she began to tremble all over again for entirely different reasons.

She was certain he would stop and return his lips to hers when he reached the thatch of curls between her legs, but to her shock, he kept going. His big hands stroked her thighs, and it wasn't until his thumbs ran along her inner thigh that she realized she'd been steadily inching her legs farther and farther apart. The realization made her tense.

"Are you all right?" he asked, pausing and raising his head. "Do you want me to stop?"

"What are you doing?" she asked in return, panting. She lifted herself on her elbows just a bit. The sight of her legs partially spread with Alex's face between them was as incongruous as it was fascinating. The ache that had been building deep inside of her grew, leaving her breathless with curiosity.

Alex grinned, his eyes flashing. "I believe the crude term for what I'm doing, or rather what I hope to be doing, is eating your pussy." A shiver of excitement zipped through Marigold. "In more technical terms, I'd like to use my mouth and tongue to stimulate your sexual organs to the point of bringing you to orgasm."

He could have been speaking Russian for all she understood from what he'd just said. It was the impish twinkle in his eyes that made her say, "Oh. All right, then," and relax back against the pillows.

"I think you will find this most enjoyable if you open as wide as you can to me," he continued in his devilishly formal tone.

Marigold nodded, then wiggled her hips. She had no idea what she was doing. Alex must have sensed that as well. He stroked his hands down her thighs to her knees, lifting them and pressing them far apart. The resulting movement left Marigold bristling with excitement, and a bit of embarrassment, as the most secret part of her yawned wide for him.

She had about half a second to consider the position the most ludicrous thing she'd ever done before Alex's hands swept up her thighs to delve into the folds between her legs. The sensations his touch evoked were so potent that she sighed aloud and gripped the bedsheets on either side of her.

"You're so wet," he growled, as if that were a good thing. "But I can make you even wetter."

He followed up his words by leaning in and raking his tongue along her opening. Every nerve-ending fired in unison as pleasure throbbed through her. She let out a long moan as his tongue continued to lick and tease, and even to thrust inside of her. She'd never felt anything like it, even in her own explorations of her body—which now seemed pitiful. Such intimate contact should have been terrifying, and indeed, fifteen minutes earlier, it would have been. But now, it was exquisite.

"Oh," she panted as the pulling, tightening sensations inside of her began to grow pitched. "I think...I feel...."

Alex shifted what he was doing, drawing the folds of her flesh aside as he moved his mouth and tongue to tease the button of pleasure nearby. The sensation topped everything else he had done, sending her body over the edge. The world seemed to narrow down to just his mouth over her, his tongue stroking patiently, and then to explode into pure pleasure. She throbbed with it from the inside out.

Alex shifted over her quickly, while she was still lost in the bliss of her body's release. The pressure of something large at her opening joined with the pleasure she already felt. A moment later, he thrust into her.

A flash of pain, like something tearing, cut through the trembling bliss. Marigold sucked in a breath with the realization that he was inside of her. Her virginity was gone. That part of Alex that had startled her so badly when she'd seen it before now stretched her from the inside. And it felt...wonderful.

"Are you all right," he asked her, tension sharp in his voice, as though he were pressed to the limit as much as she was. He held himself perfectly still as he filled her, but she could feel just how much control that took.

She drew in a slow breath, lifting her arms to hold onto him. Instinct told her to shift her legs as well. He helped her along, positioning first one leg, then the other over his hips.

"Like that," he panted, jerking slightly against her as if

failing in his attempts not to move. He bent down and kissed her, but was panting too hard to draw it out. "I need to move now, my darling. Are you ready?"

She nodded, breathless with anticipation. Was there more to mating than just being joined together as they were?

Yes, there absolutely was. Alex began to move, using small, gentle strokes at first as he guided himself in and out of her. Each thrust brought a wealth of new sensations with it. They were wonderful. The feeling of being possessed and stretched intensified as his strokes grew longer and more powerful. Pleasure began to build within her all over again.

Alex's sighs evolved into something deeper, more guttural, as whatever was driving him took over. Marigold felt the moment his careful consideration of her comfort gave way to ages old instinct. His every thrust was filled with purpose and pleasure, and she cried out in time with them, sinking into the amazing feeling of him using her body to reach for what he needed. But there was power in the way he needed her, and when at last he tensed and growled with release as he spilled himself inside of her, a second, throbbing orgasm hit her.

With completion came an enveloping sense of content-ment. Alex relaxed, his weight strangely comforting as it pressed on her. She stroked his back as he caught his breath, tensing her inner muscles just a bit to make sure he was still inside of her. She loved the feeling, now that the first shock and pain were over, and she wanted much, much more of it.

All too soon, Alex recovered enough strength to roll to the side, breaking free of her. Marigold felt his absence acutely. Her body burned from exertion, but she still welcomed Alex's arms around her as he pulled her body against his.

"What do you think?" he panted. "Should we do that again sometime when we're both not exhausted?"

"I think it would be a pleasant way to pass an evening," she gasped in reply, taking his hand from where it rested on her side and moving it to cup her breast, just in case he thought her casual sarcasm represented real indifference.

He went to work right away, kneading her breast and teasing her nipple to keep her pleasure simmering. "A few hours sleep, and we can try to reach step seven," he laughed.

"Dear heavens." Marigold tingled with need that was already renewing. "That was only six out of twelve?"

He kissed her cheek, then collapsed against the pillow. "Who said twelve was as high as the steps go?"

A shiver of anticipation shot through Marigold, even as she forced herself to close her eyes and let sleep take her. At this rate, she was going to have to name her first-born daughter Katya in honor of Lady Stanhope. She certainly owed the woman a mountain of thanks.

CHAPTER 7

*L*azy contentment greeted Alex with the morning
sun. He hadn't slept so well in years, and not just
because he and Marigold wore themselves out the
night before, and once in the middle of the night. Silence
blanketed the elaborate bedroom, broken only by
Marigold's deep steady breathing. She lay tucked against
his side, one arm draped haphazardly across his chest. Her
head rested on his shoulder, and one of her legs hooked over
his. It wasn't the most comfortable position he'd ever woken
in, at least not physically, but the intimacy and tenderness
of it warmed his heart, turning him into a sentimental
old fool.

She was his wife, something he'd never dreamed he'd
have. The bed they lay in was soft and warm, peace reigned.
It was as far from the bustle and noise and stress of Parliament as he had ever been. The world's problems seemed
distant and unimportant. It felt as though he might actually
have half a chance to be the man he'd always wanted to be, a
good husband, in Marigold's arms. He let out a long breath

and settled into the pillows, wanting the moment to last forever.

Which was why the hesitant knock at the bedroom door sent spikes of frustration through him. He tensed so hard and fast that Marigold stirred awake.

"Sir?" Phillips's muffled, embarrassed voice came from the other side of the door.

Alex let out a breath, rubbing a hand over his face. He would murder the man if his reasons for interrupting the morning after his wedding were anything other than national catastrophe.

The knock sounded again, slightly louder. "I'm sorry, sir?"

Marigold drew in a quick breath, clutching the bedcovers to her chest and burrowing against Alex's side as though Phillips could see through the door. "Who is it? What do they want?" she whispered.

"It's Philips, my soon-to-be late man of business," Alex growled, then raised his voice to say, "You'd better have a damn good reason to come knocking at my bedroom door the morning after my wedding."

There was a slight pause, then Phillips said, "Turpin has called a special session to vote on his repressive bill, sir. Rumor has it that he expects there to not be enough members present to vote it down, since so many of your key supporters were up late celebrating."

Alex growled an oath that made Marigold's eyes pop wide and pink splash her cheeks. He didn't even have time to kiss her as he leapt from the bed and marched across the room. He had to avoid piles of wedding garments as he headed to the door.

"When does the session start, and do you have any idea

when during the session this blasted bill will come to a vote?" he asked through the door.

"It's hard to say, sir," Phillips replied. "Turpin isn't following normal procedure by any means, but he has enough supporters to get away with it. They say Disraeli is willing to support him."

"Blast that man," Alex thundered.

"He was at the wedding," Marigold said.

Alex glanced over to find her sitting up in bed, the sheet held to her chest but not doing much to hide her tempting figure. Her golden hair spilled in tousled waves around her creamy shoulders. Her lips were still slightly red from their night's activity, begging to be kissed again. In spite of everything, a surge of need ran through him, tightening his groin and pushing his frustration higher.

He banged his fist on the doorframe. So much for being a good husband. "I'll be there as soon as I can," he sighed, wincing.

"Yes, sir. I'll see about rousing your supporters and getting them to Westminster immediately."

"Good man."

Alex pushed away from the door, glancing hurriedly around the room for the change of clothes Phillips supposedly left for him the day before. Knowing Turpin and his crooked ways, he wouldn't have time to bathe properly or shave before dashing halfway across town to Westminster. The blackguard would pay for this.

"Are you leaving?" Marigold asked, scooting her way to the edge of the bed, the covers still clutched around her.

A second wave of regret and frustration stung Alex. "My darling, I'm afraid I have to." He crossed to the side of the bed as she stood, and took her in his arms. The sheet fell away, leaving them skin-to-skin, which did nothing to stiffen

his resolve to rush to Parliament to defeat Turpin. It stiffened other things instead. "I'm so sorry," he said, tilting her
head up to kiss her. In their hours-old marriage, he'd already
apologized to her far too much.

"I...I understand," she murmured when their kiss ended
and he stepped away to search for his clothes. "You're an
important man. The nation needs you in vital ways."

Alex glanced over his shoulder at her as he poured
water from the pitcher on the washstand into the matching
bowl and splashed the essential parts of himself. Marigold
didn't look as though she understood at all. She looked
devastated. And she had every right to. "Today would have
been a lot of fuss and nonsense anyhow," he said,
attempting to make her feel better, certain he was only
making things worse. "While I'm working, why don't you
make your grand entrance at Croydon House and show all
my servants who their new mistress is?" He tried to make it
sound like a treat when, in fact, he'd been looking forward
to presenting her as his wife and the new mistress of the
house himself.

"That sounds lovely," she said, gathering her robe from
the chair where it was draped and putting it on. She tried to
smile, but it didn't look convincing to Alex.

He cursed himself and cursed Turpin doubly as he
dried himself off and practically threw his clothes on.
Phillips would have had a fit to see him make a mess of
things, but Marigold came over to help. Between the two of
them, he was dressed, his shoes were put on, and a comb
pushed through his hair in about five minutes. Alex
marched for the door, but paused to take Marigold in his
arms for one more kiss before opening it.

"I will make this up to you," he promised. "I swear it.
I'm so sorry." He was already picking out which jeweler he

would visit on his way home from Westminster, whenever that would be.

"Be dazzling today," she told him, stroking his stubbly cheek and kissing him one more time. "Don't let Turpin win."

"Believe me, I won't," he said, stole one last kiss, then rushed from the room.

HE WAS GONE. MARIGOLD LET OUT A HEAVY BREATH and stared at the door Alex had closed behind him when he left the room. It was the morning after their wedding. They'd spent the most magical night in each other's arms. She'd discovered things about herself that she would never had guessed at, and already, Alex was gone.

Slowly, she dragged herself away from the door to flop in the chair where her robe had been draped, wondering if mistresses and secret paramours felt the same sense of abandonment after their assignations. She glanced across to the second, empty chair, Alex's robe untouched over its back. A cold knot formed in her gut.

No, it wasn't fair of her to resent him for leaving. She pushed herself to stand, even though she'd barely settled in the chair, and moved to the washstand to clean up. The intimate parts of her still carried traces of Alex and the way he'd made love to her. She blushed hot at the realization, feeling unusually awkward as she wiped herself clean. At least it all meant there was solid evidence that she could end up with child soon, if they kept that kind of activity up.

If Alex wasn't called away to Parliament every time they got cozy with each other.

With a frustrated sigh, she pushed that thought away and focused on practicality. She did have an entire new household to introduce herself to. And her father and siblings would certainly be down for breakfast soon, even though they'd been up late reveling. She finished washing and rang the bell to call for the maid to bring a proper bath, then set about tidying the room and making the best of the situation.

She was washed, dressed, and back in her chair, lacing her boots as Judy, one of her father's maids, picked up her wedding dress and Alex's clothes from the night before when the envelope Lady Stanhope had given to Alex fell from the inner pocket of his jacket.

"I'm sorry, miss—I mean, Mrs. Croydon," Judy said with a smile and a blush. "I'll get it." She bent to retrieve the envelope.

"No, no. I'll take that." Marigold rose from her chair and crossed to take the envelope.

"It was a beautiful party, madam," Judy whispered to her, as though she wasn't sure she should be addressing a woman who had been elevated so high the night before. "You looked like a princess."

"Thank you, Judy." Marigold's first genuine smile of the day appeared. "But you don't have to be so formal with me all of a sudden. I'm still the same old Marigold I was yesterday." She winked.

"Oh, no, madam." Judy looked scandalized. "You're a married woman now, the wife of an important man." She leaned closer and whispered, "They say he could be Prime Minister someday."

"And you can say you knew me when I was just simple Miss Bellowes," Marigold teased her. She adored Judy, and Gretta and the rest of her father's servants. The fuss and nonsense of maintaining rigid social ranks had always irritated her, especially considering her grandparents had only been a half-step above the level of servants themselves.

"It's a shame that Mr. Croydon was called away, though," Judy went on, laying Marigold's dress across the bed.

"You heard about that?" A twist of uneasiness and renewed disappointment washed through Marigold.

Judy sent her a sympathetic look. "He's doing important work though, isn't he?"

"He is." Marigold smiled, but it wasn't powerful enough to drown her discouragement. She tapped the envelope against her free hand, then marched for the door. "Thank you for your hard work, Judy," she said as she exited.

Alex was doing important work, and he was an important man, but Turpin was the heart of the problem. She strode quickly through the halls of her family home one last time, heading for the breakfast room. Alex would still be in bed with her if it weren't for Mr. Daniel Turpin. She and Alex might still be doing delicious things. Alex was sensual, and he'd been skilled enough to turn what had started out as raging fear into desire that was far from satisfied. She wanted more of that, more time to explore the wonders of marriage. She wanted more of her husband, and Turpin had taken that away from her.

The breakfast room was abandoned, just as Marigold had expected. Her father usually took breakfast in his study when the entire family was in residence, and her sisters were notorious lay-a-beds, particularly after parties. Marigold's own arrival in the room was so unexpected that Clarence, their head footman, had to scramble and rush to bring enough food up from the kitchens for her to eat.

As she waited, she opened the envelope and read its contents. Within minutes, her cheeks burned pink with shock and anger. At the party the night before, all Marigold had been able to see of the papers was the name Ruby Murdoch as mentioned in a constable's report. The story spelled out in the rest of the papers was a horror.

A young woman named Ruby Murdoch had been arrested for prostitution. She had a newborn infant with her that was in a terrible state. The constable who arrested Ruby had enough of a heart to see that both she and the baby were given medical care before being shipped off to the St. Pancras workhouse.

The story had deeper, more sinister roots than that, though. Other papers in the stack Lady Stanhope had given Alex detailed reports that Ruby Murdoch had been employed at a place called the Black Strap Club, although Marigold wasn't sure that employment was the right word. The papers were cryptic, but the description of the club sent a chill down her spine. It didn't sound like the sort of place a well-born woman could even conceive of, let alone know about.

But Ruby's story went further back than that. The oldest papers in the packet were employment records from the house of none other than Turpin. Ruby had been a maid in his house. Along with the simple records was what looked like a letter from a Mrs. Yates to a Mrs. Belvedere, gossiping about the ill treatment Ruby had had at Turpin's hands. Marigold puzzled through the details as she read. Mrs. Yates had never had a bit of trouble from Ruby, and indeed, had found her to be a good, hard worker and a conscientious girl. Then all of a sudden, she was found to be with child and Turpin demanded she be dismissed.

With a gasp, the pieces flew into place. Turpin had interfered with the girl. He himself was the father of her child. And instead of taking responsibility in any way, he had cast poor Ruby off. But there had to be more to it than that. Shameful as it was, great and powerful men got their maids in trouble all the time, and the fate of those poor women was bleak as a rule. Lady Stanhope would not have presented Alex with the information about Ruby if she were just another fallen creature. There had to be something about the case that was scandalous enough to end Turpin's political career, but what?

"Good heavens, what are you doing here?" Marigold's sister, Flora, was so startled to see her as she turned the corner into the breakfast room that she jumped. "Shouldn't you be...otherwise occupied?" A sly grin spread across her face.

Marigold stood, gathering up the papers and stuffing them back in the envelope. "Alex was called to an emergency session of Parliament this morning," she explained in a rush. "And I'm afraid I need to be off myself."

"Off?" Flora blinked rapidly. "Wherever to?"

"Croydon House, of course." Marigold held the envelope containing Ruby Murdoch's story to her chest, praying her sister wouldn't ask about it. "I have an entire household to take control of, after all."

"Yes, you do." Flora swept over and gave her cheek a kiss. "I'm so proud of you, Mari. I always knew you'd make a splendid match someday and that you were just holding out for exactly the right man."

On any other day, the flattery would have touched Marigold deeply. She was grateful for her sister's support, but her mind was so far away at that moment that it was all she could do to stay focused enough to kiss her cheek in return before rushing out to the hall.

"Levins, could you call for a carriage to take me to

Croydon House?" she asked the butler when she reached the front hall.

"Certainly, miss—forgive me, madam." Levins smiled at her like a proud papa. "Shall I have Gretta bring your coat and hat as well?"

"Yes, please."

Levins bowed before disappearing down a side corridor.

Marigold was left to wait in the front hall, pacing and running her fingertips along the edges of the envelope. What could be so scandalous about a fallen maid that it would necessitate a man being removed from his office in the House of Commons? Men could get away with murder and keep their seat, and Marigold was certain some probably had. But why would Lady Stanhope consider a minor kerfuffle scandalous enough to be presented as a wedding present?

The questions were still rolling around in her head as her father's simplest, open buggy pulled up in front of the door. Gretta had already brought Marigold's hat and coat and helped her put them on, so she hurried out into the street, still puzzling things over.

"Good morning, Mrs. Croydon," Able, her father's driver, greeted her in his broad, London accent, with a cheerful grin and a wink. "I'm surprised to see you up an' about with the dawn chorus." He hopped down from the buggy to give her a hand into the back.

Marigold was done with giving explanations for not being in bed the morning after her wedding, so she cut straight to business as she settled into the seat. "I'm heading to Croydon House this morning," she told him as he resumed his place to drive. "But I'd like to run a quick errand first."

"Anything for you, Mrs. Croydon." He touched the

brim of his hat, then gathered up the reins. He tapped the single horse pulling the buggy into a walk, heading toward the end of the street, then asked, "Where to?"

"Do you know of a place called the Black Strap Club?" Marigold asked.

Able pulled the horse to an abrupt stop and turned to stare at her. His expression turned grave, and splotches of color formed on his cheeks. "Where did you hear that name, miss?" he asked, forgetting her new form of address.

Marigold suddenly felt like a young miss who had put a foot wrong. "I read about it," she said, not exactly lying, but not willing to divulge the truth. "But I'm still not sure what exactly it is."

Able glanced anxiously from side to side, as though someone on the peaceful, empty street might call for the police if he put a foot out of place. He leaned closer to Marigold and said, "It's not a seemly place, miss. Not even now you're married an' all. It's the sort of place where, if me mum heard I even knew about it, she'd box me ears."

Marigold frowned, feeling as though she were inches from discovering what Lady Stanhope knew. "Is it a broth-el?" she whispered.

Able's cheeks turned a darker shade of pink. "Worse than that, if the rumors are true," he whispered in return.

Marigold frowned. What could be worse than a brothel? Lady Stanhope must have known. But between the suggestion that such a place was even possible and the anxious look Able gave her, she didn't have the nerve to ask to be taken to Lady Stanhope's townhouse to ask about it. Besides, Lady Stanhope was probably still in bed, along with the rest of the world, after the wedding party. And knowing her, she wasn't in bed alone.

Instead, Marigold leaned forward and cautiously asked, "Could we at least drive by the...place?"

Able frowned and rubbed his chin as if considering it. "I guess it wouldn't hurt to pass through that way. Fast," he added. "Without stopping."

"Thank you, Able. And once we've seen it, you can take me on to Croydon House."

Able nodded, his humor changed to business. "Yes, Mrs. Croydon."

He tapped the horse into motion again, and they headed out onto a wider, busier road. Marigold continued to hold the envelope containing Ruby Murdoch's story tight, irrationally worried that she'd let it go and it would float away as the buggy sped on. For whatever reason, she couldn't shake the feeling that her fledgling marriage depended on bringing Turpin down with the story of Ruby.

The biggest surprise about the Black Strap Club was how little time it took to pass by it.

"There you go, ma'am," Able said with a nod, his jaw tight, as they passed a stately, unassuming Georgian edifice surprisingly close to Kensington Palace.

Marigold leaned forward to get a better look. There was nothing at all that would hint the building was anything more than a large private residence. Even the front door was boring, though it was painted with black lacquer. There wasn't so much as a sign giving the building a name.

"That's it?" Marigold let out an impatient sigh.

"That's it," Able echoed gravely.

Marigold was on the verge of believing she'd been sold a bill of goods, or that Lady Stanhope was having a laugh at Alex's expense, and that there was nothing wrong with the Black Strap Club at all, when the pale face of a young woman appeared in one of the upstairs windows. The woman couldn't have been more than sixteen, and even though she was yards away, Marigold could clearly make out a huge bruise on the side of her face. She glanced out over the garden across the street with a look of longing that broke Marigold's heart, as if she had looked out at it day after day but never set foot in it.

The woman turned her head just enough to meet Marigold's eyes. Something close to panic lit the woman's expression, and she opened her mouth. Marigold had the horrifying feeling the woman was about to cry out for help, but instead, she snapped back to face something inside the room. Then she disappeared entirely.

A chill shot down Marigold's spine. "Drive on, Able," she said, her voice hoarse.

"Yes, ma'am," Able replied, sounding as eager to get away as she was.

Marigold leaned back against her seat, hoping she hadn't been seen. Her heart raced, and her mind immediately connected the frightened face in the window with Ruby Murdoch. Perhaps there *was* something worse than a brothel. She wasn't sure she wanted to dig into the case after all for fear of what she would find.

Then again, if just a glimpse of a face could instill her with such dread, if Ruby Murdoch had ended up in that place because of Turpin, perhaps Lady Stanhope knew how to bring Turpin down after all.

CHAPTER 8

$\mathcal{I}$t was a bloody big waste of time. Alex ground his teeth in weary frustration as the hired hack carrying him home from Westminster rocked through crowded streets.

"I'm sorry, sir," Phillips apologized from the seat facing him. In spite of the man's bright ginger hair and almost cherubic good looks that made him appear a decade younger and far more innocent than he was, he looked as depressed as a thief on his way to the gallows. "I didn't know it was a ruse. If I had, I never would have disturbed you and Mrs. Croydon."

"It's not your fault," Alex growled.

In point of fact, it was Turpin's fault, through and through. The blackguard had deliberately orchestrated the charade of a vote with the expressed purpose of dragging him and the rest of his friends out of bed and making them sit in the Commons chamber looking like the dog's dinner for interminable hours of debate about sewers. Alex would have walked out—or punched the villain in the nose—but Turpin and his cronies had organized the speeches and discussion in such a way as to hint that if any of them left, the nefarious new bill would be discussed immediately.

It had all been a pointless, nasty scheme, designed to hurt and humiliate him personally, and it had worked. Alex had no idea how he would explain the whole thing to Marigold. The higher duty of politics didn't seem half as lofty as he'd always believed it to be when faced with the reality of disappointing a wife.

"Bugger all," he burst out as the carriage came to a stop in front of his townhouse, punching the seat beside him.

"What, sir?" Phillips sat up.

"I was going to stop by the jewelers to purchase some little bauble as an apology gift for Marigold." Less than twenty-four hours, and he was already a miserable failure as a husband. He shouldn't have been surprised.

"I could go for you," Phillips suggested.

Alex shook his head and sighed heavily as Long, one of his footmen, opened the carriage door. "You've been up longer than I have. Go rest."

"Thank you, sir."

Alex stepped down from the hack and glanced up at the homey edifice of his London house. He'd chosen the property in the burgeoning new borough of South Kensington for its convenience and the modern facilities being built into the new homes, but he'd come to like the warm, orange brick façade with its fiddly ornamentation. It was a far cry from the peace and beauty of Winterberry Park, but everywhere couldn't be Wiltshire.

It was an even greater comfort to step through the front door and have Marigold standing there, looking radiant in a light blue day dress that complimented her coloring, a bright smile on her face. She had a curious flash of excitement and determination in her eyes too.

"So?" she asked, striding across the front hall to take his hands. "Did you defeat Turpin roundly?"

He answered with a low, wry laugh and a shake of his head. "Turpin never even brought his damned bill up for debate." He paused then added, "Sorry, that's no excuse for language."

Marigold's brow furrowed in confusion. "Then why all the fuss?"

He brushed a hand across the side of her face, smiling wearily at her. "He was trying to keep me from you, and he knew that only the direst emergency would do that."

Marigold stared at him as though he said he'd gone to fight a dragon. "Is anyone truly that petty?"

"Yes," Alex answered without hesitation.

Marigold's frown deepened. "I suppose that does make sense, though." She indulged in a thoughtful look for a moment before meeting his eyes again. "I need to talk to you about Lady Stanhope's gift."

Alex's brow shot up. He'd forgotten about Katya's mischief, and, given the circumstances, it was the last thing he expected Marigold to bring up. "Could it perhaps wait until after I've had supper and a bath?" he appealed to her, his expression softening.

She broke into a compassionate smile. "Of course it can." She hesitated for the barest moment, then lifted to her feet to gently kiss his lips.

After the day he'd had, nothing could have been more welcome or more wonderful. In spite of the fact that Phillips was standing right there, still not resting as he'd been ordered, and Long as well, he drew Marigold fully into his arms and kissed her with all the passion of a man who had been forced away from his bride.

"Well," Marigold breathed, eyes bright, when he let her go. "Perhaps Ruby Murdoch can wait after all."

Alex blinked. "Who's Ruby Murdoch."

Marigold laughed, hugging him, then stepping back. "Why don't I explain while you have your supper?"

"Why don't you explain while I have my bath?" he countered.

Marigold's cheeks flushed a tantalizing shade of pink. "Whichever you'd like."

He'd like not to have to worry about any of it. He'd like to be in Wiltshire, with Marigold and with James—who, blast it all, he still hadn't had a chance to explain. But he was stuck with what was available to him. Long set off immediately to run a bath in the technological marvel that was the upstairs bathroom of his townhouse, while Phillips volunteered to head to the kitchen to inform Mrs. Clifford, his housekeeper, that he would take supper in his room.

"I trust you're finding your way around the house?" he asked as he took Marigold's hand and headed upstairs.

"It's a splendid house," she replied. "And your staff are all so accommodating. They were surprised when I showed up without you, but we made each other's acquaintances quite nicely."

It was a new sort of comfort to have Marigold chatter on about things he would normally never have given his attention to as he dragged his weary self up to the bedroom that he would now share with her. She helped him remove his jacket and shoes, and for a few fleeting moments, he considered forgoing the bath and just taking her to bed and making love to her for hours. But he wasn't the young man he used to be. His stomach came first. And she would probably appreciate him bathing and possibly even shaving before bedding her.

The bath was ready before his supper tray was brought up, but only by a matter of minutes.

"Have you eaten?" he asked Marigold as he stepped into the soothingly warm water of his bath.

She took her time answering, possibly because she was too busy leaning against the doorway that led from the bathroom to the bedroom, watching him with fascination. A hungry smile curved on her lips that had nothing to do with food. Alex couldn't help but gloat just a little. He may have been a few years past his prime, but he'd always taken good care of himself. If his wife enjoyed looking at him, then he'd have to find more excuses to be naked in front of her.

"Oh." She blinked, coming out of her increasingly heated observations. "Yes, I ate earlier. I didn't know when you'd be home." Her smile grew to something close to wickedness, and she stepped back into the bedroom.

Alex missed her instantly, laughing at himself for his foolishness. He sank against the back of the tub, closing his eyes and letting the steam soothe him for a moment.

"Does Turpin ever intend to bring his bill up for a vote, or was the whole thing today just a way to vex you?" Marigold called from the other room.

Alex opened his eyes and craned his neck to try to look into the bedroom, but Marigold was out of his line of sight. "Knowing Turpin's lot, they really are planning whatever measures they can to counteract what we're trying to do. But the wheels of government move slowly in the best of times." He found a cake of soap on the edge of the tub and started washing in earnest.

"But it would be nice to remove Turpin from the picture," Marigold said.

Alex stopped mid-scrub. There was a note of cunning in her tone, as if she'd discovered something. But of course, if she'd read whatever it was that Katya sent to him, she probably had.

"After today," he said, resuming his bath, "I'd go to great lengths to give Turpin a taste of his own medicine. Opposing me on political grounds is one thing, but today's nonsense was purely personal."

"And I suppose you'd like a personal way to get back at him?"

Alex frowned. Was he the sort to stoop as low as Turpin had? At heart, he had always prided himself on staying above the mudslinging free-for-all that politics often descended into. But in his current mood, considering what Turpin's trick had taken him away from, he was in the mood for revenge.

"I might consider it," he said, his words coming out darker than he'd intended them to.

A moment later, Marigold appeared in the doorway wearing nothing but a silk robe, her hair loose around her shoulders. Her curves were outlined to perfection, and the flimsy silk of her robe did nothing to hide the tight peaks of her nipples. Alex dropped the soap. His cock jerked to life as his pulse shot through the roof.

"Turpin will rue the day he tried to come between the two of us," he said, hoarse with longing.

"He will rue the day for more than just that."

There was a triumphant gleam in Marigold's green eyes as she stepped deeper into the room, toying with the sash of her robe. She hadn't needed to put it on in the first place, assuming her intentions were what he thought they were, but the anticipation of waiting for her to shed the useless garment only made Alex harder.

"As it turns out, Turpin may have been too much of a

villain for his own good," Marigold said as she neared the edge of the tub.

"How so?" His heart pounded with the need to reach out and pull her into the bath with him, even though he was thoroughly enjoying simply looking at her.

She reached the edge of the tub and sat. Her robe opened enough to give him a glimpse of her bare leg and thigh. Supper suddenly took second place to other activities.

"The information Lady Stanhope gave you was about a former maid of Turpin's named Ruby Murdoch," she said, more businesslike than flirtatious. "I haven't had much time to study it, but from what I gather, Turpin got the maid in trouble." She glanced down and away with a flash of embarrassment before going on. "She is in St. Pancras workhouse now with her infant, but she was sent off to work at a place called the Black Strap Club first."

Disgust and fear for the woman he didn't know shot through Alex, flattening his growing erection and dousing his fire. "The bastard," he growled.

Curiosity pinched Marigold's face. "I made Able drive me past the Black Strap Club on the way here, and—"

"You did what?" Alex sat up, sloshing water close to the edge of the tub.

Marigold had the good sense to blush and look ashamed. "Able warned me that it was worse than a brothel, and yes, the place felt sinister to me. I saw a girl in one of the windows...." She swallowed, but didn't go on.

Alex placed a wet hand on her thigh, both to comfort her and to remind himself that she was there with him, under his protection, and that evil like the kind Lord Shayles peddled couldn't touch her.

"It is a brothel that specializes in deviant sexual practices," he told her, needing to be honest, even though it killed him to damage her innocence that way. "Although the man who owns the place denies it, many believe the women who 'work' there are not at liberty. That is part of the appeal for the wretched souls who frequent the place."

A horrified look twisted on Marigold's face. "You mean, that woman I saw in the window was enslaved?"

Alex's stomach twisted. "Possibly."

"I should have done something." Marigold stood, in a panic. "I should have called the police or gone to her rescue somehow."

He took her hands as she moved to wring them, pulling her back down to sit. "My darling, it wouldn't have done any good. The police are aware of the establishment, but either afraid to do anything about it due to the influence of the men who patronize the place or are being paid off by its owner."

"But that's appalling."

"It is," Alex agreed. He didn't like the direction the conversation had gone in, and was no longer comfortable as he twisted in the tub, digging his knees into the side, in order to continue holding Marigold's hands. Something had to be done. "Why don't you join me, and we can wash away the filth that you've had a brush with?"

Marigold's anxious look softened as she focused on him. It was clear that she wouldn't forget what she'd just learned about the darker side of the world, but also that she was strong enough to rise above it.

"We must do something about Ruby," she said, squeezing his hands.

"The maid?"

"Yes. I haven't told you the full story yet," she went on. "Between the time she spent at that horrible club and St.

Pancras, she was arrested for prostitution. Which means that even though she did find a way to escape from that place, she fell out of the frying pan and into the fire. And while the workhouse may be a step up, those places are wretched. We need to do something."

Alex let go of one of Marigold's hands so that he could shift back to a more comfortable position and frowned in thought. Katya had given them Ruby Murdoch's story for a reason, not just to shock Marigold. If Turpin truly had impregnated his maid then sold her into slavery at the Black Strap Club, and if all of that could be proved and made public, a scandal would be the least that would happen. If the case were presented right, Turpin could end up in prison. But only if they were careful every step of the way. And the first bit of care they needed to take was to get Miss Murdoch and her child out of the workhouse and into safety and security.

"I'll send Phillips to fetch her from the workhouse as soon as possible," he said, deciding on a course of action as he spoke. He glanced to Marigold. "We can keep her here, under our employ, if that's what she wants, while the whole matter is investigated further. And if she feels secure enough, she might be willing to share her side of the story."

Relief burst through Marigold's expression, her shoulders sagging. "Thank you, Alex. Even if Turpin can't be brought to justice for his crimes, I'll feel better knowing Ruby is cared for."

Alex met her smile with one of his own. There was a slim chance that hiring a notorious maid would upset his staff, but if worst came to worst, he would relocate Miss Murdoch to Winterberry Park.

"Now," he said, his hand sliding from her hand to her thigh, fingering the hem of her robe in an effort to expose more of her leg, "why don't you take off that silly robe and join me while the water is still warm?"

Marigold's smile turned impish, and she stood, tugging at her robe's sash. "Don't you like this lovely bit of frippery my sister Flora gave me as a wedding gift?"

He was so grateful the mood had shifted back to where he wanted it to be that it made him reckless. "I like what's under it more."

She was close enough for him to grasp one end of the sash. He tugged before Marigold was ready, the sash untied, and her robe fluttered open, giving him a spectacular view of her luscious body. The skin of her stomach and thighs was pink and creamy. Her breasts were generous but still pert, and her nipples were large and a tempting shade of dark rose. The curve of her hips had blood rushing back to his groin, and the bush of curls that hid her womanly treasure left his fingers itching to explore her.

There was still a hint of nervous excitement in her eyes as she let the robe slide from her shoulders and tossed it aside. As responsive as she'd ended up being the night before, he forcibly reminded himself that she had virtually no experience and wasn't ready for the full fire of his passion yet. That didn't stop him from reaching for her waist as she stepped into the tub and drawing her down to straddle his thighs.

She made a fetching sound, somewhere between a gasp of awe and a squeak of discomfort, as she settled into the water with him. "What a strange sensation."

"Don't tell me you've never had a bath before," he teased, having a hard time focusing on levity with her breasts so close to his face. He splashed warm water, fragrant from the soap he'd used earlier, up her sides and closed his hands over her breasts.

"No," she laughed, moving uneasily above him, almost as if she were afraid to let her cunny rub against his growing erection. "But never with someone else."

"I think you'll find it's rather delightful," he teased, circling his arms to her back and swishing more water over her. "Although I'm not as nimble as I once was, so don't expect fireworks."

"Fireworks in the water?" She arched one eyebrow.

Desire shot through him. She was too inexperienced to know what a simple, teasing look like that could do to him, but she would learn in a hurry. He nudged her to lean forward enough for him to kiss her while still lounging against the back of the tub. She caught on, grasping the edge of the tub as their lips met.

Her lips held so much sweetness that he closed his eyes and reveled in their touch. Between the warm water, the depth of his exhaustion, and the glow of desire filling him, he felt no need to rush. Gently, he coaxed her mouth open and began a slow exploration with his tongue while his hands smoothed down her back to her hips. He kissed her languidly, subtly urging her to relax and bring her hips into full contact with his. He would let her take the lead this time, but that didn't mean he wasn't impatient to feel her heat against his cock.

"I like kissing you," she said after they'd been at it for several long minutes.

"How fortunate for us both," he murmured. "I hope you enjoy other things as well." He shamelessly circled his hands around her backside, guiding her to grind against him.

She drew in a quick breath and whispered, "Can you do that in the bath?"

"With enough effort, you can do that wherever you'd like," he replied, teasing her with his most sultry grin.

Her already pink cheeks flushed deeper, and sparks filled her eyes. "Show me how," she whispered, moving awkwardly against him.

"I'm not sure how comfortable it will be for your knees in this tub."

"My knees are not particularly concerned at the moment," she said.

He chuckled, adjusting to what he hoped would be the most comfortable position for her. "You'll have to do most of the moving," he explained, positioning her hips above him, then taking hold of himself to guide his way to her entrance. "Go slowly until you get the hang of it, then at whatever speed feels best to you."

She nodded, excited but hesitant, until he arched into her. She sucked in a breath, her expression turning heavy-lidded with pleasure as he penetrated her. The look made him want to thrust hard and repeatedly into her until she was crying out with orgasm, but he stayed as still as he could, moving his hands back to her hips and guiding her to press down, taking him in farther.

"Oh, my," she gasped, taking in more and more of him until he was lodged so deep he thought he might lose his mind. That feeling only intensified when she tightened her inner muscles around him, biting her lip, and clearly enjoying the sensation of sheathing him.

"You can move now," he choked out, hands still on her hips.

"Like this?"

She pulled back, and Alex caught his breath at the friction. He stopped her just before he slipped out, shifting the pressure of his hands to show her what to do.

"Oh, I see," she said with a shuddering breath and drew him in again.

She was a fast learner, although it was torture just to lay there, feet braced against the end of the tub, holding her hips while she slowly taught herself to ride him. He had to promise himself that, if he could just be patient now and let her have her way with him, he would make love to her the way he wanted to later, when they were in bed. Now it was her turn to find pleasure in him, and there was something sinfully sweet in letting her inexperience play itself out.

"This is nice," she panted as she picked up her pace. She still gripped the back of the tub on either side of his head for purchase, but had leaned forward to the point where her breasts brushed his chest with each thrust. "This is exceptionally nice."

"It is," he agreed with a moan, not sure how long he could hold out. He didn't think for a moment that he deserved the sensual sweetness of his young wife riding him in a way most society wives would never dream of. But as long as she didn't mind learning to make love like a mistress instead of the way polite and stuffy advice manuals told women they should engage with their husbands, then he wasn't going to complain.

He let her continue at her own pace until her soft moans and cries hinted she was frustrated at not quite being able to reach release. Then he tilted her back just a bit, sliding his hand between her curls, his fingers seeking out her folds. She gasped when he reached and rubbed her clitoris, and the energy in her thrusts was renewed. Suddenly, they were working for a common goal, and she arched into him, truly striving for it.

The sight of her body, wet and arched back, her breasts bouncing in the water, her nipples hard, her head thrown back with pleasure, was so potent that he almost couldn't hold out until she came. It was a blessing when she gasped and cried out as her inner muscles contracted around him. He burst a moment later, letting out a fierce cry as the water in the tub splashed every which way in response to their combined movement.

All too soon, the magical sensation passed, and they both let go of the last of their energy, sinking into the cooling water. He grabbed the edges of the tub as she let go, sagging against him. A deep sense of contentment, like every last bit of the frustration and disappointment he'd had to deal with that day was worth it, filled him.

"And now," he panted, stroking one hand down her back to squeeze her backside, "supper sounds like a good idea."

She lifted herself up to stare at him, blinking. "Will your appetites never be satisfied, my husband?" She then burst into giggles that left him buzzing with happiness from the inside out.

He arched a brow, stealing a kiss. "With you as my wife? I don't think they will."

But he was ready to spend as long as it took attempting to find out.

CHAPTER 9

*A*fter a rocky start, Marigold settled into what she considered a triumphant married life with joy, and more pleasure than she ever could have bargained for. Alex was passionate, patient, and inventive in bed. She was embarrassed to look back on those first moments of her wedding night and how terrified she had been. Lady Stanhope had been right about how delightful sexual relations could be, and for the first six weeks of wedded bliss, not a day went by when Marigold and Alex weren't wrapped up in each other, sweating and panting as they experienced well beyond twelve steps of carnal bliss.

It left Marigold in a triumphant mood, especially when it came to tackling the situation of Ruby Murdoch.

"Are you settling in well?" she asked Ruby as the young woman brought her hat and gloves to the front door, where Marigold was waiting for the carriage to be brought around to take her to the Palace of Westminster. It was late July, and Parliament was closing for the summer at last. She and Alex were heading to Winterberry Park, Alex's country house in Wiltshire, the next day, but Ruby, who had been rescued from the workhouse within days of Marigold and Alex's wedding, would be staying at Croydon House.

"Well enough, ma'am," Ruby answered with a curtsy, her eyes downcast.

Marigold fastened her hat to her elaborate hairstyle, studying Ruby as she did. The young woman had been in a terrible state when Phillips had brought her back from the workhouse. Her skin had been pale and clammy, her face sunken, and she'd flinched at even the slightest advance any man made toward her. Except, perhaps, Phillips. She'd clutched her baby—a tiny girl named Faith—close, refusing to let Mrs. Clifford take her away to be washed and fed properly.

"It's because the workhouse tried to take her away," Phillips had whispered in Marigold's ear as she'd watched, puzzled and horrified by the situation.

"I thought mothers were allowed to keep infants with them in the workhouse," Marigold had whispered back.

"They are, ma'am, but the administrators were certain little Faith would die anyhow and didn't want Ruby distracted from her work because of it," Phillips had said.

The thought of Ruby losing her baby under such uncaring circumstances had horrified Marigold so much that she had allowed Ruby to have a room of her own with Faith instead of sharing a room with another maid, and she had instructed Mrs. Clifford to ease Ruby into her duties as housemaid, and to be kind to her. In addition, she had personally seen to it that a physician came to tend to Faith. She'd even spent an hour here and there cradling and cooing over the baby while Ruby attended to her duties. Those hours had made her own longing for a child so powerful that she engaged in her and Alex's nocturnal activity with exceptional vigor.

The one thing neither she nor Alex, nor even the ever-patient Phillips, had been able to get Ruby to do was talk about Turpin or the Black Strap Club, or anything that would help Alex bring about the end of Turpin's career and interference in Parliament. But there was still time.

"I plan to return as soon as the session is over," Marigold explained to Ruby as the young woman handed over her gloves. "Although I expect Alex will stay a little longer. Lady Lavinia Prior and Lady Stanhope will be coming for supper this evening, then we are all going out to the theater one last time before everyone decamps to the country. Do you think you'll have the oriental parlor tidied up by then?" she asked, even though it was a ridiculous question. Of course the parlor would be tidied. That was Ruby's job, and she was surprisingly good at it. But the more Marigold could engage the shy woman in conversation, the closer she might come to talking about what they needed her to divulge.

But all Ruby said was, "Yes, ma'am," and curtsied, still not looking her in the eye.

The footman, Long, cleared his throat and moved to hold the door open, indicating that the carriage had arrived. Marigold sent one last smile, one she hoped was confident and caring, Ruby's way.

"I'm so glad you've come to work for us," she said. "I know things will get better for you from here."

"Thank you, ma'am." Ruby curtsied and ventured a tremulous smile in return, but she didn't say more.

Marigold tried to hold back the twist of frustration the maid's reticence caused. They could force her to talk about Turpin, to bring the whole thing to a close so that the matter could be dismissed quickly, but that would have done more harm than good. And until Ruby spoke, the most Marigold could do to help Alex advance his cause was to appear on his arm at official events, smiling and well-turned-out, and to go out of her way to be sure he was satisfied at night. While there was nothing wrong with either duty, and while she took immense enjoyment in the latter, it wasn't what she'd thought married life would be like. Her nights were dazzling, but her days felt much longer and somehow lacking.

"You have no idea how happy I am to see you," she told Lavinia as her friend hopped into the carriage once they'd driven to pick her up.

"Me?" Lavinia blinked in surprise as she settled on the seat beside Marigold. "Why ever would you be happy to see boring old me when you have a whole cadre of new, married friends to call on?"

Marigold sighed. "Because I don't truly know any of those married friends, aside from Lady Stanhope, who, as it turns out, isn't welcome in most respectable social circles."

Lavinia made a sound expressing just what she thought of anyone who would turn up their nose at Lady Stanhope. "It sounds like you're mired down in a sea of my mother's friends."

Marigold winced. "I think I *am* mired down in your mother's circles." She shook her head.

Lavinia rested a supportive hand on her arm. "They are an influential bunch, though. Which, I suppose, is why Mama is so determined to nab exactly the right husband for me."

"Wouldn't you rather choose your own?" Marigold asked.

"As if I have that option," Lavinia laughed.

Marigold sighed and slumped back against the seat as best she could with her fashionably enormous bustle. "Not that I've seen much of my husband at all since we married."

"No?"

Marigold tried not to make a face like a spoiled child. "It's like we're living separate lives under the same roof. I had hoped to...."

"What?" Lavinia pressed her.

Marigold sent her a guilty look. "I don't mean to complain, but I was hoping Alex and I could become friends as well as spouses."

"*Are* women friends with their husbands?" Lavinia blinked.

"We should be, but I'm not sure I even know mine." She paused, irritated with herself for not being content with all the wonderful things she did have. But she still felt like a puzzle with pieces missing. "Weren't our lives supposed to change and improve as we aged and married?"

"But your life *has* changed and improved," Lavinia argued. "*Because* you are married. You have a distinction now that I don't."

"I suppose."

Marigold brushed a hand over her skirt, trying not to be a sourpuss. She adored Alex. He made her feel things she'd never dreamed of. But if she were honest, she couldn't remember the last conversation she'd had with him. Parliament demanded his utmost attention. Her father had been right. Alex was a difficult man to be married to.

"Well," she said as the carriage turned onto Great George Street, and the Palace of Westminster loomed before them, "I'm not going to let the awkwardness of this adjustment phase irritate me, even if it has provoked me into a less than perfect mood. And upset my digestion."

Lavinia laughed. "Don't tell me your digestion has turned questionable."

Prickles of self-consciousness raced down Marigold's back. "Just in this last fortnight or so."

Lavinia continued laughing. "Oh dear. Mama is forever complaining about her delicate digestion." She pressed a hand to her mouth, but her eyes continued to dance with mirth. "My poor Marigold. You're already turning into one of society's properly lofty mavens."

"Lord help me," Marigold groaned as the carriage joined the queue of others waiting to disgorge parliamentary spectators.

Marigold tried to keep her spirits up by shifting the conversation to the latest gossip about the actress who would be starring in the play they were all seeing that night, but a lingering sense of dissatisfaction hung over her. Ruby was safe, but she wouldn't talk. Alex was a dream in bed, but she barely had a chance to see him during the day. Her dearest friend was no longer in the same social category she was. Every blessing she'd been handed out came with a curse. And she truly hadn't felt right in her own skin for weeks now. If married life were such a prize for a woman to win, why did nothing feel right?

When it was their turn to disembark at Westminster's grand front door, Marigold took a deep breath and pushed as much of her troubles out of her mind as she could. "I'm looking forward to Alex's speech," she told Lavinia as the two of them headed toward the entrance. "He was up late practicing it last night, and I'm sure it will leave everyone energized and excited for Parliament to resume this winter."

"If it does resume," Lavinia added. "They say Disraeli's government is on its last legs, and that there will definitely be an election next year."

"Which is precisely why Alex's speech is so—"

She stopped when they were just inside the doorway to

St. Stephen's Hall. Only a few yards away, Turpin stood glowering at her. Marigold had barely seen the man in the six weeks since he'd tricked Alex into leaving their bed the day after the wedding. Her fury was as fresh as it had been that day, but Turpin glared at her with equal disgust. It was enough to unnerve her, though she wasn't about to back down from her own anger.

"Mr. Turpin," she said, taking the lead and nodding at him.

Turpin narrowed his eyes, stepping around a group of passing young men to stand as close to her as was socially acceptable. "You won't get away with it," he growled.

Marigold's pulse shot up. The blackguard must have found out about Ruby somehow. There was no other reason she could think of that he would behave in such a threatening manner to her when he barely knew her. She wasn't about to be cowed. "You won't get away with it either, sir," she shot back, then took Lavinia's hand and marched away.

She began to tremble as they moved deeper into the hall.

"What was that all about?" Lavinia asked, breathless with awe, her eyes wide with alarm.

Marigold pressed her lips together, glancing over her shoulder to where Turpin was still watching her as if plotting revenge. "Mr. Turpin is the very worst of men," she told her friend, careful not to damage Lavinia's innocent sensibilities the way hers had been damaged by the revelation of Ruby. "He's done something despicable, and Alex is determined to bring him to justice for it."

"That sounds exciting," Lavinia said, though her enthusiasm shifted to worry when Marigold turned back to her. "Doesn't it?"

Marigold was spared having to explain when she

spotted Alex striding up the hall toward them. Her heart leapt with relief in her chest, and it was all she could do not to run up and throw her arms around him as if he were her knight in shining armor, come to vanquish their mutual foe. It didn't even register that Lady Stanhope was with him.

"Are you ready for your dazzling speech?" she asked, pushing the encounter with Turpin out of her mind as fast as she could.

Alex must have suspected something, however. He glanced to the side, meeting Turpin's gaze with the ferocity of a tiger protecting its territory. The fact that Turpin was still watching them did nothing to settle Marigold's nerves.

"Did he accost you?" Alex asked, narrowing his eyes at Turpin.

"Only to tell me I wouldn't get away with it," Marigold replied. At the very least, she wanted to take Alex's hand to seek comfort from his touch, but he was focused on staring daggers at Turpin instead.

"I was afraid of that," he said.

"Come along, Lady Lavinia," Lady Stanhope said, reaching for Lavinia's hand. "Let's give your poor Mama the vapors by sitting together at the very front of the gallery. We'll save a seat for Marigold as well."

"But...I...shouldn't we...." Lavinia's protest went unheeded as Lady Stanhope dragged her off toward the gallery stairs, leaving Marigold and Alex alone.

"I should explain," Alex said, taking Marigold's arm at last and leading her across the hall to a side corridor with long, quick strides.

"Explain what?" A sense of dread pooled in Marigold's stomach.

Alex didn't answer until they were several dozen yards

along a dim, narrow corridor. Then he stopped and turned to her with a sigh, pushing a hand through his hair.

"Turpin was behaving like an ass this morning," he said. "He was being insufferable about the clout he had and the influence he would bring to bear on any vote about the rights of women that we put forward, whether today or next year. Things became heated."

A slightly sheepish look brought a blush to Alex's face. Marigold could only imagine the resemblance Alex and his friends might have had to brawling schoolboys in the heat of the moment.

"I told Turpin flat-out that he may soon find himself forced to resign his seat in Commons," Alex went on.

Marigold frowned. "Did you tell him about Ruby?"

Alex winced.

For a moment, Marigold wasn't sure if she should take him to task for putting Ruby in danger or congratulate him for setting things into motion. "How did he react?" she asked instead.

Alex's lips turned up in a triumphant grin. "He flinched like a thief before a magistrate."

Marigold's brow lifted, and her spirits with it. "So he knows that his actions were deplorable enough to cause a scandal."

"He must." Alex nodded, inching closer to her. "Which means we're on the right track." He slid an arm around her waist, drawing her flush against him.

Marigold giggled, glancing around to see if anyone was watching them. The corridor was blessedly empty, but the hullabaloo in St. Stephen's Hall was still close enough to make her feel deliciously wicked.

"So Lady Stanhope was right, and Ruby *could* bring

Turpin down, thus striking a blow to those opposing your bill?" she asked, clutching the lapels of his jacket.

"It would appear so," he said, his voice lowering to a sensual purr. Heat filled his eyes as he stared at Marigold's lips. "Lady Stanhope was right about a great deal of other things as well."

"Such as?"

He answered by surging forward and slanting his mouth over hers in a kiss that was as far from appropriate for the halls of Westminster as could be. Marigold gasped in shock, but was quickly overcome by the triumph of having her husband all to herself, even if they were in the middle of one of the busiest buildings in London, and even if it was just for a moment. She sighed as she leaned into him, returning his kiss with equal ardor, wishing it could be more.

"I miss you," she sighed. Her heart fluttered and her chest squeezed as she heard her own words. She hadn't meant to sound so vulnerable.

"I miss you too," he echoed, cradling the side of her face as he kissed her with mounting passion. "All I want is to spend days in your arms instead of arguing with bullish rogues and blackguards."

None of the flowers he'd brought her or jewels he'd clasped around her neck in the last six weeks could hold a candle to those simple words. The only gift she wanted was him, and it made her reckless. She threw her arms around his shoulders, kissing him with a scandalously needy sigh. And he kissed her in return as though the world had dissolved around them.

Until someone cleared their throat at the end of the hall.

Marigold gasped and twisted to see who it was, but they

hadn't stayed long enough to be seen. Her body buzzed with desire and embarrassment, and she could feel the heat of scandal rising up her neck.

Alex wasn't as flustered.

"Over here," he whispered, taking her hand and crossing the corridor to a small, unassuming door.

Marigold blinked as he pushed it open and pulled her into what appeared to be a small closet filled with ledgers and stationary. The whole thing had a musty, papery scent. There was only one tiny window at the top of one wall to let in light, and not much at that.

Alex shut the door and turned the lock. "We have about ten minutes before I need to be in chambers," he whispered, sweeping toward her and taking her in his arms.

"Ten minutes for what?" Marigold panted as he backed her toward the small, square table wedged between the closet's two crowded shelves.

"For stage twenty-four," he whispered.

She didn't have a chance to reply. His mouth was over hers, kissing her into dizzy desire within seconds. Confusion mingled with excitement, swirling through her gut to set the most intimate parts of her throbbing. She kissed him with as much enthusiasm as he showed, all while her mind was reeling. He couldn't possibly mean to take things further than an ardent kiss, could he?

With a sudden movement, he lifted her by the waist, sitting her on the edge of the table. Then he started to gather her skirts, lifting them up and bunching them around her middle.

"Alex," she whispered between clumsy kisses. "What on earth are you doing?"

"Making love to my wife in a closet in the Palace of

Westminster," he growled in return, fumbling with the fastenings of his trousers.

Shock and deep, pulsing excitement zipped through every nerve and fiber of Marigold's being. "We couldn't possibly," she gasped, even as she wriggled to spread her legs apart. "This is ridiculously dangerous."

"I know," he replied. She could just make out the spark of wickedness in his eyes in the dim light.

"If we're caught, we'll never live it down," Marigold went on, gasping as Alex shifted closer, stroking his hands along her thighs and between the split in her drawers to touch her intimately.

"Then we'll have to be very, very quiet to be sure we aren't caught," he murmured, voice thick with desire, his breath hot against her ear.

Any further protest was cut short as his thick, hot length thrust suddenly inside of her. She gasped, only swallowing her moan of pleasure at the last moment, and arched her hips into him. It was wild and surreal. She was fully dressed, hadn't even removed her hat, and he was moving inside of her, stretching her to the fullest. Heat suffused her as he thrust harder and faster. She clung to his shoulders, biting her lip to keep from crying out in ecstasy at the sensations he ignited in her. Her body responded hungrily to his aggression, and he was mating with her far more demandingly than he ever had. She was surprised that she enjoyed it so much and was spilling over the edge into orgasm with lightning speed. Staying silent and swallowing her cry of pleasure was next to impossible.

Moments later, his body stiffened, and he muffled a cry against the shoulder of her gown as he came. The shift in tension was palpable as he sagged with release. They were both left spent and panting. Marigold blinked in disbelief as she clung to him, her head still spinning. The whole thing seemed to be over before it began. She might not have believed anything had happened, but for the distinct slip of something liquid against her inner thigh as Alex moved away from her and set about righting himself.

Hot embarrassment at the slippery sensation kept her blazing as she hopped off the table and straightened her skirts around her. She wore enough layers of fabric that the liquid wasn't there for long, but without a doubt, everyone who looked at her would know she'd just been well and truly ravished. In a closet.

"I feel as though I could conquer the world now," Alex growled, taking her into his arms once his trousers were fastened and kissing her soundly.

She had to laugh. There was no other response to the outrageous thing they'd just done. She wasn't sure whether she felt triumphant for helping him screw his courage to the sticking place, as it were, or tiny and insignificant in the face of his experience.

"Will we be seen leaving the closet?" she whispered instead.

"Not if we act as though nothing is out of the ordinary," he said.

They gave each other a final look-over, straightening rumpled clothing, then Alex turned to the door. He unlocked it and stepped out of the closet as though leading Marigold into church.

Blessedly, the corridor was deserted, but as they headed toward St. Stephen's Hall, it was clear they'd taken more time than they should have.

"Blast. They might have already started," Alex hissed, picking up his pace.

They made it to the hall just in the nick of time. The

last of the MPs were filing into the chamber, and the attendant at the stairs leading to the Strangers' Gallery had started turning people away. Alex didn't have time to do more than raise Marigold's hand to his lips before being forced to let it go and jogging to slip through the door before it was closed.

"Lady Stanhope is saving a seat for me," Marigold told the attendant at the stairs, who she was certain could see right through her blush to the reason she was late.

Surprisingly, he let her by without comment. Marigold rushed up the stairs, then down through the rows of seats to the front row, where Lady Stanhope and Lavinia were waiting. She took her seat beside Lady Stanhope with a stunned look, still feeling tender in intimate places. As proceedings began on the floor below, she continued to feel dizzy, blazingly hot, and just a bit sick to her stomach. And that was before she noticed Lady Stanhope watching her with unconcealed delight.

"Well done, my dear," Lady Stanhope murmured in tones that were as congratulatory as they were sly.

"What? I...it's...." Marigold stammered to come up with some explanation for her state.

Lady Stanhope leaned closer, eyes fixed on proceedings below, and said out of the corner of her mouth, "I know the look of a woman who's just been run up the flagpole and saluted when I see it."

Marigold hadn't thought she could blush harder or hotter, but she'd been wrong. She clapped a hand to her mouth to stop herself from laughing...or perhaps vomiting. Both seemed equally likely all of a sudden. She leaned against Lady Stanhope, praying the nausea and dizziness would pass quickly.

Lady Stanhope still wore her knowing grin as Alex took

the floor below, but she dragged her eyes away from him—even as Marigold attempted to straighten and pay attention—to study Marigold.

"Gentlemen," Alex began in an energetic voice, wearing a wide smile. "We cannot leave our duties and close this session of Parliament without discussing once more the plight and the rights of women."

Marigold swallowed hard, breathing deeply and willing the nausea to pass.

"Well, well, my dear," Lady Stanhope said, circling a motherly arm around Marigold's back and rubbing it, even as she pretended to be focused on Alex's speech. "Are double congratulations in order?"

"Is Marigold feeling unwell again?" Lavinia whispered.

They were starting to draw angry looks from the men in the gallery with them.

"I'll be fine," Marigold gulped. She sat straighter. "Look, it's already passing." Although whether it was or wasn't had yet to be determined, as far as she was concerned.

"You'll be fine." Lady Stanhope continued to rub her back. "I went through it three times and came out none the worse for wear."

It took Marigold a moment before Lady Stanhope's words sank in. As soon as they did, she sucked in a breath and snapped to face the older woman, eyes wide. She immediately started counting the days since her wedding night.

"But it's only been six weeks," she whispered in disbelief.

Lady Stanhope leaned close. "It was less than a month for me. I think you'll find that for most healthy young women in their prime, it doesn't take long at all."

A smile spread across Marigold's face, and she glanced down to the chamber, where Alex was powering through his speech. "For we cannot hold ourselves up as a model society if half our population is given no rights at all," he was in the middle of saying. His supporters nodded and cheered their agreement, while his opposition, particularly Turpin, glared at him and shook their heads.

"Oh my," Marigold whispered, pressing a hand to her stomach. Beside her, Lady Stanhope chuckled before returning her arm to her side. In spite of the twinge in her stomach, Marigold's spirits rose to towering heights. She'd told Alex that she wanted to be the mother of the Prime Minister's son, and it seemed she was already well on the way to doing her part to achieve that goal.

CHAPTER 10

*A*lex had never left the closing session of Parliament on a higher note. His final speech had been well-received, both by members of his own party and by those packing the gallery as witnesses. No doubt that was because of the vigor and conviction with which he delivered it. And that was the direct result of the vigor and conviction with which he'd delivered something else just before his speech.

As the heat of passion—quite literally—faded, sheepishness over the risk he and Marigold had taken and doubt as to whether he'd pushed her into something she might not have wanted rushed in. In retrospect, Marigold might have been more alarmed by the suddenness of his lust and the clandestine nature of his means of assuaging them than she was aroused. He promised himself that he would make it up to her, though, and nipped into the jeweler on the way home to purchase a stunning pair of diamond earrings.

"They're lovely," Marigold said with a smile, then promptly set them aside to slide her arms around his shoulders. "But you're the only gift I need."

"What a charming sentiment," he replied, bringing her

close for a kiss. But a whisper of panic kept him from enjoying the moment entirely. Violetta had always adored jewelry. With her, it had made up for all his many short-comings. But the rules of the game were different with Marigold, and he wasn't sure he knew how to play anymore. The thought terrified him.

He tried to justify his choice of gift by saying, "You'll have quite a bit of opportunity to wear all sorts of jewels while we're in Wiltshire."

"Oh?" she asked, taking his hand and leading him deeper into their bedroom, sitting on their bed and gesturing for him to sit with her. She wore a mysterious smile, and her cheeks were a tempting shade of pink.

"I may not be a titled gentleman," he explained, "but those in Wiltshire who are consider me one of their own. They are forever teasing me that if I play my political cards right, I should be rewarded with a title before too long."

"That would be splendid." Marigold brightened, pressing a hand to her stomach. "That would mean your heirs would join the ranks of the high and mighty."

He smiled, liking the thought of their children being lords and ladies. Although that thought came with the worry over what that would mean to James. The poor boy would have noble half-siblings while he would be normal old Mr.... They hadn't even decided on what his surname should be.

"I've already received an invitation from someone called Caruthers for next Friday," Marigold went on. "I wasn't sure I should accept it until talking to you about it."

Her eyes lit up with an eagerness that warmed Alex's heart. Surely, she was just eager to please him. She couldn't possibly want to waste her precious time doing something as boring as talking to him.

"Accept whichever invitations you'd like." He inched closer to her on the bed, circling his arms around her waist and pulling her onto his lap. That was the sort of congress he knew and understood. "I'm sure everyone in Wiltshire, in the entire western part of the country, will be falling all over themselves to see you at their gatherings."

She laughed and shook her head, but whether out of modesty or because she didn't believe him, he couldn't tell. There were so many things about his young, exciting wife that he couldn't begin to fathom. He wasn't sure if he'd taken on more than he could handle or if marrying her was the wisest decision of his life. Even if it had been more Katya's decision than his own. At least there was one thing he could do to recommend himself to Marigold.

He kissed her, reaching for the hem of her skirt and sliding his hand up her stockinged leg. She gasped and shivered in response, threading her fingers through his hair. He was instantly at ease. They worked so well together in a horizontal position that it almost made him forget he had no idea what to do with a wife.

They made love slowly and sweetly, which made them so late for the theater that they decided to forgo the outing all together. But it was worth it. He had so much to make up for after their quick assignation in the closet. Marigold's sighs of pleasure reassured him that he was good for something where she was concerned, and by the time they fell asleep, sated and content, he was back to feeling triumphant one more.

Although the feeling didn't last long, considering how early they had to get up the next day in order to catch the first train to Wiltshire from Paddington Station. Phillips knocked on their door early enough to give them a leisurely amount of time to wash and dress, but they both slept right through it. He knocked several more times before boldly sticking his head around the door and saying, "Sir, you have less than an hour before your train departs."

It was as though he'd fired a cannon into the room. Alex jerked fully awake, rousing Marigold as he did. She was even more alarmed than him at how little time they'd left themselves to prepare for their journey. The two of them flew through their morning routine, cutting corners and helping each other throw on their traveling outfits while Phillips tapped his watch and frowned.

By some miracle, they made it to Paddington with time to spare. Of course, Alex was well aware that that miracle's name was Gilbert Phillips.

"Your trunks have already been handed over to the porter," Phillips explained, handing Alex and Marigold their tickets. "Noakes is sending a footman to fetch them from the station in Lanhill."

"Thank you, Phillips." Alex thumped his man on the back. "You'll come along by Thursday?"

Phillips grinned. "Just as soon as I finish sleeping my way through the week."

Alex chuckled. Phillips so rarely took a holiday that as far as he was concerned, he could spend the week gaming and whoring and Alex wouldn't blame him one bit. But Phillips was an upright soul and would probably spend his free time staring at landscapes in the National Gallery.

"Do keep an eye on Ruby," Marigold said, casting a worried look Phillips's way. "She's still skittish."

"I'll guard her with my life, ma'am," Phillips replied in a tone that had Alex's brow rising to his hairline. He'd never suspected Phillips of harboring any special feelings for a woman before. If he were honest, the prospect of his man of business forming an attachment to a woman who had been so badly used by Turpin, and who was vital to any case he might mount against his enemy, was unsettling.

As if thoughts of the case summoned him, Alex glanced across the crowded train platform and spotted Turpin and his wife harassing a porter. Alex narrowed his eyes. Turpin's home constituency was in Worcester, and as the Parliamentary session had ended the day before, it wasn't out of the question that their paths would cross at the station, but he wished they hadn't.

"Is it time to board?" he asked Phillips, taking Marigold's arm in an attempt to escape Turpin's notice.

He wasn't fast enough.

"Croydon," Turpin boomed. He broke away from his wife and the porter, marching toward them.

Marigold hissed out a breath. "What could that odious man possibly want with us?"

Her question was answered a moment later as Turpin came to a glowering stop in front of them. "Don't think for a moment I will be cowed by your libelous scheme."

Alex's gut clenched. He tugged Marigold protectively closer, regretting that she had to look at the man's sour face. "I don't know what you're talking about, Turpin."

Turpin stared at him as if judging how much Alex knew. "If you use that little whore against me, there will be consequences."

Phillips stiffened, color splashing his cheeks. Marigold glared at Turpin with admirable ferocity.

Alex attempted to remain calm and in command of the situation. "A young woman's life was ruined."

"By her own stupidity," Turpin growled. "If a word of this gets out, all I need do is make public her low character."

Alex leaned closer to him. "If word of your involvement with the Black Strap Club gets out, along with your mistreatment of Miss Murdoch, voters in Worcester will be made aware of your own low character. And with hints of an election in the air...." He left his threat hanging.

Turpin turned a deep shade of puce. "Consequences, Croydon. Mark my words."

Alex stood taller and huffed a laugh, shaking his head. He was saved having to draw the confrontation out when the conductor called for first-class passengers to board. He nodded to Turpin with a curt, "Good day," glanced to Phillips, then led Marigold away to their train.

"That man makes me sick," Marigold grumbled as they settled into their private compartment. "How can he live with himself, much less walk around in public?"

Alex sighed. "Men like Turpin see themselves as a cut above their fellow men and as an entirely different, superior species to women in general. He most likely thinks of Miss Murdoch as an inhuman object, born to be at his disposal."

"It's sickening," Marigold said, pressing a hand to her stomach. She looked sickened indeed.

"Are you feeling quite all right, my dear?" he asked as the whistle sounded at the front of the train and the whole thing jerked into motion.

"I—" She stopped, her mouth open, a flash in her eyes. For a moment, she seemed to be thinking something over. Then she closed her mouth, shook her head with a smile, and patted his arm. "It's nothing."

Alex arched a brow, not quite believing her. But whatever it was, he trusted she would tell him in her own time. Instead, he blew out a breath, finally letting the tension of the whirlwind their morning had been slip away. "At least we have an easy journey ahead of us. We'll be at Winterberry Park by late this afternoon. I can't wait for you to see the place and to meet the staff."

"I've been looking forward to it all month," she replied, her smile as wide as ever.

The way she looked at him and the way she looped her arm through his gave Alex the bolstering feeling that she'd been looking forward to actually spending time with him for a month. The six weeks since their wedding had passed in a parliamentary blur, and only with her sitting there in the train compartment with him did he realize he'd barely spoken more than a few words to his wife since their wedding. No wonder she wanted to talk to him.

"Have you spent much time in the country?" he asked. It was a question that newly acquainted people would have discussed, but in their haste to the altar, they'd left a lot of ground uncovered.

"Not really," she began, snuggling closer to him. "Papa's business dealings keep him in London year-round out of necessity. But my younger sisters married men who have country estates, and for these last few years, I've spent a fortnight or two visiting each of them during the summer."

Alex smiled, enjoying the easy way she talked about her sisters and their families. She didn't stop talking after exhausting the subject of her infant nieces and nephew. In fact, they managed to keep the conversation going through the hours of their journey. All of his concerns about the bill for women's rights, all of his frustrations about Turpin and his cronies, and all of his anxiety about his shortcomings as a husband faded away. His wife was, surprisingly enough, a brilliant conversationalist. He found himself talking to her as if she were a lifelong friend and not simply the woman who made his blood run hot again at his age.

"So by the time we came down for supper, Lavinia was frozen solid, and I could barely feel my feet." Marigold laughed, recounting a story from her school days, as they stepped down from the train in Lanhill.

"You stayed up there that whole time?" Alex laughed along with her, his heart lighter than it had been in years.

"What else could we do?" Marigold took his arm, leaning close to him. "We'd made a bet, after all."

"And bets must be honored, of course," he agreed with a broad grin.

It was a beautiful afternoon. The sun beamed down from a clear, blue sky. Lanhill's station was a tiny one, and Mr. Bolton, the stationmaster, spent his time between trains tending the magnificent garden that greeted weary travelers. Benjamin Connors and Robby Deane, two of his footmen, were already receiving their trunks from the train's porter, and he nodded to them in greeting. The quaintness of the old station was a hallmark of the entire region, and Alex felt right at home in it as he escorted Marigold toward the platform exit.

"Lavinia seemed so much younger than me then," Marigold went on, smiling at the beauty around her as if she too were coming home. "That difference hardly matters now, since our positions are so—oh."

"What?" Alex glanced to her as they stepped through the barrier to the street, where one of his larger carriages was waiting for them on the curb.

"Well, Lavinia and I aren't of the same station anymore," Marigold went on. "Although her mother is bound and determined to marry her off to the highest, most well-placed gentleman she can. So we will be again soon."

"Isn't marrying their daughters to distinguished men the aim of all mothers?" Alex commented as he nodded to his driver.

"Lady Prior is more determined than most," Marigold

said with a sigh. "She has already turned down two suitors who Lavinia rather liked, but who didn't quite live up to her standards. I'm afraid at this rate, poor Lavinia will end up on the shelf if her mother doesn't—" She stopped, spotting something farther down the path leading from the station into town and said, "Well, hello. Who are you?"

Alex turned out of mild curiosity. That instantly turned into a burst of overwhelming, conflicted emotion.

James stood at the edge of one of Mr. Bolton's gardens, his two chubby hands full of freshly turned dirt. His short pants and round-collared shirt were smudged with more dirt, but he wore a broad smile, as though he were the happiest child on earth. The sunlight played off of the highlights in his dark, tousled hair. The whole sight filled Alex with the purest burst of love that he'd ever known.

James spotted him a moment later, and burst into a smile of pure joy. "Macky!" he shouted, throwing his dirt aside and running headlong at Alex.

After all the turmoil of Violetta's death due to complications from James's birth, after months of bitter sorrow and regret, and after years of guilt for farming his son out to Arthur and Clara Fallon, Alex had found himself in the uncomfortable position of loving his little bastard more than he'd ever thought it was possible to love. He let go of Marigold's arm and rushed to meet him.

Though not quite three, and having lived somewhere else for all that time, James understood there was a connection between them, though Alex doubted he knew the truth of what it was, and when he was close enough, James jumped toward him. Alex scooped the boy into his arms, hugging him close.

"What are you doing here?" he asked once James had

lifted his head from his shoulder, where it rested during their hug.

"Choo-choo!" he declared, pointing through the garden fence to the train, which was just rolling into motion to move on.

"Are you all by yourself?" Alex looked around, searching for Clara or one of the village children, anyone who could have been minding the boy. Surely *someone* had to be minding his son.

His glance landed on Marigold, standing stock still where he'd left her. Her eyes had gone round, and the color had drained from her face as she stared at him and James. Alex's heart sank like a rock into his stomach. She knew. She hadn't even had to guess. James resembled him so much that there'd been no point even trying to conceal his origins from local people, and apparently the truth was obvious to all. Including Marigold.

An even harder truth was suddenly obvious to Alex. No amount of jewelry would be enough to buy his way out of neglecting to tell his wife about his son.

CHAPTER 11

*A*t last, everything had seemed perfect. She and Alex were talking. They'd spent the day together in an upright position, sharing tidbits of themselves that had nothing to do with making love. She'd finally felt as though her marriage could truly start on a meaningful level.

Then, in an instant, all that was gone. The truth hit her harder than the train she'd just stepped down from. She'd married a complete stranger. She didn't know the first thing about Alex or his past or his character. The man he was in Parliament was only a fraction of the man standing before her, a man who had a child.

The boy looked so much like him that it had knocked the air out of her lungs. The two were clearly on familiar terms, otherwise the child wouldn't have run straight into Alex's arms the second they stepped out of the station. Most telling of all, Alex clearly loved the boy. She'd never seen such joy in his eyes or so bright a smile on his face. Certainly not when he looked at her.

She pressed a hand to her stomach, to the spark of life

growing inside of her. Her baby was barely formed, and it already had competition.

"James, would you like to meet someone very special to me?" Alex asked the boy in his arms, his question hesitant.

Marigold blinked rapidly to tamp down her sudden urge to weep. There wasn't anything to weep about, or so she tried to tell herself. Alex *had* mentioned a previous relationship. Once. Briefly. Anger welled up in her all the same. They'd been married for six weeks, and not once in all that time had he thought to tell her he had a son.

The boy, James, shifted in Alex's arms to look at Marigold. He raised a dirty hand and flapped it. "Bye-bye."

"No, no, *hello*," Alex laughed. "It's hello when we meet someone."

"Hello," James said. He turned to Alex. "Cake?"

"We can have cake later," Alex told him, beaming. "Right now, we need to take you home."

Marigold swallowed hard, her heart twisting in her chest. The scene in front of her was unbearably sweet. Alex was clearly besotted. But she had never felt more alone. The world she'd entered by marrying Alex wasn't at all what she'd thought it was. No wonder he'd barely spent more than two minutes talking with her in the past two months. Her father had hinted there was something Alex hadn't told her, which begged the question, did everyone know about his son but her? Was she a laughingstock? She'd believed she could be the fulcrum of Alex's universe, his equal partner in all things. Now she felt like an afterthought, an intruder in a world that was already fully formed and functioning without her.

He sent her a guilty look, his smile dropping. "I can explain," he said, darting an anxious glance to the footmen and carriage that had come to meet them. "Truly, I can. But I need to take James home first."

"Doesn't he live at Winterberry Park?" Marigold asked, her voice fragile and wispy, blinking rapidly.

Alex let out a breath. "No, he lives with Rev. Fallon, the local vicar, and his wife and children."

Marigold swallowed, unsure what to do with the added information. Alex had a child he'd never bothered to mention, and he'd foisted the boy off on another family. The nausea of her own pregnancy swelled, and she felt dizzy.

Alex let out a breath, some tension leaving his shoulders. He stepped closer to Marigold. "Why don't you take the carriage back to Winterberry Park. I'll take James home, then I'll come along and explain."

Marigold shook her head tightly, not trusting herself to speak until she'd taken a few more breaths. "I'll come with you," she said hoarsely.

Alex pursed his lips, looking as anxious as if she'd asked him to walk across fire into a pit of vipers. He glanced to James—who appeared to be more interested in the pin stuck through Alex's tie than the drama enfolding the adults—then sighed in resignation. "It's just up this way."

He marched past Marigold up a gently-sloping hill. His hand moved toward hers, as if he would escort her, but Marigold deftly backed too far out of his reach for him to touch her. His expression hardened as if he knew what that meant, and he walked on.

"We're going up to the vicarage to return James," he told his footmen and driver.

"Would you like us to follow you, sir?" the driver asked.

Alex shook his head. "No. Take the trunks home, then bring the buggy 'round the Fallon's to pick us up."

"Yes, sir," all three of the young men replied. They

glanced worriedly toward Marigold for a moment before moving on to do as they were told.

The walk up the hill and through the small town of Lanhill was a surprise boon for Marigold. She needed time to steady her breathing, to gather her thoughts, and to pray that her stomach would settle. She needed time to shift her entire world to fit into the new reality that had been thrust upon her. Alex was a stranger. She knew less about him than she did about the clerks who worked in her father's office. She'd had more conversations with Lavinia's driver than she had with her own husband. And yet, she'd married Alex. She'd given her body to him—in a closet in the Palace of Westminster, even—she'd conceived his child...and he'd barely told her anything.

Part of her wanted to be furious, but she was beyond even that. She was numb, and felt as though she were walking through a dream, someone else's dream, as she followed Alex and James through what could have been a charming and beautiful town, if she'd had the focus to take it in. James chattered to Alex with youthful exuberance and a toddler's vocabulary. It should have been wonderful. It should not have brought Marigold to the edge of tears.

"There you are." A woman's alarmed shout jerked Marigold out of her thoughts as they neared a cozy, country church with a house off to one side.

Marigold snapped her head up to find a tall, dark-haired woman with not one, but two newborn infants in her arms. She had circles under her eyes, but still managed to be striking in appearance.

"Clara," Alex greeted her with a smile. "Having a bit of a rough day?"

"Mr. Croydon, I'm so sorry." Clara looked as though she might drop from exhaustion and shame. "I don't know how he slipped away. For once, I thought we had everything under control."

Marigold's brow went up slightly at the woman's accent. She was American, which was unusual enough to break through the shock she was lost in.

"Did you find him?" A man with a strong, English accent was heard just before he stepped through the front door of the house beside the church.

Marigold blinked again. The man wore the high collar of a minister, but his sleeves were rolled up, and he too carried a baby in each arm, somewhat older than the other two. They were both in tears, and as the man joined them on the pavement in front of the house, they set the smaller babies in Clara's arms to crying as well. Marigold suddenly had an idea why the couple looked so worn out, and how James could have escaped their notice.

"Alex," the reverend exclaimed with a combination of welcome, panic, and exhaustion. "I'm so sorry. We've been looking for James everywhere, but the twins have been a handful today."

"All of them," Clara added with a weary laugh, trying to rock both of her infants at once. "Oh, this will never do. Come inside so we can put these ones down and greet you properly."

"I heard about the new arrivals," Alex said as he followed the frazzled couple through their front garden and into the tiny cottage. He glanced to Marigold, his expression apologetic. She followed, her lips pressed tightly shut. As soon as they were through the door, he went on with, "For some reason, I didn't realize it was twins again."

The reverend laughed humorlessly. "Punishment for our sins, eh?" He broke into a smile as he glanced to the babies in his arms. "And an outstanding blessing."

"But we didn't mean to lose track of James," Clara added as she shifted the two newborns into a wicker bassinet sitting on a table filled with piles of folded nappies. Marigold could only imagine how many they went through in a day with four babies, none of whom looked older than a year and a half.

"Clara, Arthur, I'd like you to meet Marigold Croydon, my beautiful bride."

Alex's introduction took Marigold by surprise, and she had to blink herself into full focus. She could only just manage a polite smile. "How do you do?" She began to extend her hand, but wasn't sure who to offer it to.

"It's a pleasure to meet you." Clara came forward, a warm and welcoming smile on her weary face. She took Marigold's hand and shook it with American enthusiasm. "We were so pleased when we heard Mr. Croydon was marrying at last."

"We've been looking forward to meeting you since we heard," Arthur added, handing the two older babies to Clara when she stepped back so that he could shake Marigold's hand as well. "This is Bonnie and Amelia," he gestured to the two wailing babies in Clara's arms. "And causing havoc in the bassinet over there are George and Miles."

"They're delightful," Marigold said, utterly over-whelmed.

"No, they're not," Clara laughed. "At the moment, they're a pack of howling wolf pups ready for their supper. You've caught us as a bad time, I'm afraid."

"Not at all," Marigold lied, falling back on every bit of rigid politeness that had been drummed into her in finishing school. She wasn't sure she could have withstood the chaos

—both of the Fallons' house and of her own inner turmoil—if she hadn't.

Alex had set James down, and the boy had immediately grabbed his hand and dragged him to one side of the room to see a collection of stuffed toys. His full attention was on his son's jabbered explanation. Both sets of twins were screaming and crying, reflecting everything Marigold was trying so hard to hide.

"Oh, dear," Clara murmured. "Arthur, take the girls." She shuffled the babies back into Arthur's arms, then rushed forward to put an arm around Marigold's shoulders. "It's a lot of noise and mess, I know. The kitchen is much tidier, and I need to feed everyone anyhow."

Before she knew it, Marigold was swept out of the main room of the cottage and into the kitchen off to one side. It may have been tidier than the rest of the house, but that wasn't saying much. Dishes and pots sat on the counters, clean but not put away. The table held an army of bottles and a rack of drying, rubber nipples. Piles of laundry sat in one corner. A steaming pot of something was cooking away on the stove.

"We do have help," Clara explained. "But Missy has gone home for the day. That's why supper is always the trickiest time."

It was too much. The mess and the noise, the unfamiliar surroundings and the faint smell of burning. It piled in around Marigold, making her feel like a fish that had been wrenched out of water and left to flap away on land without notice.

"He didn't tell me," she gasped, her face pinching as she fought desperately not to burst into tears in front of yet another person she didn't know at all. "He didn't say a bloody word."

"He didn't what?" Clara glanced over her shoulder from the stove, where she moved the pot to a cooler burner. She let go of the pot and rushed back to Marigold. "Oh, no." She threw her arms around Marigold as if they'd been friends their whole lives.

Marigold wasn't sure she liked the sudden, stifling embrace of a strange woman who was nearly a foot taller than her, but she would take whatever comfort she could get. "He didn't tell me he had a son."

Clara made a sound of sympathy and hugged her tighter. As much as she appreciated it, Marigold had to wrench free of her embrace to stop the wave of nausea that threatened to embarrass her.

"We rushed into everything," she went on, just needing to get it out at once. "I barely know who he is. What was I thinking?" Panic rose through her so fast that she had no choice but to lunge forward, darting through the door that stood open, leading out to the back garden, where she promptly tossed her stomach onto the grass.

Clara rushed after her, gathering her into her arms and leading her a few steps farther into the garden to a bench in the shade of a tree. She'd thought fast enough to bring a damp rag with her, which Marigold used to wipe her mouth, and then her tears.

"I don't know how a man could marry a woman without disclosing his son," Clara said, somewhat awkwardly. She rubbed Marigold's back. "But Mr. Croydon is a good man. I'm sure everything will be all right."

Marigold shook her head, squeezing her eyes shut and praying that one short burst of crying was enough to get it out, and that she could summon the strength to make it through at least the rest of the day in once piece. "I've only known him since the beginning of May," she said, her shoulders sagging. "I was flattered by his attention and aroused by his presence." She'd just vomited in Clara's garden and wept all over her while spilling her unfortunate business. There didn't seem much point in holding the truth back from the woman. "I don't really know who he is, and I'm married to him."

"Poor dear." Clara continued to rub her back. "Marriage is such a gamble to begin with. But maybe it's not as bad as all that."

Marigold glanced wearily toward her.

"At least he only failed to mention James," Clara went on. "It's not like he failed to mention a mistress and six kids, all of whom depend on him."

It was not what Marigold wanted to hear. She stared at Clara in disbelief...then laughed. The reaction came out of nowhere. It wasn't truly a reflection of how she felt. But Clara's statement had been so baldly American and so blunt that Marigold couldn't help but laugh until her tears were flowing again. And oddly, it was just the thing she needed to break through the overwhelming shock that had her in its grip.

"It will be all right," Clara laughed along with her. "And if it isn't, well, we could use an extra pair of hands around here, if you need somewhere to go to get away from it all."

Marigold gulped in a few breaths and wiped her face with the damp rag once more. "Thank you. And where are my manners? Can I help you with supper?"

They both stood. Clara looked bashful as she said, "Under normal circumstances, I wouldn't dream of asking the wife of a wealthy MP, who obviously comes from class herself, and who is so distraught, to help with my meager supper preparations...."

"But you could use an extra hand," Marigold finished for her. "I'm glad to help."

They headed back into the kitchen. It was completely mad. She was utterly out of her depth. Clara was exactly the opposite of every richly born woman who had ever been her friend and her kitchen might as well have been a different planet. But as she helped Clara spoon out porridge for the older babies, cooling and fortifying it with milk, then cutting vegetables for the stew Clara and Arthur would eat for supper, the initial misery of her sudden shift in reality smoothed out.

By the time the buggy arrived from Winterberry Park and she returned to the main part of the cottage to face Alex again, she felt far more in control of her faculties and far less likely to either beat Alex senseless or collapse into a veil of tears. She said goodbye to Clara and Arthur, their babies, and James with the politeness that had been instilled in her, then followed Alex out to the buggy.

Alex remained silent as he handed her into the buggy and settled beside her. Marigold didn't trust herself to look at him, so kept her gaze straight forward as the driver flicked the reins and they lurched forward. Her arm was pressed against Alex's out of necessity in the small buggy, but she couldn't quite stomach the thought of him touching her.

"His mother, Violetta, was an Italian actress with whom I had a long-lasting relationship," Alex said at last with a heavy sigh. "She died nearly three years ago, due to complications after James's birth. Something about the placenta not being fully expelled and rotting inside of her."

Marigold's body went rigid, and she clutched her hands in front of her. "Did you have any other children?"

"No," he answered quietly. "To be honest, she didn't think she could. James was a surprise to both of us."

Silence fell between them. Marigold's heart pounded against her ribs. With every beat, she ached to demand why he hadn't told her sooner, why she'd had to find out without a shred of warning or preparation. She was too overwhelmed to form the question, though.

"It was years ago," Alex resumed, rubbing a hand over his face and resting his elbow against the edge of the buggy. "Violetta is the reason I never married, or the reason I didn't marry sooner."

A fresh wave of anger and despair swept through Marigold, heating her face. Had he loved her? Did he love her still? Would he always love her?

"I should have told you sooner," he murmured.

"Yes, you should have," Marigold said with a burst of vehemence. She squeezed her eyes shut and looked away from him, out over the sun-kissed, Wiltshire countryside. It was beautiful, but they might as well have been in a bog in the rain. A rush of homesickness for London and the familiar threatened to crush her. "What else don't I know about you?" she asked through clenched teeth.

"Marigold," he began, both apologetic and impatient, reaching for her hand.

She tugged hers out of his grasp. "What else have you failed to mention to me? Do you have a harem of dusky beauties in your back garden? Do you keep elephants in your stable? Have you penned a series of scandalous novels under a secret name?"

"I'm sorry," he implored her. "I am completely at fault here. It's unforgivable that I forgot to tell you about James. I've been so swept up in parliamentary business lately. The bill for women's rights is so important to me, and Turpin has been such a thorn in my side that I—" He gave up his explanation with a sigh, shaking his head and burying his face in his hand. "I'm sorry."

Marigold remained silent. Her anger faded quickly. He truly was a busy and important man, and she'd known that from the day she met him. She hadn't exactly been reasonable and circumspect when it came to planning their wedding, and she hadn't been pushed down the aisle. Lying by omission about his son was Alex's fault, but rushing into a marriage with a man she barely knew was hers. And of course a man of Alex's age and experience would have a past and its consequences.

That didn't lessen the sting of her situation, though. Her shoulders sagged as they approached a palatial mansion set on a gentle slope. Winterberry Park was surrounded by trees, and Marigold caught glimpses of vast gardens stretching out to either side. Under any other circumstances, her new home would have filled her with awe and excitement. She was to be mistress of everything before her. But all she could feel was a longing for London, for her father and Lavinia and the things she knew.

"Welcome home, sir," a stately, grey-haired butler greeted them as the buggy stopped at the bottom of a wide staircase and patio that led to the house's massive front door.

"Thank you, Noakes." Alex hopped down from the buggy, then turned and offered an anxious hand to Marigold.

For the sake of the servants, Marigold took it with a plastered-on smile and stepped down to the gravel drive. She let Alex tuck her hand into the crook of his arm, even though the rest of her was still stiff with betrayal. A deep weariness was swiftly pressing down on her as well.

"We're so pleased to welcome you to Winterberry Park,

madam," a non-nonsense woman in a housekeeper's simple black dress greeted her.

"This is Mrs. Musgrave," Alex whispered to her, leaning closer than Marigold was comfortable with.

She smiled all the same, greeting Mrs. Musgrave, and then the rest of the staff, all of whom were lined up in starched uniforms, their expressions eager and friendly. Marigold knew the first impression was more important than anything else in her life at that moment, and drew on every bit of her schooling and acting ability to appear as the affable, charming wife of an important man. It saw her through the introductions and into the house for the briefest of tours. She was able to keep her smile in place and appear interested in the house and its operations all the way until Alex finally led her to their bedroom and closed the door.

Then she nearly fell apart.

The room was large and comfortably furnished, with a sizeable bed draped with a blue coverlet. A small desk rested under one window, and a nightstand with a clock and bowl of biscuits sat next to the bed. Two doors in the far wall must have led to dressing rooms or closets, or perhaps even an elaborate washroom, like the one Alex's townhome had. But Marigold ignored all of it, heading straight to one of the overstuffed chairs on either side of an empty fireplace. She sank into the chair, every bone in her body weary to the core, rested her head against the side, and closed her eyes.

Alex stood still for a long time. So long Marigold was tempted to open her eyes. At last, he moved, sitting on the bed and taking off his shoes, if the sounds she heard were right.

"I can have Mrs. Musgrave prepare one of the other

rooms for you if you'd like," he murmured, tired and defeated.

Marigold's chest tightened. "Giving up so easily?" she asked, eyes still closed.

He stopped moving. Only then did she open her eyes to find him studying her, a look of exhausted bafflement in his eyes.

"Only if it's what you want," he said at last, finishing with his shoes.

She shook her head. "What I want is to know who I've married," she said. She wanted to be fair. More than anything, she wanted to be fair with him, even if he hadn't been particularly fair to her. They'd conceived a child together, after all. James or no James, their child would be his heir.

She wriggled in the chair, straightening. If she wanted to be fair, she should tell him she was pregnant then and there, but the words stuck in her throat.

Alex stood with a sigh and walked to her chair. He crouched in front of her, which didn't look particularly comfortable for him. "I swear to you, I did not forget to tell you about James from any malicious intent. And I know it sounds just as bad for me to admit that my duties in parliament and my troubles with Turpin caused me to forget my own flesh and blood, but we're away from all that now. Would you please allow me the chance to start anew and to make things right between us?"

Marigold had cried so much in the last few hours that she didn't think she was capable of more tears, but they stung at her eyes anyhow. What choice did she have but to say yes, seeing as they were already married, and marriages couldn't easily be undone? But more than that, the sputtering embers of everything she'd felt for him in their short, fiery marriage were still burning. She *wanted* to love him. She *wanted* to have the perfect marriage with him. But they'd made such a mess of things.

In the end, she couldn't find the right words to answer him, so she reached for his hand. He took it with a relieved exhale. Neither of them moved beyond that, though. Not for what felt like an eternity.

At last, Alex stood, his knees cracking. "I'll ask Noakes to send supper up here, since I'm sure we're both too undone to take it downstairs."

"Thank you," she said, pushing herself to stand so that she could remove her hat and gloves. She was suddenly anxious about removing her traveling clothes with him in the room, though. One afternoon, and they were suddenly miles away from being in the right state for intimacy. Surely that would come again in time, though. But not until she'd discovered exactly who she'd married.

CHAPTER 12

*A*lex had no one to blame but himself. Although it would have been nice if he could blame Turpin or Parliament in general, or even Katya for pushing things along faster than they should have gone. But as handy as it would have been to foist the disastrously rough patch his new marriage had hit on someone else, it was his own failure to pay attention that had landed him in the mess.

Just as it was his failure to pay attention that had depressed Violetta's spirits, casting her life in shadows that she never recovered from. She'd probably been happy for the first time in years when James came along. How ironic that the one thing that could have brought her joy was the thing that killed her. He was responsible for that too.

That thought wouldn't leave him as he paced the platform at Lanhill's train station, waiting for Phillips to arrive. There was no need whatsoever for him to be there to meet his right-hand man, but the silence at Winterberry Park for the past week was beginning to grate on his nerves. Marigold had much to learn about managing a country estate, and spent the bulk of her days with Mrs. Musgrave, getting the hang of things. Either that or she resented him so much that she couldn't bear to be in the same room with him beyond meals. They certainly weren't intimate in bed, which he didn't blame her for one bit.

He sighed and rubbed a hand over his face as the incoming train's whistle split the air. A twist of irony tugged at the corner of his mouth. He ignored his age as much as possible and still believed himself to be in the prime of his youth, but nothing made the years seem heavier than being at odds with a woman. He had to make it up to her. He wouldn't be able to live with himself until he did. But he'd been saying that since even before he married her, and he had yet to figure out how one made so many things up to one's wife.

The train rolled into the station, screeching to a halt, and half a dozen passengers disembarked. Lanhill was a tiny station, so it wasn't difficult to spot Phillips's distinctive ginger hair the moment he stepped down. Surprise relief spilled through Alex as he marched over to greet the man.

Phillips blinked at him, startled. "I didn't think you'd actually come all the way here to meet me, sir."

"Yes, well, I was in the area and knew you'd be arriving," Alex lied, shaking Phillips's hand. "I wanted to hear how everything went with the revelation."

Phillips's expression hardened to business as Alex walked him to the baggage car, where the porter was unloading a handful of suitcases and trunks. "I leaked the information about Miss Murdoch to *The Times* and *The Observer*. *The Times* wasn't inclined to malign someone so closely associated with the political leanings of its owners, but they have the story. *The Observer* published a small piece three days ago," he reported with a triumphant grin. "So the truth is out there. I expect *The Times* will be forced to address it this summer, if rumors develop the way they usually do."

Alex thumped Phillips on the back. "Good man."

He'd been uncertain about playing his trump card where Turpin was concerned so quickly, but frustration and impatience had pushed him to do something, anything, that might brighten Marigold's mood. She genuinely cared about Ruby Murdoch's fate, and if Turpin could be brought to justice, perhaps she would forgive him.

"How is Miss Murdoch?" he asked after Phillips collected his suitcase and the two of them headed out of the station to the street, where his buggy was waiting.

Color splashed Phillips's face, though his frown was troubled. "She's been through the ringer, sir. She knows she's had a lucky break by being taken in at Croydon House, but it'll take her time to trust again." He paused for a moment before adding, "It might be best to bring her and Faith, that is, her baby, out here to Winterberry Park for the summer."

Alex raised an eyebrow. Something in the too-flat expression Phillips wore hinted he was hiding something. Alex had known the man for years, and suspected that he'd developed an affection for the poor young woman. Phillips wanted Miss Murdoch near him.

"I'll speak to Mrs. Croydon about it as soon as possible," he said, his heart lifting. At last, he had something important of a tender nature to discuss with Marigold. A spring filled his step as he climbed into the buggy. This could have been the opening he needed to start things on a positive path.

He didn't have a chance to raise the question with Marigold until much later that day, though. It was James's day to spend at Winterberry Park—something he'd agonized about all week. Would it be more or less hurtful to keep James at arm's-length for a time? Would Marigold flinch at the sight of his son, or would she think he was a blackguard for banishing his own child? He debated the issue back and forth with himself right up until the last minute, when he decided to keep to his original plan and have James for the day. Lucky for him, James was a charmer, and Marigold seemed to be the kind of woman who loved all children, no matter how disgraceful their fathers were.

"It almost seems a shame to send him back to Clara and Rev. Fallon," Marigold commented as she waved goodbye from Winterberry Park's front steps as the sun began to set.

Alex's heart shot to his throat. She was speaking to him. He had a chance to fix things after all. "Arthur and Clara have managed well so far," he said carefully.

Still watching the maid who walked James down Winterberry's long drive and not looking at Alex, Marigold said, "They have their hands full, though, Clara and Rev. Fallon. Two sets of twins within a year of each other would be a daunting task for the most experienced mother." Her hand drifted absently to her stomach.

Alex's brow twitched into a frown. Did she still want a child with him, in spite of his utter failures as a husband? Heaven knew that making her pregnant was the one thing he could competently manage. She'd been perfectly satisfied with his performance before he'd ruined things. But if he was going to save their marriage, he would have to do better than giving her what any lover could.

He must have stayed silent, studying her too long. She sent him a sideways glance, then blushed and lowered her eyes. "I wouldn't object if you chose to bring James to Winterberry Park for a while," she said in a quiet voice.

"With the right nursemaid and this lovely estate to wander, he may be quite happy."

Alex drew in a breath, the thrill of victory coursing through him. With it came a flash of inspiration. "Funny you should mention that."

Marigold turned fully to him. "Mention what?"

"A nursemaid."

She stared at him as if she had no idea what he was on about.

He shook his head slightly and changed his stance. "When Phillips arrived this morning, I asked him how Miss Murdoch was faring." Just as he'd predicted, Marigold's expression filled with interest. "Phillips seems to think Miss Murdoch would be happier here, at Winterberry Park, especially since the scandal is about to break."

"The scandal is about to...what?" Her eyes flared with alarm.

Alex winced. It seemed he had yet another thing on his hands that he hadn't quite thought through. It was damn difficult to remember to consult someone else in his decision after nearly fifty years of being his own entity.

"I've made sure that two key newspapers are aware of Miss Murdoch's story and Turpin's involvement in it," he told her. "One of them, *The Observer*, published a piece about it on Sunday. So the ball has been set into motion."

"And how does Ruby feel about all this?" Marigold crossed her arms.

Alex cleared his throat. Blast him, but he hadn't thought to ask. "I don't know," he admitted. "But it strikes me that we could kill two birds with one stone by bringing Miss Murdoch here so that she could serve as James's nursemaid for a while."

Marigold's eyebrows shot up. "You would trust a

woman with Miss Murdoch's past, a woman who has a child of her own, with the care of your son?"

It was next to impossible for Alex to tell whether the flash in Marigold's eyes was offense at the suggestion or approval of his outlandish idea. The rest of society would think he had lost his mind to violate the rules of acceptability so grievously. He hesitated for a little too long before answering, "Yes?"

For a few, terrifying heartbeats, Marigold simply stared at him. Then she relaxed into a pleased smile. Alex was so relieved that he could have fallen to his knees and wept.

"I think that's a wonderful idea," she said. "Especially if Turpin's crimes become public knowledge. I'm sure Ruby would feel much safer in the countryside than in the thick of things in town."

"My thoughts exactly." Alex stepped toward her, resting a hand on her arm.

Marigold's smile faltered, and she stared at his hand. He pulled away, regretting that he'd crossed the invisible boundary between them. But at least she hadn't wrenched free of him and marched back into the house. It was a step in the right direction, even if it was a tiny one.

"We should sit down and discuss the parameters of James's extended visit," he said, praying that she would take the bait and spend more time with him.

She hummed and nodded. "I think we'll need to be careful how we approach Clara and Rev. Fallon with the idea. We don't want them to think you've lost faith in their ability to care for James."

"Precisely." Alex took a deep breath, bristling with nerves as he took a chance and asked, "Would you like to stroll through the garden and discuss it? August sunsets are lovely at Winterberry Park." Although if he were honest, he would be much happier watching the sun rise, through the window from his bed, with her tucked happily in his arms.

All the same, he hesitantly offered her his arm. After a long, heart-stopping breath, she reached out and tentatively rested her hand in the crook of his elbow. Alex was so relieved that he nearly tripped down the stairs on the way to the garden path. Perhaps his failures weren't so unforgivable after all. Perhaps he could start over and spend the kind of time with his wife that he should have before proposing to her. For once in his life, he had a chance to make things right. An old dog could learn new tricks.

For as long as she could remember, Marigold had listened to the tales of her friends with houses in the country and longed to have that kind of escape herself. Now that she was firmly settled in Wiltshire with a vast estate of her own—or rather, Alex's—to manage, she longed for the faster pace and familiarity of London. Winterberry Park was perfectly lovely, and she and Alex were in high demand at parties and gatherings all across the county. But since her arrival two weeks before, she hadn't felt grounded or focused.

She settled onto the stool in front of the vanity in the dressing room Alex had encouraged her to set up across the hall from their bedroom. The fashionable gown she'd donned for the soiree at Alex's brother Edward's house that night swirled around her in a cloud of peach chiffon, but she could have been wearing sackcloth for all the joy it gave her. What use were beautiful gowns when nothing felt right?

"Would you like to wear the diamond earrings or the

sapphire, ma'am?" Ada, the housemaid who had been elevated to her lady's maid asked, holding up both pairs.

Marigold dragged herself out of her thoughts, glancing between the two stunning sets Alex had given her in the weeks after their wedding. Each was gorgeous in its own way, but they held little interest to her. She could see now that Alex had bought them out of a sense of guilt, or worse, obligation.

"It doesn't matter," she said with a sigh. "Whichever you think would look best."

Poor Ada's shoulders slumped, and her brow creased with worry. "The sapphire would be more dramatic, I think, ma'am," she said, returning to the bureau, where all the rest of Alex's guilt offerings were stored, to put the diamonds away.

Marigold's gaze shifted to the view out the open window. Wiltshire really was lovely. Alex had been spot on the other day when he told her that August sunsets were beautiful. Their walk through Winterberry Park's gardens had been enjoyable, even if it hadn't been particularly comfortable. She sensed that Alex didn't really know what to say to her, and if she were honest, she hadn't been much better. The worst of it was that she couldn't, in all honesty, say that the awkwardness between them was new or unexpected. It was merely what was left over when the excitement of making a rash decision wore off.

"There we go, ma'am." Ada brought the sapphire earrings to Marigold with a smile.

"Thank you, Ada." Marigold returned the maid's smile, then faced the mirror to put the earrings on. "How is James settling in?" she asked Ada's reflection.

The young woman's smile brightened. "He's making himself quite at home, ma'am. Though it'll be a blessing when the nursemaid you've sent for arrives. The maids have their hands full minding a little tike with Master James's energy. He does so like to wander off."

Marigold managed a tired smile. "Little boys are always a handful, I suppose." She stopped short of saying she looked forward to having one of her own. It was too soon for her to have the slightest hint about whether the babe she was carrying was a boy or a girl.

The baby. She took a shaky breath as she finished fastening her earrings. She still hadn't told Alex. She should have said something that evening when they strolled through the garden, discussing James's visit. Not coming out with the truth made her as guilty as Alex was for failing to mention James. Well, not *quite* as guilty. But really, how did one find a smooth and natural way to inform one's husband that they were about to become a father? Legitimately.

Marigold stood, blowing out a breath and smoothing her skirts. "Thank you for your help, Ada. I expect we'll be back from this party rather late tonight."

"I'll wait up for you, ma'am." Ada curtsied.

Marigold fetched her beaded reticule from the vanity and headed for the door. If she were counting her blessings, she would have to count Ada among them. She was a cheerful young woman with a smile that put her at ease. And heaven only knew how much she needed that.

As she reached the top of the stairs and started down to the front hall, where Mr. Noakes was waiting to see her and Alex off, James burst out from one of the drawing rooms, laughing and shrieking. A moment later, Alex stomped into the hall behind him, arms outstretched, a comical snarl on his face.

"Beware, Sir James! The vicious dragon is going to snatch you up," Alex called.

James rolled with laughter. "Macky! Macky, no!" He spotted Marigold and charged up a few stairs to hide in her skirts.

Marigold's heart leapt, then flopped into her stomach as James grabbed her leg through the layers of her skirt. She couldn't have stopped herself from laughing if she'd tried, and rested a hand on his head. "Don't worry, Sir James. I'll protect you."

She turned to Alex, but he had dropped his dragon stance. Now he just looked like a slightly sheepish gentleman dressed in a fine evening suit, with grey in his hair. All the same, Marigold's heart leapt again.

"Ah, Lady Marigold, this dragon has been slayed by one look at your radiant beauty," he said.

It wasn't so much his words as the hope in his eyes that sent heat and color straight to Marigold's cheeks. She hid the reaction by finding James's pudgy hand in her skirts and walking down the last few steps with him.

"Mari go out?" James asked as they crossed to Alex.

"I'm afraid so," she said, crouching and cradling his face with one hand. "But Macky and I will come home later, and when you wake up tomorrow, we'll have eggs and toast."

"Mmm." James rubbed his belly.

A thousand conflicting emotions welled up in Marigold's chest. As frustrated as she was with Alex, it was impossible not to love James. He was just a child, after all. His origins weren't his fault. She kissed his cheek and stood, feeling unaccountably misty-eyed, and handed him over to Martha, one of the housemaids.

"Your carriage awaits, my lady," Alex said, offering his arm and continuing the charade.

She smiled at him and chuckled as she took his arm. A moment later, she sucked in a breath. It was the first time she had genuinely laughed at something Alex had said in two weeks. If the sting of his betrayal was already fading, perhaps they had a good chance of making something of their marriage after all. She touched a hand to her stomach. Of course, they'd already made something of their marriage.

"Why does James call you Macky?" she asked as Alex handed her into one of his more formal carriages. It was drawn by two powerful horses instead of one, like the buggy.

Alex let out an ironic laugh. "He calls me Macky because we were all too silly and indecisive when he was learning to speak to come up with anything better."

Marigold stared blankly at him as the carriage lurched into motion.

"We couldn't very well have him call me Papa," he said, a flush painting his cheeks in the evening light streaming through the carriage window.

"I suppose not." Marigold nodded.

"Clara began teaching him to call me Mr. Croydon, and Arthur kept calling me Alex. I suppose James gathered up what syllables he could from those names and came up with Macky."

"The logic of a child." Marigold smiled.

"He's a clever boy," Alex agreed with a father's proud grin.

"I'm sure he'll make quite a name for himself," she said.

He didn't reply, and she couldn't think of anything else to say. As clever as James was, Marigold couldn't help but wonder what kind of place he'd have in the world, especially as younger siblings came along. Perhaps Alex was thinking the same thing, because he stayed quiet for most of the rest of the journey.

In the two weeks since they'd been in Wiltshire,

Marigold and Alex had dined at Edward's house twice. Edward was younger than Alex by almost ten years, and although he admitted freely that he wasn't half as ambitious as Alex, or nearly as good with money, he had a wide circle of friends and entertained frequently at his cottage, as he called it. Though "cottage" wasn't quite what Marigold would have called the stately, ten-bedroom house in the town of Frogwell, adjacent to Chippenham. Edward was a bachelor who enjoyed life, and in her two previous visits, Marigold had met everyone from the Bishop of Swindon to famous cricketer W.G. Grace.

"I'm told Lady Evangeline Gilchrist will be in attendance tonight," Alex finally said as they neared the lights of the town. The sun had set during their half-hour journey. "I think you'd enjoy her company."

"I look forward to meeting her, then," Marigold answered, feeling doubly awkward, since the conversation had lagged for so long. At any point, she could have given Alex the good news, but she hadn't.

Alex smiled at her in the dimming light and took her hand. She didn't pull away. "Edward is particularly fond of Lady Evangeline. So fond, in fact, that I hope we'll have a wedding to go to next spring."

Marigold's lips twitched. Her insides quivered. She simply couldn't resist cracking a joke at their expense. "Good for them for waiting more than three weeks to become engaged," she blurted before she changed her mind.

Alex turned his head to stare at her, his eyebrows lifting. Slowly, a smile spread across his face, reaching his eyes so that they caught what little light there was and glittered. "Smarter than we were, eh?"

"Infinitely."

It felt as though someone had opened a window and let

the air in. Alex's chuckle was low and subtle, but he was definitely laughing. She couldn't keep her own laugh from escaping, though she tried to by pressing her free hand over her mouth.

By the time the carriage pulled up in front of Edward's house, Marigold felt lighter than she had in weeks. Things were progressing. They weren't perfect, the mistakes were all still there, but they were moving forward. It was more than she could have hoped for.

"Alex," Edward greeted them with a loud, cheerful shout as they were shown into the large sitting room where two dozen guests at least were already gathering. "And my darling sister-in-law. What a pleasure to see you here."

Marigold's laughter continued to bubble right under the surface. Edward held a large glass of wine, and it was clear he'd already enjoyed at least one other. Alex shared a long-suffering look with her and rolled his eyes, which only spurred her to laugh more.

"Edward," Alex greeted his brother with a handshake and a thump on his back. He leaned closer. "Shouldn't you save the wine until after supper?"

"Of course not, old chap," Edward replied, loud enough for everyone in town to hear, let alone everyone in the room. "This is a celebration."

"What are we celebrating?" Marigold asked, pressing a hand to her stomach. It fluttered with the wild thought that somehow Edward had found out about the baby, even though she hadn't told anyone other than Lady Stanhope.

But Edward shouted, "Turpin's downfall!"

Several of the other guests raised their glasses and echoed, "Turpin's downfall!"

"Why? What happened?" Alex asked, his eyes suddenly bright.

"Haven't you heard?" A beautiful woman in what Marigold recognized as the latest Paris fashion swept forward to join her. "*The Times* came out with a salacious story about him and a maid he supposedly dishonored."

"Marigold, I'd like you to meet Lady Evangeline Gilchrist," Alex said, though his eyes were alight with more than just the introduction of a woman who could end up as Marigold's sister-in-law. "Lady Evangeline, this is my beautiful bride, Mrs. Marigold Croydon."

For the first time in weeks, it felt good to be introduced as Alex's wife. "How do you do?" She nodded to Lady Evangeline.

"Splendidly," Lady Evangeline replied, a little too enthusiastically, making Marigold wonder just how much wine had been poured all around before they arrived. "That horrible toad, Turpin, is about to get his comeuppance."

"Today it's *The Times*," Edward said, "and tomorrow it will be every other newspaper in Europe."

"It's scandalous what he did to that poor woman," Lady Evangeline followed on top of Edward's words.

He returned the favor by rushing on with, "Of course, Turpin will claim it's all hearsay and nonsense, but if they can find what happened to the girl and get her to tell her story in court, why, this will be the end of that blighter's career."

Marigold sent a sideways look to Alex, who was grinning like a cat with a canary. It was the same mysterious, wicked sort of grin that had drawn her to him in the first place, and it made her toes tingle. Better still, she could tell that he wasn't about to burst out with the truth of how the story had made it to the papers or where Ruby Murdoch was. He would let the whole thing play out without taking credit for a bit of it. And although that was brilliant strategically, it raised him in her estimation as well.

"You're a little late," Edward went on. "We're all just about to sit down to supper. Come along."

Marigold exchanged a full glance with Alex and squeezed his arm before they followed the rest of the crowd through the parlor and into the dining room.

Supper truly was a celebration, although Marigold wasn't convinced Edward and his friends needed something like Turpin's scandal to burst into bacchanalia. They were in high spirits, and managed to lift hers with them. Or perhaps it was the way Alex laughed and carried on with the rest of them that warmed her heart. She hadn't seen him so relaxed since the night before they left for Wiltshire. His smile was easy, his manner was charming, and as the meal progressed, a whisper at the back of her head reminded her that this was why she'd fallen so hard and fast for him. How could a woman not throw caution to the wind when a man was as charming as the devil himself? It made her wonder if perhaps the time had come to put everything on the table, tell him about the baby, and take their marriage back to where it had been before hitting the bump.

"Do you know," she whispered to him as everyone rose from their places at the end of supper and prepared to adjourn to the ballroom, "I think I might be a little too tired for dancing tonight." She glanced up at him with confidence, hoping he would understand that she was promising something more when they returned to Winterberry Park.

"Are you sure?" Alex began. "Mr. Holbert over there is an excellent—" He stopped abruptly and did a double-take as soon as his eyes met hers. "I'll have the carriage brought around," he said in a suddenly hoarse voice.

Marigold stifled a giggle, glancing around to see if any of

the other guests had noticed the exchange or interpreted what it foretold. They were all too busy laughing and chatting and pushing their way through the hallway to the ballroom. Alex dodged through a few of them to have a quick word with his brother. A very quick word. He broke away from Edward after only a few seconds.

Edward raised his hand and shouted, "Good night and Godspeed, Mrs. Croydon."

"God speed, Mrs. Croydon!" several others echoed.

Alex's carriage was brought around with surprising speed. The driver remained in his seat, his cap pulled low.

"I would have expected Henry to be carousing with the other servants downstairs," Alex said as he helped Marigold to climb inside.

"Do they have their own parties here in Wiltshire the same way they do in London?" Marigold asked, excitement buzzing through her as Alex settled on the seat beside her, closing the door.

"Of course," he smiled. "What's the point of driving your employers to a revelry like this one if you can't enjoy the leftovers yourself? Drive on, Henry," he called. The carriage lurched into motion.

Marigold grinned from ear to ear, even though she wasn't sure Alex could see it. "In that case, I hope Henry isn't too put out to have left the party early."

"If he is, I'll make sure there's something in his pay packet to compensate him."

He leaned closer to her, sliding his arm around her waist. A thrill of temptation like she wasn't sure she'd ever feel again zipped through her as they sped away from the lights of Frogwell and into the darkness of the countryside. They slowed for a moment, and the carriage dipped slightly, but it rushed into motion again, picking up speed, in no time.

"And now, my darling wife, was there something you wanted from me?"

Marigold's heart beat as fast as the carriage raced through the night, and both were racing with incredible speed. "There's something I need to tell you," she said, barely able to suppress a giggle. This was why she'd waited to say something about the baby. After two weeks of misery, she finally felt as though she and Alex had reached common ground. Things were exactly the way they should be for news like hers.

But before she could say a word, Alex pulled her closer, resting his hand on the side of her face. "Are you going to tell me you forgive me?" he asked. Even in the darkness, she could see the light of hope in his eyes. "Because I know I've been a wretched fool. But I promise I can learn. I may be an old dog, but I want more than anything to learn new tricks. Teach me."

Excitement blossomed in Marigold's chest, leaving her breathless. She felt dizzy and out of control, and not just because of the way the carriage rattled and jolted as they charged over country roads. She wanted him. She wanted her husband, faults and all. The shock was over, and her heart longed to be with him.

She surged into him, which felt like being thrown against him the way the carriage jostled. He caught her tightly in his arms and kissed her. Everything else disappeared. All Marigold felt as his lips parted hers and his tongue invaded her was promise and hope. She had never been so grateful to discover that anger could be temporary and peace could be restored. His hands caressed her curves over the layers of her dress, and she unbuttoned his jacked to reach for his warmth. They could mend the wrongs between them after all.

Thoughts of the closet at Westminster came back, and heat poured through her. If they could make love in a closet, surely they could make love in a speeding carriage too. She reached for the buttons of his waistcoat—then let out a sudden yelp as he bit her tongue.

"Sorry," Alex gasped, leaning back. "Sorry, it wasn't me. This bloody carriage."

He was right. The carriage was knocking around wildly. She'd been too caught up in the return of passion to notice at first.

"Henry!" Alex leaned forward, banging against the top of the carriage near where Henry sat outside. "Slow down, man. Are you trying to get us all killed?"

He was answered with a jolt of stunning force. To Marigold, it felt as though they'd run over something, but kept on going. Fear replaced desire in a split second, and she grabbed the edges of her seat as hard as she could.

"Henry!" Alex shouted, banging for all he was worth.

It did no good. The carriage tore on, hitting every rut and bump along the way. In fact, without being able to see through the night, Marigold would have guessed they'd left the road entirely and—

She didn't finish her thought. With a loud crack, the world tipped sideways. Seconds later, she was slammed against the front of the carriage. Then pain. Then blackness.

CHAPTER 13

*a*lex drifted through the darkness, hearing nothing but the roar of blood pounding in his ears. Slowly, groggily, the world came into partial focus around him. His head pounded. His body ached. His left arm in particular throbbed. He clawed his way up through the blackness, noticing small details. A horse was crying in pain nearby. Tiny shafts of moonlight stabbed down through cracks that shouldn't have been where they were. And in the distance, he heard faint shouts of alarm.

The temptation to give up and fall back into the darkness was overwhelming. If he could just relax and sleep, the pain would go away, and—

"Marigold."

The single word spilled clumsily from his lips, but it was enough to snap him to full attention. They were in the carriage. The carriage had crashed. That was the only explanation. He pushed away from a padded surface, possibly the back of a seat, but it was in the wrong place. One of the carriage doors was above him, and what had been the front was shattered.

"Marigold," he repeated, more urgently, and reached in the darkness to find her. His hands closed around warmth and fabric, what might have been her arm or her leg, he couldn't tell. Everything was topsy-turvy.

Careful not to crush her because he couldn't see her, he twisted, reaching for the handle of the door above him. His heart pounded in his chest and his breath came in painful, shallow gasps. He pushed the door up and open, letting in enough moonlight to see.

Marigold lay in a crumpled heap on the floor. Blood streaked across her pale face. She wasn't moving.

"No." The word came out as a sob. He reached for her, bracing himself against the odd angles of the wrecked carriage and gathering her in his arms. "No, oh, no. Marigold."

Desperation ripped through him as he hugged her close, cradling her and rocking. He wiped the blood from her face, kissed her cheek, felt for her pulse. It was there, faint and thready, but it was there.

He had to get her out, get her to a doctor. With every ounce of effort he could manage, he pushed his way to a standing position, struggling to lift Marigold high enough to get her through the door and onto the side of the carriage. One of the horses continued to make horrible, shrieking sounds, but the other was silent. As he pulled his way through the door to perch on the side of the carriage by Marigold's side, he searched through the darkness.

"Henry!" he shouted, wincing as he moved into position to climb down from the wreck. "Henry!"

His driver was nowhere in sight, but a pair of shadowy figures were running toward the wreck in the dark.

"Hello! Hello there," a man with a rural accent shouted. "Are you all right?"

Alex grimaced as he struggled down the overturned carriage, pulling Marigold toward him, then into his arms. He wasn't stable enough to support her weight on legs that were more injured than he'd accounted for, and they both spilled to the ground.

"Fetch Dr. Miller," the voice shouted, much closer to them. Moments later, heavy footsteps reached the wreck, where Alex lay, cradling Marigold against him. "We saw the carriage tearing through the night without a driver," the man said. "Saw it run off the road, hit something, and go flying through the air."

The words barely registered. "My wife," Alex panted, trying desperately to push through his pain. "My wife."

The man—a farmer, judging by his dress, or what Alex could see of it in the moonlight—jumped into action. He scooped Marigold up in his beefy arms, then paused to see if Alex needed help as well. Alex considered it lucky that he could power his way to his feet on his own, though he leaned against the man's shoulder until he was certain he was steady.

"My home's just this way," the farmer said, starting slowly across the uneven terrain of the field they'd crashed in. "I'll send me son to take care of the horse."

Alex had no idea how long it took to trudge across the field to the tiny, thatched cottage. It could have been an hour or a minute. He was grateful for the light and the simple bed that the farmer lay Marigold on.

"I'll fix some tea," a woman who must have been his wife said, crossing herself.

"Dr. Miller is on his way," the farmer assured them.

Alex nodded, but his full attention was on Marigold. He'd never seen anyone look so pale, at least not since

Violetta's last days. The horrific, helpless memories of those days pounded through him with every beat of his heart. He couldn't lose another one. Every woman he'd ever loved died.

As soon as the thought came, he pushed it away, crouching on the side of the bed and gathering Marigold in his arms. "Marigold," he murmured, then louder, "Marigold. Wake up."

She was so still. Blood stained her fine gown from more than just the cut across her forehead. Her arms and a good deal of her chest were exposed by the summer fashion, and cuts, scrapes, and bruises marred her perfect skin. But there was still more blood, on her skirt and what he could see of her ankles. He reached for the hem of her skirt, anxious to see if she'd somehow cut her legs, even with layers of skirts and petticoats.

A deep, sick feeling formed in his stomach as he bunched up her skirts. The tiny bit of blood on her ankles was nothing to what he discovered the higher up her legs he went. By the time he made it to the top of her thighs, he choked, dizzy with panic. Her drawers were soaked with it.

"Where's Dr. Miller?" he bellowed, panic sucking him under.

"He's on the way," the farmer's wife called from the other room.

Marigold stirred, groaning with pain. Her eyes fluttered, but didn't quite open. She writhed, trying to roll to the side and curl into herself, clutching her stomach.

"Marigold," Alex panted, eyes wide, heart racing. His hands shook as he brushed her forehead, not sure if he should hold her or keep his distance. But no, he couldn't let her lie there in pain without knowing how desperately he loved her. "Marigold, hold on. The doctor is coming. I'm here. Hold on."

She groaned louder as sweat broke out on her forehead. Alex hunched over her, hugging her and trying to keep her from moving too much or too hard. Instinct told him to keep her as still as possible, whether that was the right thing to do or not.

"It's all right," he whispered to her, shaking as he held her, eyes blurry with tears. "You'll be all right. Everything will be fine."

Time seemed to drag and fly at the same time. He held Marigold as she groaned, never quite coming around. That was easier than when her eyes rolled back in her head and she stopped moving or crying at all. The best Alex could hope for was that she would continue to breathe.

At last, Dr. Miller arrived.

"What happened?" he asked as he marched into the room, setting his bag on the side of the bed. He pushed Alex aside as he sat to examine her.

A rush of anger at being cast off so cavalierly kept Alex from answering immediately.

"The carriage wrecked," the farmer said. Alex hadn't noticed him stepping into the doorway. "We saw it from the garden. Tore through the night like Satan himself were on its heels, then smashed when it hit a rock or some such."

Dr. Miller nodded, grasping Marigold's head and turning it this way and that. He felt her pulse and checked the cuts on her arms, humming and grunting the whole time. When he palpitated her stomach, Marigold let out a pained groan.

"Marigold." Alex rushed forward, but Dr. Miller held out an arm, glaring at him, and holding him back. Alex licked his dry lips, unable to catch more than a shallow breath. "There's more," he said, feeling sick. "Blood. Under her skirt."

Dr. Miller frowned at him, pursed his lips, and lifted the hem of Marigold's skirt. As soon as he saw what Alex had seen, his irritated expression burst into alarm. "Out!" he shouted, standing and reaching for his bag. "Everybody out of here. Get him out and keep him out."

"No, I won't leave," Alex said, even as the farmer grabbed both of his arms from behind and wrestled him out of the room. "I won't leave my wife. Marigold! I won't leave her side."

He had no choice. The farmer was younger and much stronger than he was, and in spite of all his effort, Alex ended up standing in the main room of the house as Dr. Miller slammed the door on him. He yanked and struggled and did everything he could to break free of the farmer's grasp, but all too soon, he realized how futile his efforts were. There was nothing he could do but wait.

"Have a cuppa tea," the farmer's wife said gently. Her expression was painfully sympathetic. "You could use a few sticking plasters on your face yourself, sir," she added.

Alex lifted a hand to his forehead. It came away bloody. It hadn't dawned on him that he was injured too, not when Marigold was in such dire circumstances. The tension drained away from him, and the farmer finally let him go. All the pain and exhaustion he'd kept at bay pressed in on him, and it was all he could do to make it to one of the rough chairs by the cottage's fireplace before collapsing.

He let the farmer's wife bring him tea and tend to his wounds. She suspected his left arm was broken, and as soon as his fear for Marigold lessened, the pain was bad enough for him to agree with her. She splinted it while they waited for Dr. Miller to finish with Marigold.

That wait stretched on and on. Alex's initial panic gave way to a fresh, more potent wave.

"What's going on in there?" he shouted after what felt like an eternity of waiting. He tried to push himself up from the chair to go find out, but between the way his entire body ached and the warning glance of the farmer, all he could do was shout from where he sat. "I demand to know what's wrong with my wife."

"I'll go and check," the farmer's wife said with a pitying half-smile.

She walked to the door, knocked, then poked her head in. But instead of asking questions or saying anything at all, she let out a sudden, horrified gasp and backed into the main room, snapping the door tightly shut behind her. She whipped around, all color drained from her face, and pressed her back to the door.

"What?" Alex demanded, leaning forward in spite of the pain it caused. "What is going on in there?"

The farmer's wife raised a trembling hand to her chest, then her mouth. Then she let it drop. "Th-the doctor has everything under control," she squeaked.

Alex surged forward, not believing a word she said, but the farmer blocked him before he could stand.

"I demand to know what's going on with my wife," Alex shouted, feeling right on the edge of madness. He couldn't catch his breath, and his heart felt as though it were about to leap from his chest. "Goddammit, tell me what's going on."

"I-it'll be all right," the farmer's wife said, utterly unconvincing. "I'm sure Dr. Miller knows what he's doing."

The only thing that stopped Alex from ripping the farmer and his entire house apart to get to Marigold was the commotion caused by Henry, Edward, and one of Edward's servants bursting through the door.

"We heard what happened," Edward said, slurring his words.

Alex glared at Henry. "The devil take you," he shouted. "Your incompetent driving might cost me my wife. You're dismissed without a reference this minute."

"It wasn't me," Henry gaped in return. "It wasn't me. I didn't even know the carriage was gone. It was another bloke, the one who was skulking about at the party."

"It's true, sir," Edward's servant backed Henry up. "We all assumed he was someone else's driver. There were so many people at the party."

"I've sent people to look for whoever it was," Edward went on, looking as though he were struggling mightily to be sober enough to handle the situation, but not succeeding. "The constable and his men are out looking too, but the bastard can't be found."

Alex stared at his brother. The information coming at him was slow to sink in. Someone other than Henry had driven off with them and somehow deliberately set the carriage on a path to destruction. It hadn't been an accident at all. It was attempted murder. His gaze snapped to the closed bedroom door. It very well could be murder, depending on what was happening in that room. And as far as Alex was concerned, he knew of only one man who had reason to murder him. Turpin.

"There's tea enough for everyone," the farmer's wife spoke wearily into the stunned silence. She moved away from the bedroom door, disappearing into the kitchen.

Alex slumped back in his seat, eyes still glued to the door. His wife could be in that room dying while Turpin likely laughed and bragged to his friends about getting rid of their chief opposition. He would murder the man. If

Marigold didn't make it through, he would kill the man with his bare hands.

Time stretched on again—or not, Alex still couldn't tell —before the bedroom door opened at last. Dr. Miller stepped through, but the sight of him wasn't a comfort at all. He'd donned an apron, with was splashed with blood. His hands were stained with it. Alex's chest constricted to the point of agony, and it felt as though his heart stopped completely.

"I'm afraid she's lost the baby," Dr. Miller said.

The whole world stopped. Alex's vision went black at the edges. His stomach roiled and his lungs wouldn't draw in air.

"And unfortunately, there were complications when I attempted to ascertain whether the entire fetus was expelled or, like before...." His words faded away, and he waved a hand. For some reason, he couldn't quite meet Alex's eyes. "We'll speak about this some other time, when you're well."

"What complications?" Alex demanded, surging forward. He still didn't have the energy to stand. "Is she alive? Will she live?"

"Your wife is alive, sir," Dr. Miller said wearily. "She is young and strong, and I believe that, with time, she will make a full—" He stopped and shook his head with a weary sigh. "She will recover."

If anything, Alex's alarm doubled. "What are you saying, man? Will she be all right or not?"

Dr. Miller sighed harder. "As I said, there were complications with...with my examination."

"Dammit, man!" Alex pushed himself to stand. The farmer looked like he might block him yet again, but

Edward and Henry stepped in, supporting Alex under his arms. "I demand you tell me what you're refusing to say."

"It's too soon to tell," Dr. Miller reeled back, raising his bloody hands as if to defend himself. "It may be nothing. The bleeding has stopped, for the most part, although there may still be—"

"What did you do to her?" Alex roared. The dragon he'd pretended to be with James that afternoon raged within him.

"There was scarring," Dr. Miller said at last, as pitiful as a terrified child. "At least, there will be. My instruments...it was difficult to see what I was doing...I was only trying to make sure that the incomplete expulsion of the placenta that happened to Violetta didn't happen to this one."

"Women don't need fancy doctoring when they lose a baby," the farmer's wife said, gaping at Dr. Miller. "Nature takes care of the loss. You didn't try to interfere with it, did you?"

"I want to see my wife," Alex demanded, pulling away from Edward and Henry.

No one tried to stop him as he marched into the bedroom. Whatever Dr. Miller had done, he'd tried to clean up from it, or hide it. Marigold was covered with a blanket, but flecks of blood were still visible here and there. A pile of linen that looked as though it also contained the skirt and petticoat of Marigold's dress sat in a corner, discreetly covered with a towel. Alex only gave it a cursory, horrified look before flying to the bed and sinking to sit by Marigold's side.

He grabbed her limp hand and held it to his cheek. At least she was breathing, though she was still as pale as the sheets around her. A bottle of laudanum sat on the table beside the bed.

"Oh, my darling," Alex choked out as tears stung his eyes. "I'm so sorry. I'm sorry that I did this to you. Just stay with me. Stay with me."

He kissed her hand, his tears dropping on her fingers, then curled forward to shelter her body with his. If only he'd been able to shelter her from everything else.

CHAPTER 14

She couldn't pick up her fan. She wasn't sure why she'd dropped it in the first place...or where it had gone...or why everything around her was so dark and misty. All Marigold knew was that every time she bent to pick up her fan, searing pain shot through her middle. And yet that urgency, that sense of having lost something, pressed down on her, urging her to try again and again and again. But she couldn't bend, couldn't pick up what she'd lost. She didn't even know where she was.

The terrifying, frustrating void stretched on and on, until she felt as though she'd been searching through the darkness, looking for what was lost, bending to reach for it, and crying out in pain for years, an eternity. And it was hot. Not just because August was upon them. Everything was hot, no matter which way she turned.

At one point, she thought Alex was there, murmuring soothing words to her. She clung to him as the pain and heat rose to a fevered pitch. For a moment, she opened her eyes and was left with the uncanny impression that she wasn't on some black, misty plane looking for her fan at all, she was lying flat in the bed of a wagon, the scent of the hay packed around her thick in her nostrils. Alex held her, stroking her forehead and murmuring, "We'll be home soon, we'll be home soon."

But that felt like a lifetime ago. The swirling darkness returned, as hot as an inferno, and once again, she twisted and turned, aching every time she bent, unable to reach what she'd lost, or even figure out what it was.

And then the heat faded away. The pain dulled to a constant ache, and the restlessness of her search calmed to deep, deep sleep.

It felt as though she were rising from some sort of evil enchantment when, at last, she pried her eyes open. Bright sunlight streamed in through curtains that billowed in a summer breeze. She recognized the window. She was in bed, in the bed she shared with Alex. Something cool and wet was being daubed on her forehead by unskilled hands. She blinked, drew in a breath, and forced her eyes to focus.

James. James sat on the bed by her side, patting her forehead with a wet rag. He wore a serious look on his cherubic face, which was less than a foot from hers. As soon as Marigold's eyes fluttered open, he drew in a breath and let go of the rag, leaving it on her forehead.

"Mari," he shouted, clapping his hands. "Mari awake."

A shuffle and snort sounded from one of the chairs beyond the foot of the bed. With what felt like immense effort, Marigold shifted her head to find Alex lifting from what looked like a sleeping position. One of his arms was bound in what looked like a sling.

"Mari awake! Mari awake!" James called out, bouncing his way down the bed. His every movement sent dull, throbbing pain through Marigold, but she couldn't find the energy to care.

"Marigold?" Alex leapt from the chair. If he had been snoozing, he was fully awake now. He darted to the side of the bed, jostling it and sending a spear of pain through Marigold's stomach and hips as he sat, and grabbed her hand from where it rested on the bedcovers with his uninjured hand. "Thank God, Marigold."

He lifted her hand to his lips, covering her knuckles with kisses, then pressed it to his forehead as he bent over and sobbed.

"No cry, Macky," James said, scrambling over Marigold's legs and causing a fresh wave of pain that darkened the edges of her vision. "Mari awake."

"Yes," Alex said, relief thick in his voice. "Marigold is awake, but we must be careful with her."

He let her hand go so that he could lift James off of her legs and into his good arm. The other one was definitely broken and healing. Marigold watched the two of them, focusing on her breathing and how good something so simple felt.

"What happened?" she asked, surprised at how weak and rough the words sounded.

Alex hesitated, wiping tears from his face, then dodging James as he tried to continue wiping them. He gently caught James's hands and held them so that he would stop. "There was an accident. The carriage crashed," he began reluctantly.

Memories flooded in on her. She'd been in the speeding carriage, kissing Alex and contemplating doing much more. She'd been about to tell him she was pregnant. Then came the crash, the blackness. All she remembered after that were flashes of pain, a bedroom that wasn't her own, and someone forcing her to drink what felt like a gallon of foul-tasting medicine. Then came the fog and darkness.

"I remember the carriage." She tried to move, to sit up, but could barely manage to shift a few inches.

"Don't try to move," Alex said, setting James on the floor and scooting closer to her. He stroked her face, caught her hand and kissed it again. "You've been through a lot. The doctor...he had to...and then...and...infection set in."

Marigold blinked, not sure whether something was still wrong with her and she wasn't catching everything he was saying or whether he was choking up and unable to speak. Her body felt as though it had been trampled by horses and dragged halfway through Wiltshire. She wanted to sleep again.

"It's been over a week," Alex choked out with a combination of relief and sorrow. "Dr. Miller didn't think you would last through the fever."

Marigold wasn't so weak that she didn't note the rush of fury in his words. He was so angry that she blinked and tried to move instead of relaxing back into sleep.

"I'll have his license revoked," Alex went on, fuming. "I'll have him strung up as the quack he is." He glanced to her, and his demeanor instantly changed. "I'm sorry, my darling. There will be time for that later. All that matters for now is that you made it through the fever. You're here, you're alive, and Mrs. Canny believes you won't relapse. You're here to stay. So rest now."

He kissed her hand again, holding it to his cheek. Marigold stared at him, unable to comprehend what she was seeing. She'd never witnessed any man, let alone Alex, so overly emotional. She must have skated all the way to the doors of Hades and back for him to be weeping openly in front of her. That's all that mattered to her. The rest would have to wait.

She closed her eyes, and within seconds had fallen into

a heavy, dreamless sleep. There was no telling how long it lasted or what was going on around her, but unlike her previous sleep, it was restful, healing.

When she awoke again, the window was still open and the curtains still billowed, but the sunlight was dimmer, as if it were morning instead of afternoon and cloudy. Alex was gone, and so was James. A maid was busy arranging something on a small table on the other side of the window, but Marigold couldn't make out who she was until she turned to face her.

"Ruby?" She blinked the sleep away, pushing herself up a few inches on the pillows.

"Mrs. Croydon." Ruby's face lit up, and she left was she was doing to rush to Marigold's side. "You're looking so much better, ma'am," she smiled.

Marigold gaped at the young woman. She wasn't sure she'd ever seen Ruby smile. The sight was as welcome as the breeze blowing through the window.

Ruby bent to help Marigold sit, piling pillows behind her and adjusting the bedcovers as she did. "It's so good to see you awake, ma'am," she said as she worked, fussing over Marigold like, well, like she had nearly died. "Everyone's been so worried. Not a living soul could convince Mr. Croydon to leave your side for an entire week. And Mr. Edward has visited every day. Rev. and Mrs. Fallon have come every day as well, and the village children all made cards to wish you well. They said they're learning a song to sing to you once you get better. And Gilbert, that is, Mr. Phillips, has been running back and forth between Winterberry Park and Chippenham and London every few days in his efforts to catch the man who did it."

Marigold blinked and shook her head, which ached after the onslaught of information. "I...what...how...."

187

She couldn't form her thoughts into a single question. Too many questions rattled in her brain. But it felt good to sit up, strangely enough. Even though her entire middle ached and she was so weak she felt in danger of sliding and falling over at any moment.

"Could I have some water?" she asked instead, her thirst suddenly overwhelming.

"Yes, ma'am. Right away, ma'am. Then I'll fetch Mr. Croydon right away." Ruby skipped to the table where she'd been working before and poured water into an infant's porcelain cup with a spout. "Your father and sisters have been telegraphing like mad," she went on. "And Lady Lavinia, and Lady Stanhope too. I've never seen so many messages flying around."

She brought the cup to Marigold and held it to her mouth. Marigold was about to insist she could manage on her own, but when she lifted her arms, it was a shock to realize she would likely drop the cup if she tried to hold it. A simple porcelain cup.

"Master James has been as eager to wait on you as Mr. Croydon has," Ruby said as Marigold finished drinking. "He's such a darling. Thank you so much for thinking to send for me to mind him." Her cheeks were rosy with delight. "I'll fetch Mr. Croydon now."

With a short curtsy, she sped out of the room, leaving Marigold alone. Marigold blew out a breath, shaking her head in bewilderment. They'd barely managed to get Ruby to say three words together in London. Alex could hardly be bothered to spend an hour on end with her, let alone sit by her side for days when she wasn't even conscious. The Fallons barely knew her, and for all she knew, the village children hadn't even heard of her. She felt as though she'd gone to bed in one world and awakened in an entirely different one.

Footsteps charging up the hall alerted her to Alex's arrival before he burst through the bedroom door. "You're awake," he said, his voice heavy with relief as he rushed to sit on the side of the bed. His left arm was still secured in a splint and sling.

"For the time being," she said, using all of her effort to raise her hand.

He took it, kissing it as he had the last time she woke up. He seemed rested and well put together at first glance, but the more she studied him, the easier it was to see the lines in his face, the grey at his temples, and the exhaustion in his eyes.

"How long was I asleep this time?" she asked, already tempted to return to sleep.

"Just since yesterday afternoon," he said. "It's late morning now." He paused, then added, "Do you feel up to trying some broth or tea? I've been worried sick that you wouldn't get enough nourishment these last ten days."

Marigold blinked at him, wondering how on earth she'd been nourished at all in that time. That explained the cup with the spout, at least. "I could eat something," she said.

Alex turned to Ruby, who was standing in the doorway. "Tell Mrs. Carlisle to send up broth, soup, anything."

"Yes, sir." Ruby curtsied, then rushed off.

Marigold wriggled against the pillows, trying to find a more comfortable position. Her back was in agony, and every way she turned brought a new wave of aches. "I never thought I'd look forward to eating so much," she laughed weakly. Alex leaned forward to help with her pillows, eventually giving up and twisting on the bed so that he could hold her against his side with his good arm. "I suppose I should keep my strength up," she went on, "since...." A flush of excitement and guilt splashed through her. "Alex, there's something I need to tell you."

"No," he said with a surprising catch in his voice. His arm tightened around her. "There's something I should tell you."

She turned her face slowly to him. There was so much pity and anger in his expression that dread trickled through her, making her dizzy. "What?" she whispered.

He drew in a long, shaky breath. "The impact of the crash," he started, then stopped and swallowed. Marigold's dread grew, as did the horrible suspicion that she knew what he was about to say. "You were very badly injured," he went on, barely able to get the words out. "Even before Dr. Miller got ahold of you."

An icy chill joined the gnawing dread filling her, as if she were drowning from the inside. "Just tell me," she whispered.

Alex swallowed again, licked his lips, blinked rapidly. "You lost the baby," he said in a hoarse rush.

Marigold gasped, her eyes instantly stinging with bitter sorrow. If he hadn't been holding her up, she would have collapsed and not been able to right herself. Too many things made sense—the aches and soreness all through her stomach and hips, the dream that she had lost something, the hollowness.

"We'll...we'll try again," she said, working to swallow her tears. "As soon as I'm recovered, we'll have another one."

Alex shook his head, looking downright ashen. "No," he whispered. "Not after what...."

Between his words and his expression, Marigold went numb. "It can't be that bad," she whispered. "I made it through the fever. I'll work hard to get well again. Surely we can—"

He pressed his fingers to his mouth, then took a deep breath. "When Dr. Miller saw you'd miscarried, he attempted an examination to be certain everything was expelled."

Marigold frowned in confusion and mounting fear. "Why?"

Alex shook his head. "It was bloody foolish, unnecessary." For a moment, he was angry beyond the ability to speak. Marigold felt his body heat around hers. But he gathered himself enough to go on. "No one was in the room with him, and he'd given you laudanum, so there's no way to know for sure. And then the fever set in. Mrs. Canny, the midwife, says it's a miracle the infection wasn't worse, but she...." He drew in a shuddering breath.

Marigold had gone rigid at the story. Her stomach twisted, but she forced herself to say, "Please just say it and get it over with."

Alex shook his head. "It's a miracle you're alive," he said, "but that's the best miracle we can hope for. Mrs. Canny says the damage is irreparable. There won't be any more babies. There can't be."

Marigold nodded slowly, her gaze losing focus. The numbness had spread through her body and into her heart and mind. She should have been wailing with grief and fury, as angry as she could tell Alex was. She should have been weeping for her lost baby, for all the babies she would never have. Instead, she felt nothing.

She turned her face away from Alex. "I don't think I can eat after all," she murmured. Her voice felt a thousand miles away.

"You should at least try to eat something," Alex said, cradling her tenderly.

She could barely feel his touch. What was the point of eating when there was nothing to eat for? She didn't make any effort to wriggle out of Alex's arms, though there didn't seem to be a point in taking comfort in his embrace either. There wasn't much point to anything.

The silence between them stretched on, until Ruby arrived with a tray carrying two steaming bowls. "Mrs. Carlisle sends bone broth and chicken soup," she announced with a smile. That smile vanished as soon as she glanced in Marigold's direction. "I'll just put it on the table," she whispered, depositing her load on the table, then rushing out of the room again.

Alex waited several more seconds before saying, "Please try to eat something."

Marigold didn't move, didn't react at all. Part of her argued that she should at least try, that life wasn't over yet. A greater part of her wondered if, in fact, it was. She'd all but demanded to marry Alex because she wanted to be the mother of the Prime Minister's son. She'd failed miserably at that. What was she supposed to do now?

"Here." Alex set her gently aside, then got up and fetched the bowl of broth and a spoon from the tray. He carried them to her, barely managing with one arm in a sling, then dipped the spoon into the broth. "I have it on good authority that Mrs. Carlisle's bone broth is infused with magic. She sent bowl after bowl of it up after Violetta died." His voice flattened on the last two words, as if he hadn't thought his sentence through and shouldn't have said it to begin with.

Indeed, his whole countenance sagged so much that Marigold shifted, pushing herself to sit straighter. Damn it all, if she couldn't have Alex's children, the least she could do was pay him the respect of not dying the way his mistress had.

"Let me taste it," she sighed, as if telling him to go ahead and chop her hand off.

Alex perked up a bit, bringing the bowl and a spoonful to her mouth, even though the effort with his broken arm made him grimace in pain. Marigold sipped gingerly, surprised to find the warm, salty liquid actually didn't taste half bad. She let him feed her another spoonful, then another.

By the time they made it to the sixth spoonful, her mind was beginning to work again. "What did Ruby mean?" she asked. "That Mr. Phillips is trying to catch the man who did it?"

Alex let out a heavy sigh. His shoulders sagged so much that he set the bowl and spoon on the bedside table. "Henry wasn't driving the carriage that night. An unknown man who infiltrated the party picked us up. The police have done as much investigating as they can, and as near as they can figure, the man hopped down from the carriage just outside of Frogwell." He hesitated, then pushed on. "Burrs were found under the horses' harnesses. The local constable believes they were put there to make the horses run mad. He's surprised that they got as far as they did before the carriage wrecked."

Marigold's eyes went wide. "Someone tried to kill us?"

Alex nodded. "Several men at the party saw the driver, but no one has been able to identify him yet. No one has been able to trace how he got to Edward's house or where he went afterwards. And unless they find him, there's no way to tell if he was acting alone, what his motives were, or who hired him." His expression hardened.

It didn't matter that Marigold had spent the better part of ten days unconscious and on the brink of death. She knew in an instant what he was thinking.

"Turpin," she whispered.

Alex nodded. "Who else? He had the motivation, and heaven knows he has the means."

"Surely investigators will be able to find a link, to prove he is responsible."

"We can only hope," Alex said. "And even if Scotland Yard turns up nothing, Turpin is a marked man." His face clouded with fury so potent that Marigold felt it down to her weary, broken bones. Alex's gaze shifted to her, stark with determination. "After what he did to you, if the law doesn't bring him to justice, I'll kill him myself."

CHAPTER 15

*A*ugust moved slowly. Marigold could hardly believe she slept through most of it. Her body needed to heal, though, and if she were honest with herself, so did her heart. Even when she reached the point where she could sit up in bed herself and eat increasingly solid food from the tray Ada or Ruby brought to her three times a day, she couldn't summon the motivation to get up and resume her life. What was there to resume?

As soon as she was no longer experiencing pain every time someone bumped or sat on—or in James's case, jumped on—the bed, Alex began sharing it with her at night once more. Marigold was ashamed to realize that she hadn't once stopped to wonder where he was sleeping while she recovered. She hadn't stopped to wonder what he must think of her, now that she was barren. But as soon as the thought occurred to her, she couldn't think about anything else.

She lay on her side as Alex slept behind her, his deep, steady breathing a constant reminder of the problem that now faced her. She could never give him what he wanted, what he needed. The room was dark, just the first hints of sunrise creeping through the open windows. She watched the curtains stir in the faint morning breeze. As much as it went against conventional wisdom, she liked having the windows open, especially since the weather had been so warm. She needed the fresh air to settle her thoughts.

All her life, she had dreamed of being a mother. Everywhere she'd turned, from her schoolbooks to the lessons she'd learned in finishing school, a woman's destiny as a mother had been drilled into her. That was why God had created women, and that was why men married them, especially men of Alex's importance. The role she'd seen herself playing in his world was gone.

She reached under the sheets to rest her hand on her stomach, her face pinching in agony. The physical pain had been gone for days, but the bitter sting of failure twisted through her. It wasn't fair, not to her and not to Alex.

As if he could hear her thoughts, Alex stirred, stretching out of sleep. He inched closer to her, closing his arm around her. It was still in a sling, but healing enough for him to use it to draw her close, her back against his chest. Marigold sucked in a breath, her body going rigid. He couldn't possibly be interested in making love to her, could he? What would be the point? Besides which, her body was far too fragile for that sort of activity.

But no, he simply held her, settling back against the pillow. At least until she let out a breath of relief.

"Are you awake?" he asked, voice thick with sleep and surprise.

Marigold hesitated, not knowing what he would do if he knew she was. But there was no tension in his body, no suggestion of need, only warmth. "Yes," she answered at length.

"Good," he said in a soft hum, cradling her closer. "I've

wanted to watch the sun rise with you since the day we came home."

Marigold blinked, holding her breath. That was it? He wanted to watch a sunrise with her? It didn't make sense. She let out her breath, but had a hard time relaxing into his embrace.

"I'm glad you insisted on keeping the windows open," he went on groggily. "My nanny believed fresh air was bad for children, which meant I spent my summers stifled and...."

His voice drifted off. Marigold was certain it was because remembering his own childhood only drove home the point that there would be no children for the two of them. She waited, expecting him to push her aside at any moment.

A long, rumbling snore answered her worries instead. She shifted her head slightly, glancing over her shoulder. Alex had fallen back to sleep. She blinked, baffled, and glanced out the window once more. The sky was brightening. From the bed, she could just see the tops of hazy hills, bathed in coral light. The longer she watched, the warmer the light became, and the clearer the countryside appeared. A pang formed in her heart that, for a change, had nothing to do with the loss she couldn't shake. Alex's snores continued. Part of her wished he were watching Nature's brilliant show with her. An even greater part of her knew that even if he was watching, his affection wouldn't last. Not now. Now, she was alone.

Perhaps it was that hollow feeling that spurred her to get out of bed a few hours later, after Alex had risen, washed, dressed, kissed her, then gone about his day. She'd recovered as much as she could in bed. And the balmy, August morning called to her. So when no one else was around, she scooted to the edge of the bed, threw back the covers, and swung her legs over the side to stand.

She'd gotten up to use the chamber pot for the past several days, but this time, instead of climbing back into bed, she walked to the window. Her body was stiff and weak, but that wasn't about to stop her. If anything, it pushed her on. Her stupid, useless body that was no longer able to do what it was supposed to do. She would demand that it at least carried her to a better view.

The result of her efforts was the reward of gazing out over Winterberry Park's gardens and the sun-kissed Wiltshire countryside. She perched on the windowsill and took a deep breath of country air. To her London-raised eyes, the green and blue of hills and sky was something out of a fairy world. It didn't matter how wilted or crushed she felt on the inside, the world of Winterberry Park was verdant and thriving.

"Oh! Ma'am, you're out of bed," Ada exclaimed as she came through the door with a tray containing Marigold's breakfast. "Are you sure that's wise, ma'am?" she added as she rushed the tray to the table, then strode to Marigold's side, as if she might fall over any minute.

"I'm tired of being in bed," Marigold said with a sigh.

Ada greeted the comment with a wide smile. "That's a very good sign, ma'am."

Marigold dragged her eyes away from the view out the window to give Ada a weary smile. "Is it?"

"Yes, ma'am. It means you're well on your way back to normal."

Marigold continued to smile, but her heart felt heavy. Normal for her now was as unfamiliar as darkest India. "I think I might like to get dressed today," she told Ada, pushing herself to stand and walk to the table where her breakfast waited.

"Yes, ma'am," Ada replied, her smile so joyful Marigold couldn't help but match it. "I'll pick out something soft and comfortable for you."

"Thank you, Ada."

Marigold sat to eat as her maid flittered across the hall to her dressing room, leaving both doors open. Marigold uncovered her breakfast and found that she had far more of an appetite for the sugared oatmeal and buttered eggs than she thought she'd have. Her tea tasted surprisingly good as well.

So this is what recovery feels like, she thought to herself as she poured herself a second cup.

She was nearly finished, with Ada waiting patiently in the doorway, when the sound of James's laughter drifted up from the garden. Her chest squeezed tight, and sadness poked holes in the contentment Wiltshire and breakfast had given her. She forced herself to stand, feeling somewhat stronger for the meal, and walked back to the window.

James was playing in the garden below while Ruby watched him, her little girl sitting on a blanket beside a bed of August blooms. James was dressed in short pants and a short-sleeved shirt, and appeared to be imitating a frog. He jumped around the fountain that splashed in the center of the garden, his dark hair, so much like Alex's, catching the sun and shining.

Marigold swallowed, tears stinging at her eyes. If she didn't do something, James would be the only child Alex would ever have. A child he couldn't publicly acknowledge was almost worse than having none at all.

She took a breath and turned away from the window, facing Ada. "I'm ready to dress now."

"Yes, ma'am. I'll help you across if you need it."

She stepped forward, but Marigold waved her away. She would have to learn to stand on her own, starting immediately. And as soon as she was dressed, she would have to make her way downstairs so that she could find Alex and do what was right by him.

ALEX LIKED TO TAKE HIS PRECIOUS TIME AT Winterberry Park easy. He valued his few months of peace and quiet more and more as his position in the government grew. On an August day as pleasant at the one that had dawned that morning, he would normally have gone out riding or dropped in at the local cricket club to see if they needed a middle-order batsman. But with Turpin still walking free after what he'd done to Marigold, the sunny summer day was his battlefield.

"Has *The Times* printed its follow-up piece yet?" he asked Phillips as he paced in front of the large desk in his study, rubbing his still-healing arm. He was healing fast enough to find the splint and sling a damn nuisance.

"They printed a piece about the search for The Turpin Maid, as they're calling her," Phillips reported, hands behind his back like a good soldier. "But they don't seem willing to accuse Turpin outright."

"And what about the missing driver?" Alex asked on, switching directions to pace the other way.

Phillips let out a frustrated breath. "Scotland Yard is still searching, but Commissioner Stokes is wary of looking for a criminal from Wiltshire when their jurisdiction is London."

"Did you tell him that the crime almost certainly originated in London?" Alex demanded, stopping his pacing to glare at Phillips as though he were the gum in the works.

"I did," Phillips answered with equal irritation, not taking the intense questioning personally. "And while he agrees that what happened here is consistent with other complaints and suspicions he's had about the likes of Lord Shayles, he can't prove anything, so he can't do anything."

"Turpin and Shales are as thick as thieves." Alex rubbed a hand over his face. "If one is involved, I'd bet my life that the other is as well."

"I can attempt to investigate on my own," Phillips began.

Alex held up a hand. "It's too dangerous. As much as I appreciate your enthusiasm, efforts like this are best left to Malcolm Campbell."

"Yes, well, if he ever needs a dogsbody...." Phillips crossed his arms and glared.

Alex sent him a weak smile and a nod. "Thanks, but I need you to keep me in touch with the political climate in London. I won't leave any stone unturned until Turpin is stripped of his office, at the very least. I—"

He stopped dead, his jaw dropping and his heart racing. Marigold had stepped into the doorway to his office. She was dressed, though the simple gown hung awkwardly on her frame, emphasizing the weight she'd lost. Her golden hair tied back in a braid, and her skin was pale with splotches of pink on her cheeks. She stood on her own, but Ada hovered behind her, looking ready to catch her if she fell over.

Alex didn't want to wait for that to happen. He rushed forward. "What are you doing?" he asked as he reached her side, scooping her into his arms and carrying her to the leather sofa near the empty fireplace.

"I wanted to dress," she explained. "And come downstairs. It's been nearly a month since I set foot outside the bedroom."

"You need to rest and regain your strength," Alex argued, bristling with worry. He wasn't sure he could take it if she had a relapse.

Whatever her physical state, she was well enough to send him a flat, almost irritated look. "How am I supposed to regain my strength if I don't test it?"

"Slowly," he answered, as firm as she was prickly. "By changing rooms upstairs or practicing walking up and down the hall. Not by coming all the way down here."

"But I needed to talk to you," she said, lowering her eyes. The pink of her cheeks grew even more pronounced.

Alex glanced to Phillips, then on to Ada.

"I'll take this opportunity to strip your bed, air things out, and put new sheets on, ma'am." Ada spoke quickly, clearly flustered, then fled the room.

"And I'll check on the business we discussed, sir." Phillips bowed, then strode out of the room.

As soon as he was alone with Marigold, Alex moved to draw her into his arms, but she pushed away. A stab of disappointment hit him, and while he could easily have overpowered Marigold in her current condition, he respected the boundaries she was setting and scooted to the other side of the sofa.

"What did you want to talk to me about?" he asked, snakes filling his stomach. He didn't like the sober look on her face.

"I've been giving this a lot of thought," she began, quiet, still staring at her hands as they twisted together on her lap. It was so far from the bold, vibrant Marigold he had married that pain radiated through his chest. She left a long silence between them before she continued. "We haven't been married long, so I don't think it would cause much of a scandal. Especially since your entire purpose in marrying me is now...defeated."

The snakes in his gut writhed as dread filled him. "I don't understand."

Slowly, painfully, she dragged her eyes up to meet his. "I can't give you the heir you need, Alex. A man in your position, in the position you could soon hold, needs an heir. Especially if your political contributions are deemed valuable enough for you to be granted a title, which I'm certain they will be. Since I have been rendered useless to you," she paused to swallow, glancing down again, "I think that you should divorce me so that you can find a wife who can bear your children." She gulped for breath as she finished, blinking back the wetness that had formed on her lashes.

Alex gaped at her, dread turning to horror, not so much over the suggestion she had made, but because of the potent grief that radiated from her. "Marigold...." He shifted toward her, reaching for her hands with his good arm.

She backed way with a gasp, still not looking at him. "We are fortunate, I suppose, that your grand bill supporting the rights of women has not yet become an enacted law. There are far more ways for a man to divorce his wife at present than there are options in the other direction. I shall return to London, to my father's house, and after the appropriate time, you can claim abandonment and—"

"No." He clasped his hand around hers in spite of her efforts to pull away. Her eyes fluttered, and she looked up at him, her expression helpless and hopeless. "No," he said, louder and more insistent. At last. With his heart in pieces and his gut tied in knots, he knew how to be a good husband. "Marigold, I will *not* divorce you."

"But I'm a complete failure as a wife," she argued, emotion overcoming her, tears making her green eyes shine. "I can't do the one thing that I wanted to do for you more than anything else. What's the point of us continuing on when I'm useless now?"

Pain far greater than any he'd suffered in the wreck clawed at him. It tore him apart to see her laid so low, to see his beautiful wife questioning everything about her that he loved. He cursed his broken arm, as it kept him from embracing her as fully as he wanted to, but circled his right arm around her as intimately as he could.

"You are not useless to me." His voice was hoarse and his emotions intense, but he knew beyond a shadow of a doubt that she needed to hear him say it. More than she needed jewels or platitudes or anything that money could buy, she needed to know how much she meant to him. "You are beautiful and witty and clever."

She shook her head, tried to wriggle away from him, then gave up. "How can you say that when we barely know each other?" she asked, staring at him incredulously. "Wasn't that the problem between us to begin with? We rushed headlong into this marriage based on a physical attraction that serves no purpose now."

His instinct was to explain to her that sexual intimacy served a great many more purposes than reproduction, but sense kept his mouth shut. That wasn't what she needed to hear. "I won't deny that we were hasty on our way to the altar, but I married you with the full intention of staying married to you for the rest of my life."

She didn't seem at all convinced. In fact, she shook her head, shoulders slumping.

He brushed his good hand under her chin, tilting her up to face him. A confidence that he'd never felt with Violetta, that he'd never felt at all, filled him. "I want to be married to you," he said. "Not any other woman, even if she's as fertile as a rabbit in springtime. I can't imagine any other woman being as bold or passionate as you. I can count the number of women I've known who match your intelligence on one hand with fingers left over. And buried in the volumes of things we should have come to know about each other before marrying is the fact that there have been shockingly few women in my life that I have cared for enough to make my own."

It wasn't exactly an admission of love. He wasn't sure it would be right to bandy about with those words when they truly hadn't known each other long enough for them to be as true as she would need them to be when he said them. But he could feel it coming. Love was creeping up on him like the sunrise, inevitable and beautiful, and with it came everything he felt he'd been lacking in his life.

"I will not divorce you," he repeated. "And perhaps you're right. We are fortunate that the law will not let you divorce me so easily. But I promise you." He cradled her hot cheek with his good hand. "I will move heaven and earth in my position within this government to give you the right to do just that if you so choose."

She let out a breath that was halfway between a sob and a cry of joy, slumping against him.

Alex gathered her into his lap as best he could with one broken arm. "We're partners, my darling," he said, brushing her hair away from her face and kissing the remnants of the scars and bruises from the wreck that marred her beauty. "We may have entered into that as foolishly as two obstreperous children, but it's too late. The deal is done.

We're a unit now, and we still have to take the political world by storm. Together."

"I don't deserve you," she sniffled, burying her face against his neck.

Alex let out an ironic laugh. "Believe me, my darling, you do."

She burst into another strange sound, almost like a laugh, but wet and sniffley, and threw her arms around his neck. They sat there like that for a while, just holding each other. It was more than Alex ever could have asked for. His heart slowed to a strong, steady thump, and the snakes in his gut slithered away, leaving him with a sense of peace. At last, he could see the way forward. He could see himself as the man he'd always wanted to be. He only hoped that Marigold could feel half of the relief he felt, in spite of the suffering she must still be going through.

"If you think it would help," he said quietly after a time, "I could ask my friend, Armand Pearson, to visit."

She blinked and sat straighter. "The doctor? The one who inherited an earldom when his brother died?"

"That's the one." Alex nodded and smiled. "We served together in the Crimean all those years ago. He was part of our motley band of friends. Most of us were injured at Sebastopol, you know. Armand struck up a friendship with Florence Nightingale herself, and when he returned home, he left the army to study medicine." He paused, stroking the side of her head, feeling more awkward than he should have. "Armand has become particularly interested in women's medicine these last few years. He's been corresponding with an American, Dr. J. Marion Sims, in regards to women's reproductive issues. He may have some insight on the situation."

"Do you trust him?" Marigold asked, looking as though she wasn't inclined to herself.

"With my life," Alex reassured her.

She nodded. "Then if he has time to visit, and if it's what you want, please, invite him."

"I will." Alex smiled brushing his thumb across her cheek.

On a whim, he leaned close and kissed her lips, lightly, tenderly. They had so much to build back up between them that it would be tragic if he pushed things and ruined them.

But Marigold kissed him back, as tentative as a new lover. It was a far cry from what they had shared in the early weeks of their marriage, but beneath the hesitation, he sensed hope.

CHAPTER 16

"*J*'m afraid the scarring is extensive," Dr. Pearson
said with a long exhale, removing the frighten-
ing-looking instruments he'd used to examine Marigold.

She lay on her back on top of the bed, her legs propped
awkwardly on pillows so that Alex's friend could perform
his examination. Dr. Pearson's assistant hovered in the
corner of the room, ready to assist. It had been a strange,
embarrassing, and awkward examination, but Alex sat on
the bed with her, her back supported against him, holding
her hands to reassure her. He seemed to trust Dr. Pearson—
or Lord Helm, she wasn't sure which title took precedent—
so she swallowed her fear and told herself she should
as well.

As soon as Dr. Pearson shifted her skirt back into place
and stood, walking to the wash-table to scrub his hands and
instruments, she pushed the pillows aside and sat as
demurely as she could in Alex's arms.

"Was it that bastard Miller's fault?" Alex asked in a
resentful growl, holding Marigold close.

Dr. Pearson frowned, finished scrubbing his hands, then

turned to them. "I believe it was. To attempt any kind of examination or so-called treatment on a woman in the midst of miscarriage is incompetent at best and barbaric at worst. And going by what you've told me about the resulting infection, one can only assume this Dr. Miller is woefully uneducated about Dr. Lister's advancements in sterilizing medical instruments or the use of carbolic acid before examinations or surgeries." He was clearly furious at the thought.

Caught between two men fuming over the blatant incompetence of a third and the consequences that incompetence had wrought on her, Marigold sighed. "What's done is done," she said, pulling out of Alex's arms and standing.

Weeks had passed since the first day she'd gotten out of bed, August had given way to September, and the misery she'd first felt at her body's new, useless state had faded into a dull ache deep in her gut. The same way that Alex still winced and complained of weakness and an ache in his left arm when it rained, even though his bone had healed and the splint and sling had been removed.

"I am truly sorry," Dr. Pearson said, drying his hands.

Marigold sent him as much of a smile as she could manage, considering how embarrassing it was to be around him, now that he'd examined her in such an intimate way. She liked Dr. Pearson. She had the feeling he was the sort of man everyone liked. He was tall, and in spite of being slightly older than Alex, his blonde hair had only faded a bit, and the lines around his eyes indicated he was the kind of man who smiled often. His shoulders were broad, and his physique that of a man half his age. She could see how he and Alex were friends.

"So there's nothing at all that can be done?" Alex asked, standing and moving to Marigold's side to take her hand.

"No surgery or treatment that you can devise to reverse the damage Miller has done?"

Dr. Pearson shook his head as he unrolled his shirt sleeves. "I'm afraid not. I deeply regret telling you that the damage is permanent." His look of sympathy was so genuine that Marigold found herself wanting to console him instead of the other way around.

"I'll have Miller's license revoked," Alex growled. "I'll make sure he's run out of town, that he never practices medicine again. I'd string him up by his—"

Marigold rested a hand on his arm to stop him. "There isn't any other doctor nearby to help locals with their sniffles and fevers. If you banish Dr. Miller, they'll suffer."

"Then I'll hire another doctor to take his place."

Marigold couldn't argue with that. In fact, she preferred that idea to simply giving up and letting Dr. Miller's incompetence continue unchecked. But since she couldn't change what happened to her, she needed to move on to preserve her own sanity.

"We have an exhibition this evening to prepare for," she reminded Alex.

Alex let out a breath and rubbed a hand over his face. "We do."

"Exhibition?" Dr. Pearson raised his brow.

"The village children have been putting together a show for weeks," Marigold said, leading Alex away from the bed and heading toward the door. Dr. Pearson followed. His assistant stepped forward to continue cleaning his instruments. "Ever since they heard I was ill, they've been wanting to perform for me."

"How sweet," Dr. Pearson smiled.

"They were going to perform in the village hall, but

Alex is still anxious about me over-exerting myself." She sent him a mock irritated look.

He answered it with a lop-sided grin. In the last few weeks, a shift of grand proportions had happened between the two of them. The blazing fire of the first weeks of their marriage had been thoroughly extinguished, but from that, a few embers had survived. Marigold had been certain it was only a matter of time before they went out as well, but after Alex's refusal to divorce her and marry a woman who could bear him children, it was as if someone had blown on those embers, causing them to grow.

She held his arm as they descended the main stairs into the front hall. "We'd be honored if you'd stay for the performance," she told Dr. Pearson. "It's bound to be a treat."

"Stay the night," Alex added. "We've got plenty of room. You aren't needed back in London immediately, are you?"

"I'm not," Dr. Pearson said, looking delighted with the invitation. His smile faded as they reached the hall and walked on through the drawing room and out to the garden. "To tell you the truth, I wouldn't mind staying out of London for a while."

"Why?" Marigold frowned. Her whole world, up until a few months ago, had revolved around London. "What's wrong with it?"

Dr. Pearson let out an ironic laugh. "It's a cauldron of accusations and incriminations this summer, what with the Turpin Maid Case."

Marigold nearly missed a step as they passed through a set of French doors to the garden patio. "How so?"

Alex looked just as confused as she did. Dr. Pearson glanced between the two of them, surprised. "You haven't heard?" He glanced to Alex.

"Heard what?" Alex asked, taking Marigold's arm and leading her along the gravel path that wove through beds of late-summer flowers.

Dr. Pearson stopped and turned to them. "The Turpin Maid case is all anyone can talk about in London. It's stirred up every kind of scandal you can imagine. Turpin's name is being dragged through the mud for his treatment of Miss Murdoch. A few other young women have come forward as well, accusing him of inappropriate behavior."

"I haven't heard about the other women," Alex said. The light of triumph shone in his eyes.

"I'm not surprised," Dr. Pearson said. "You've had quite a bit else on your mind."

"How deep does the scandal run?" Alex asked, continuing down the path.

"Many are beginning to demand Turpin step down from his leadership position in Parliament," Dr. Pearson said. "Several members of his own party are calling his fitness for office into question. Turpin denies it all, of course, and is spitting mad over the whole thing. He claims the whole story is a fabrication and that there's no proof of any misconduct on his part, particularly since the maid in question, Miss Murdoch, is nowhere to be found."

Marigold exchanged a wide-eyed glance with Alex, glad they'd thought to bring Ruby out to Wiltshire. Alex met her glance with equal gravity. She glanced around, wondering if Ruby was nearby with James. It was likely that Dr. Pearson wouldn't recognize her if he saw her, but the need to keep Ruby safely out of sight was huge.

"Anyhow," Dr. Pearson went on, "the scandal is bad enough that Turpin has returned to London instead of biding his time in Worcester."

"Has he?" Alex looked equal parts victorious and anxious.

Dr. Pearson nodded. "He's kept himself to himself, though. I heard whispers at my club that he was hell-bent on revenge against whomever started the rumors."

Marigold's heart leapt to her throat, beating as furiously as the butterflies in her stomach. As far as she was concerned, Turpin had his revenge. But if there was more coming, she would need to be wary.

They turned the corner, walking into a scene that was the complete opposite of Turpin and everything he stood for. At least three dozen children, ranging in age from three-year-old James to a pair of girls that looked ready to leave the schoolroom, were scattered across the wide lawn that stretched away from the raised patio at the back of the house. The older girls were minding the youngest children, but the middle ones tore across the grass, the boys using sticks as pretend rifles to wage war, and the girls picking daisies and chrysanthemums from the flower beds to make crowns and chains. A harried-looking woman who was slightly too old to be a student attempted to chase some of them, while the schoolmaster was busy chatting with Ada as she laid out refreshments.

"Good heavens," Marigold laughed in spite of the chaos. It was such a change from the stilted silence of the last six weeks that she couldn't find it in herself to be upset.

"Grimes is going to have a fit when he sees his gardens," Alex muttered, though humor shone in his eyes as well.

Sure enough, within seconds, the weathered, old gardener marched around the corner, saw the girls picking his flowers, and flew into a rage, shouting, "Get away from there, you little strumpets!"

The girls screamed and scattered as Mr. Grimes ran at them, shaking his fist.

"It's all right, Grimes," Alex shouted across the lawn. "Let them have the flowers."

"But...but, sir," Grimes started.

He didn't have a chance to finish. James popped his dark head up from a group of younger children and shouted, "Mari!"

He broke away from the other children to come charging at Marigold and Alex. Ruby sat on the grass with the other youngsters, but jumped up to run after James.

"Mari outside," James shouted with delight, crashing into Marigold's legs and hugging her through her skirt.

Marigold was knocked sideways into Alex, but laughed all the same. "Good afternoon, Master James," she greeted him, resting a hand on his sun-warmed head.

"You come to watch me sing?" he asked, glancing up at her with hopeful eyes.

"Yes, dear, I have."

A sudden whim seized her, and she let go of Alex's arms and picked James up. He was heavier than she expected him to be, but her arms ached to hold him, and she was eager to test how much strength she'd regained. To her delight, James settled onto her hip and threw his arms around her neck. A throb of affection shot straight to her heart.

"Easy, easy there," Alex said, reaching out and hovering over both of them, as if they would fall apart within seconds. He glanced over his shoulder to Dr. Pearson. "Should she be exerting herself like this?"

Dr. Pearson shrugged. "The danger is long past. Mrs. Croydon is well on her way to healing. If she feels whole enough to resume normal activity, then I have no reason to forbid it." He leaned closer to Alex, and Marigold was certain she heard him mutter, "That goes for other activities too, in case you were wondering."

Her cheeks flared pink with embarrassment, so she focused on James to brush it aside. "What will you be singing for me today?" she asked.

"Songs," James declared proudly.

Marigold laughed. "Which ones?"

"All of them." James laughed with her.

"Ma'am. I'm so sorry, ma'am," Ruby said, coming to a breathless stop in front of them. "I shouldn't have let him get away."

"It's all right, Ruby," Marigold laughed. She stopped abruptly with the realization she'd given more away to Dr. Pearson than she'd intended to.

Dr. Pearson's only reaction was to raise one eyebrow and glance to Alex. Alex replied to that look with a clever grin. Apparently, that was all Dr. Pearson needed to put two and two together.

"I can take him if you'd like, ma'am." Ruby tentatively reached for James. "It's just that Mr. Turnbridge, the schoolmaster, is a bit busy at the moment." She glanced across the lawn to where Ada was giggling over something handsome, young Mr. Turnbridge had said. "And Miss Goode—she's Mr. Turnbridge's new assistant at the school—has her hands full with the other children."

Ruby nodded to the young woman who was trying to get the boys to stop waging war and trampling the shrubs in the process. Miss Goode glanced their way and smiled at Ruby. Ruby waved back.

"She's ever so nice," Ruby said. "Turns out we both grew up in Limehouse."

"Limehouse?" Marigold blinked. "What's she doing all

the way out here in Wiltshire, working as an assistant in a country school, then?"

"She's escaped a man," Ruby whispered, glancing anxiously to Alex and Dr. Pearson. "But it wouldn't be right of me to say more."

Marigold nodded in understanding. She didn't have a chance to ask more questions anyhow. James wriggled in her arms, eager to get down. He left dirty footprints on her skirt before she could bend over and let him go.

"I get flowers for you," he said, then tore off to where Mr. Grimes was grumbling as he patched up the flower beds.

Ruby exclaimed wordlessly, then chased after him, no time to beg Marigold's leave. Marigold laughed anyhow. It was just so wonderful to see Winterberry Park's garden swarming with children, even if it did cause a pang in her heart.

"We should do something for them on a regular basis," she said, thinking out loud.

"Whatever you'd like, my dear." Alex stepped toward her, placing a hand on the small of her back.

Warmth seemed to spread through her from the point of his touch. It wasn't the same thrill of excitement as she would have felt when they were first married, but in a way, it was even nicer. She turned to Alex with a smile, pleased to find him smiling back at her. He was so much more relaxed in Wiltshire. His shoulders were less bunched, and the energy in his eyes was more from simple enjoyment of everything around him instead of battle-ready power. The London version of Alex was thrilling, but a part of her was becoming more and more convinced that she liked this content, rural version of her husband even more. He was the one who had wiped the tears from her eyes and refused to cast her aside, after all.

"Would you like some tea?" she asked, brushing her hand along the lapel of his jacket to remove a fluffy seed that had landed there. "It looks as though Ada has brought some out."

Alex smirked, humor and hunger in his eyes. "It looks as though Ada is a bit busy to pour tea for us." He darted a look to the side.

Mr. Turnbridge had shifted to lean closer to Ada, whose cheeks were as pink as roses. Marigold giggled, touching her fingers to her lips, both to hide her amusement and because they longed for a kiss.

"Ah, the foolishness of the young," she said, leaning closer to Alex by a fraction.

"The young aren't the only ones who are foolish," Alex replied.

He swayed closer to her, and for one, glorious moment, Marigold knew he was going to kiss her. Then Dr. Pearson cleared his throat.

Alex stepped back, turning to send a scolding look to his friend. "I'm beginning to wonder if I should have invited you to stay after all."

Dr. Pearson laughed and slapped Alex's shoulder. "I wouldn't have missed this for the world."

Marigold smiled and took Alex's arm as they headed across the lawn to treat themselves to tea. The feeling that everything would work out came as a shock to her, but Winterberry Park felt so far removed from the tension and conflict of London that she was beginning to think anything was possible.

That feeling expanded through her as James came

rushing back to her with flowers in his hand when they reached the tea table.

"For you," he said, presenting her with the wilting bouquet.

"They're beautiful. Thank you, James," she said, smelling them to show how much she liked them.

James threw his arms around her legs, burying himself in her skirts once more. Marigold laughed, but her laugh was cut short by a gasp. A thought occurred to her. James was the only child Alex would ever have, but he'd been born on the wrong side of the bed. Alex would never be able to publically claim him, even though the truth was obvious to anyone who saw them together.

Unless there was a way for them to formally adopt James. Families had been adopting children for centuries, after all, and while there were probably rules and laws in place for titled members of the upper class, no matter how wealthy or important he was, Alex wasn't titled. At least not yet. Perhaps there was a way for him to give legal status to what was obvious in every other way. They could be a family.

"I'll take him, ma'am."

Marigold's heart thundered against her ribs as she looked up to find Miss Goode striding toward her. Her mind rang as though someone had clanged a gong next to her ears. She would never have children of her own, but that didn't mean she couldn't be a mother.

"It's no trouble, really," she answered Miss Goode, breathless and flushed with possibility.

For a fraction of a second, Miss Goode looked put out. She snapped back into a smile a moment later, and said, "Mr. Turnbridge wants the children to gather for practice now. And besides, James and I are good friends. Aren't we, James?" She knelt and grinned at James, taking his hand.

"We sing now?" James asked.

"Yes, Master James. We sing now," she said with a laugh.

Marigold let Miss Goode lead James away to join the other children and Mr. Turnbridge as they gathered on the patio steps. "Has James been attending Mr. Turnbridge's school?" she asked, turning to Alex.

"To be honest, I'm not sure," Alex said. "I suppose Arthur and Clara could have taken him there now and then when things became too overwhelming for them."

"That or he became friendly with Miss Goode thanks to Ruby."

"Your Ruby's last name wouldn't happen to be Murdoch, would it?" Dr. Pearson asked with a sly grin.

Alex narrowed his eyes. "I trust you'll keep that information to yourself."

"Absolutely." Dr. Pearson nodded. "Something tells me the woman is much safer here than in London anyhow."

"Precisely," Alex said.

They finished their tea, and Dr. Pearson took his leave to check on his assistant and to make arrangements to stay the night. That gave Alex and Marigold a chance to stroll through the rest of the garden until the children were ready to perform.

"What was that all about?" Alex asked as they reached the tree-lined path that curved down to the river.

"What was what about?" she asked, her thoughts still distracted as they raced through the possibilities for James.

"When James gave you those flowers," Alex went on. "You looked...I'm not sure." He shrugged. After a moment of hesitation, he went on with, "If it's too painful for you, I can have Arthur and Clara take James back." He winced even as he made the suggestion.

"No." Marigold said, stopping and holding his arm with both hands. "In fact, I was thinking of something exactly the opposite." Ripples of excitement coursed through her.

Alex studied her with a lop-sided grin. "Judging by that look in your eyes, I'm not sure whether I'll like what's behind that sparkle, or if it'll be the end of me."

"It's James," she said, the full importance of the moment pressing down on her and making her insides buzz. "He's your son."

An uncertain look came over Alex. "He is."

"Is there...have you ever heard of...." She bit her lip, too excited by her idea to form it into words. "Would it be possible for the two of us to legally adopt him?"

Alex stared, his eyes slowly widening. Shock spread across his face.

"He's enjoyed his time here," Marigold rushed on, feeling as though she had to prove her reasoning. "He belongs here. All of this is his by right. There has to be some way to make that official. And I could...." She lowered her head, the emotions coursing through her too powerful to face head-on.

Alex took her hands, pressing them to his chest. His heart was thundering madly. Marigold looked up at him, dizzy with hope.

"There is nothing I would love more," he said at last, letting out a breath. "But only if it's what you honestly want as well."

"It is," she hurried to say. "James is delightful. He has me utterly charmed. And he needs a mother." She didn't realize how close she was to tears until she had to blink to keep them back.

"Then I'll move heaven and earth to make sure he's yours," Alex said, his eyes filling with as much emotion as Marigold felt. "Although hopefully, it won't be that difficult. I assume all it will take is a bit of paperwork or some sort of proclamation by the courts."

"Do you think that will be all?"

"Most likely. I could send Phillips back to London with Armand tomorrow to get the process started."

"So soon?" Marigold could hardly catch her breath.

"If I could make us all a family tomorrow, I'd do it," Alex said then kissed her hands.

That didn't seem to be enough for him. He let her hands go so that he could draw her into his arms, until their bodies were flush against each other. Then he kissed her like he hadn't for months. His mouth slanted over hers, drawing pure desire up from the bottom of Marigold's soul. She wasn't sure how much of that desire she was ready to embrace, but the heat of promise between them was delicious. She kissed him back, happier with the man in her arms now than she ever thought possible. Happiness burst around her like the sunrise of a new day about to dawn.

CHAPTER 17

There were many things about growing older that Alex could have done without. Knees that creaked and popped when he bent over James to show him how to hold a cricket bat and hit a ball, for example. But age had also brought with it a degree of patience and circumspection that he never would have appreciated as a younger man.

"Set your stance a little wider and angle the bat like this," he told James, holding his hands over the bat's handle. "Get ready...."

He glanced up at Marigold, who stood several yards in front of them, both hands wrapped around a cricket ball. "I don't want to throw it too hard," she said, her face shining with happiness.

"Throw it underhand, then. We'll hit it. Won't we, son."

A zip of pride shot through Alex's heart. Finally, he was able to openly call James his son. Phillips had shuttled legal papers back and forth for weeks, everything had been signed that needed to be signed, and as soon as the courts finished with their duties, James would be an official Croydon. Not that any amount of paper could make him more of a Croydon than he already was.

"Here goes." Marigold swung her arm back, then forward, tossing the heavy cricket ball toward them.

"Ooh!" James exclaimed, putting every bit of his three-year-old effort into swinging. Thanks to Alex's guidance, he managed to hit the ball, sending it loping off to the side.

"Run, run!"

Alex let go of James, and off the boy shot. The rules of the game were still fuzzy to his young mind, so instead of racing to the wicket where Marigold stood and turning to score another run, he threw aside his bat and charged face-first into Marigold's skirts, shouting, "Mari!"

Marigold stumbled back a step, laughing, as she caught him and hugged him. The sight was so heart-warming that Alex was in danger of melting into a puddle where he stood. To fight the feeling, he straightened and beamed at his beautiful wife and adorable son, feeling like the luckiest man alive.

Of course, he'd feel even luckier once he and Marigold crossed over the last remaining hurdle between them and became lovers again. That was where his newfound patience turned into his best asset. She would come to him when she was ready, and he wouldn't push her until she was. Even if it killed him. Which it was getting close to doing.

"And now for the best part of the game of cricket," he said, striding toward the pair.

"Don't tell me you're going to make me have a go," Marigold laughed, ruffling James's hair as he clung to her leg.

"Not unless you want to," Alex said. He grinned and kissed Marigold's cheek. "The best part of cricket, of course, is tea." He nodded toward the house, where Ruby and her new friend, Miss Goode, were setting up tea.

"Can I have a biscuit?" James asked, batting his long, dark lashes up at Marigold.

"Only if I can have one too," Marigold answered, bending to kiss his forehead.

"I get one for you," James said before tearing across the lawn toward the tea table.

Marigold laughed and watched him run. Alex watched her, his heart expanding until it felt too big for his chest. He took Marigold's hand, simply enjoying the way it felt in his as he walked with her to the tea table.

"And they say the Prime Minister hisself is demanding Turpin give up his seat," Miss Goode was whispering to Ruby as they reached the table. "Word is that Turpin is bloody angry about it and out for—" She clammed up the moment Alex looked directly at her.

"Don't let me interrupt your gossip," he said with a broad happy smile, although inwardly his gut tightened. The price of his happiness for the past few weeks had been neglecting to stay on top of what was happening to Turpin. A little bit of servant's gossip was always the best way to wriggle back into the know.

Both Ruby and Miss Goode blushed and hurried to supply him, James, and Marigold with tea and biscuits, but their expressions hinted at drastically different emotions. Ruby seemed edgy, making Alex wonder if Miss Goode knew that she was the one at the heart of the Turpin Maid Scandal, or if Ruby was holding on to that secret. Miss Goode, on the other hand, had the usual look of a servant who had been caught whispering about her betters.

"I'm sorry, sir," Ruby murmured as she handed him a cup of tea, keeping her eyes downcast. "We're talking out of turn."

"Not at all." Alex smiled, hoping they would continue. "I haven't heard much about the scandal for weeks. Is Turpin still in London?" he asked Miss Goode.

"I'm sure I don't know, sir," Miss Goode said, curtsying several times in a row and keeping her head tilted down.

Frustrated that the woman would choose now, of all times, to hold her tongue, Alex softened his smile and went on. "I suppose the papers are still full of stories. Is that where you're getting your information?"

Miss Goode's cheeks turned a brighter shade of pink. "Me sister," she started, then bit her lip. "I'm sure I don't know, sir," she repeated.

"Never mind, then." Alex took a sip of tea to hide his irritation. He would have to ask Phillips for a full report later, when he finished sorting through Alex's wardrobe. Now that the business of adopting James was well under-way, Phillips had turned to his more valet-oriented duties and had been inventorying Alex's clothing to see what needed repair and what could be given away and replaced. It was a waste of Phillips's talents, as far as Alex was concerned, and he had half a mind to set Phillips the task of finding his own replacement as valet so that he could shift to strictly being a man of business.

"Mari, look. Two biscuits!"

James pulled Alex out of his thoughts and back into a smile as he proudly held up two chocolate-dipped biscuits for Marigold to see.

"They're lovely, dear," she smiled. "Are you going to eat one?"

"I eat both," James told her.

"Just one, sweetheart," Marigold laughed, taking the second biscuit from him and nibbling on the side. She sent Alex a tempting glance, as though there were other things she'd like to be nibbling on too. The look sent Alex's pulse pounding.

"You're about ready for your nap, Master James," Ruby said, crouching and holding her arms out.

"No," James declared with a frown. "Play with Mari."

"I think you should let Mrs. Croydon and your papa have some time to themselves," Ruby laughed.

"No!" James insisted, clinging to Marigold's skirts. "Mari."

"It's all right," Marigold smoothed James's head, removing his hand from her skirt. "You go with Ruby, sweetheart. I'll see you after your nap."

James fussed, and for a minute Alex wondered if he'd have to step in, but Miss Goode inched forward.

"We all have to take naps, Master James," she said. "Do you want to run around the garden with me a few times to get good and tuckered out?"

James glanced suspiciously at the hand she held out to him. "I like run."

"Then come on, I'll race you." Miss Goode burst into a short run, turning to glance back at James as she reached the corner of the house.

James giggled and raced after her. He caught up to her and took her hand, and together, the two of them tore around the corner of the house and out of sight.

"It's a good thing Molly was here," Ruby said, turning back to straighten the tea things. "She's been so helpful this past week."

"Doesn't she have duties at Mr. Turnbridge's school?" Marigold asked.

"She does," Ruby said. "But now that the older kids are helping out with the smaller ones and the very youngest are staying home with their mamas, she says she has a bit more free time."

"How fortunate for all of us," Alex said, setting his teacup aside and taking Marigold's hand. "It gives the rest of us time to ourselves."

He glanced to Marigold, certain that everything he wanted to do with that time was plain as day on his face. Even Ruby grinned and shook her head at him.

"Don't feel the need to stay here on my account, sir, ma'am," she said with a curtsy. "I've got things well in hand here."

Alex nodded to her, took Marigold's teacup from her hands and set it on the table, then looped her arm through his and started off along the lawn, past their abandoned cricket game, and to the path that wound through the meadow in the direction of the river.

"DO YOU THINK JAMES IS HAPPY AT WINTERBERRY Park?" Marigold asked as she and Alex strolled along the river path. The late-September sun shone down, filling her with warmth and making diamonds on the lazy river. Alex was a strong and steady presence by her side. After such a long time, everything felt right with the world.

"I think he's overjoyed to be where he is," Alex replied, hugging her arm against his side as he escorted her. His smile was free and easy, making lines around his eyes. The grey at his temples stood out in the sunlight, lending him a distinguished air. "I think he adores having a mama," he added with a wink.

Marigold's heart leapt in her chest, and she felt splashes

of pleased pink flood her cheeks. "I think it would be very easy to love him as my own," she said in a reverent voice. She would have to remember that he wasn't hers. Part of her thought it would be a grave disservice to poor Violetta to wipe her away from James's life completely, even though she'd never met the woman. But there would be time to address weighty issues like that in the years to come. For now, James needed a mother, and she would fill that role to the best of her ability.

"I hope Clara and Arthur don't mind," she added, a flash of guilt upsetting her happy mood. "I can't help but feel as though I took him away from them."

Alex let out a breath and shook his head. "Years ago, when Violetta died and I was incapable of taking care of James myself or making any decisions about him, they stepped in like guardian angels to care for him. But they did so with the understanding that I might want him back someday."

He paused. Marigold studied the firm lines of his jaw and his frown for a moment before he went on.

"I think they knew what I didn't back then. James is my son. He's a part of my heart. In the end, I can't live without him. I believe Arthur and Clara knew they were temporary custodians."

"We need to be sure to thank them a thousand times over," Marigold said. "And to invite them and their family to the house whenever possible so that they can continue to be a part of James's life."

"Yes," Alex said, glancing to her with a fond smile. For a moment, Marigold thought he would stop and kiss her. In fact, she wanted him to stop and kiss her. Her insides fluttered at the thought. There had been far too few kisses during her recovery, as though he were afraid she'd break if he touched her. At first, she'd been grateful for his restraint. Lately, however, she'd been growing impatient with it. But still, he walked on.

She drew in a deep breath, glancing around at the cheery countryside. A small cottage was set back from the river a hundred or so yards ahead of them, adding to the quaint, peaceful feel of the scene.

"All the turmoil in London seems so far away on an afternoon like this," she sighed, swaying closer to Alex. "I could almost forget we have any troubles at all."

"We don't have any troubles," he insisted, a sly sparkle in his eyes. "Not now. We couldn't possibly."

Marigold laughed. "I suppose Turpin and this war he's started with you can give us this one afternoon to be with each other."

"He damn well better," Alex replied with exaggerated irritation.

Marigold laughed harder. It didn't seem possible that just over six weeks after her world was turned upside down by the crash that she could glow with such contentment as she enjoyed something as simple as a walk with her husband. She still wasn't entirely certain where things stood with Alex, but every new day that dawned with both of them smiling and at peace with each other and their own decisions, every simple conversation they had over a meal, every time they played together with James or discussed plans for his future, made her feel closer to him in ways that truly mattered.

"I was hoping Ruby's friend would be a bit freer with information about London." Alex's frown deepened as they walked on. "To tell you the truth, I've been uneasy at the lack of news about Turpin's actions."

Marigold shrugged. "Perhaps he's as tired of it all as

anyone else and has chosen to ignore the rumors instead of feeding into them."

Alex rolled his shoulders, clearly uneasy. "Perhaps."

Eager to get his mind off of Turpin or anything to do with him, Marigold went on with, "I'm more concerned that Miss Goode is shirking her duties at Mr. Turnbridge's school by visiting with friends in the middle of the day."

"Yes, I'll have to have a word with Ruby about that," Alex sighed. "I know she's been through a horrific ordeal, but Mrs. Musgrave is about ready to have my hide for being so lenient with her." His smile returned in the form of a guilty grin. "She lectured me about morale and fairness among the servants the other day."

Marigold giggled. "Mrs. Musgrave should know that it's not her place to scold you." She paused before adding, "I'm the only one who has the privilege of scolding you."

"What do you have to scold me about?" Alex asked, his expression brightening.

Marigold stopped and faced him. "It's been weeks since the accident, since I was an invalid." Heat and mischief coursed through her, and she glanced up at him with a coquettish look. "You haven't kissed me nearly enough these past few weeks."

His fond, indulgent smile took on a more wolfish glint. "Well then, my darling, I'll have to do something about that."

He slid his arms around her, pulling her close and slanting his mouth over hers. His hands spread across her back as she slipped her arms around his waist under the folds of his jacket. The feeling of his mouth teasing and testing hers was divine. He ventured further, brushing his tongue along her bottom lip, then exploring deeper.

It was a different kiss from the mad, passionate ones that had left her so dizzy in the early days of their marriage. Then, she had felt as though she were caught up in a hurricane of passion. Her body had ached and tingled, desperate for his touch. Now, the fire was just as intense, but it burned deeper, slower. The need that spread through her consumed her from head to toe instead of merely flaring in her most intimate places. All the same, she longed to feel his skin against hers, to be consumed and invaded by him.

He leaned back to take a breath, studying her as he did. He wanted her. That much was clear. But along with the need in his eyes was a question. She answered it the best way she could, by lifting to her toes and kissing him with as much energy as he had kissed her.

His body relaxed against hers as he threw everything he had into kissing her, as if he were finally letting a heavy burden go. One of his hands dropped to her hip, caressing her backside as intimately as he could with the slight bustle of her day gown. It didn't matter that clothing got in the way, his intention was clear. It'd been so long since Marigold felt the full force of his desire that she didn't know whether to weep or to moan.

And then he broke away and took her hand. "I've just realized something," he said, his words thick with desire.

"What?" Marigold asked, breathless.

He set off down the river path at a pace so fast Marigold had to jog to keep up with him. "I just realized that cottage belongs to me."

Marigold blinked in confusion, skipping along at his side. Only when they approached the beautiful little cottage looking out over the river did she realize what he meant. "This is yours?"

He sent her a quick look, one that hinted there was a much larger, perhaps painful story behind things, but only said, "Yes, it is."

He let go of her hand as they ventured off the main path and onto an overgrown footpath that wound through a neglected garden to the cottage's front door. It was locked, but within moments, Alex had uncovered a key from a pile of stones near the door. He fit it in the lock, turned it, then let them in.

The cottage was clearly vacant. But at the same time, it hadn't fallen into complete decay. The front room contained a worn and faded sofa, a table and chairs, and a cold fireplace. A layer of dust covered everything, but someone had obviously cared for the place at some point. Alex shut the front door behind them, then took her hand and led her through to a small bedroom.

A shiver passed through her, swirling down to the parts of her that felt neglected. A fair-sized bed was tucked into the corner of the room. Its coverlet and pillows looked a bit dusty, but in good condition. The rest of the bedroom furniture had a thin film of dust on it, but she barely had time to look at any of it before Alex swept her into his arms again.

His kiss was far more powerful this time. The energy that coursed through him as he explored her lips and mouth was captivating. It occurred to Marigold that he had missed making love to her as much as she'd missed it, perhaps more so. Already, she could feel heat radiating from him, and the thick firmness of his staff pressed against her hip.

"I've missed you," he whispered, breaking away from her lips to kiss her cheek and her jaw. His hands moved restlessly along her back, as if searching for the fastenings of her bodice.

"I've missed you too," she sighed in reply, boldly undoing the buttons of his jacket and waistcoat to unfasten his shirt. She glanced up at him. "You didn't have to wait so long, you know."

His hands circled down to her waist as he leaned back a bit. "I wanted to be sure you were ready," he said. "I didn't know...that is, I wasn't sure if you felt...whole enough." His brow creased in concern.

She laid her palms flat against his chest with just the cotton of his shirt separating her from his skin. "I will only feel whole with you inside of me," she whispered.

His breath rushed out in a triumphant growl, and he surged forward to kiss her once more. His hands moved to the buttons running down the front of her bodice, and with swift, not entirely graceful movements, he popped each one free.

Undressing with Alex in the cottage bedroom, the hint of naughtiness that went along with their actions swirling through her, was irresistible. They were clumsy with each other's clothes, more interested in getting them off than in folding anything or being tidy at all. Each piece that came off was tossed aside, puffing up dust where it landed. At last, as Marigold sat on the end of the bed to undo the laces of her boots, Alex stripped off his drawers and pulled back the bedcovers.

It was the most glorious thing in the world to slide between the sheets with him, their bodies fitting together perfectly.

"I love the feel of your body touching mine," Marigold sighed. She was sure she sounded like a ninny, but she couldn't help it. She arched her hips into him, reveling in the hot spear of his erection between them.

He jerked his hips in imitation of what she was so hungry for, sighing loudly at whatever sensations the friction caused in him. "I love everything about you," he said before rolling her to her back and dipping down to kiss her.

The pleasure of his kiss combined with his hand cupping her breast was nothing to the swelling of affection in her heart. If he loved everything about her, perhaps he loved her as well. Just the thought of Alex loving her sent prickles of pleasure across her skin, heightening every sensation his body caused. Especially when his hand brushed its way down her abdomen and his fingers delved into the curls between her legs. She gasped at the shock of pleasure as he stroked her.

"I want to spend my whole afternoon making you come," he rumbled, nibbling on her earlobe. "My whole life."

She couldn't think of a reply—she couldn't think at all—so she sighed and arched into his touch.

He drew in a breath at her eagerness. "Do you like this?" he asked, reaching to circle her wet opening, then to slowly thrust a finger inside of her.

A brief moment of panic hit her. After everything her body had been through, she wasn't sure how intimacy would feel. What if everything had changed down there and the sort of pain she'd felt their first time returned?

He must have sensed her hesitation, because his touch slowed and grew more tender. "Are you certain you're ready?" he asked.

Her lips twitched, and for a moment she worried she'd let panic get the best of her. But with a quick breath, she forced herself to be as honest with him as possible. "I'm worried. I don't know if it will feel the same."

He nodded, kissing her lips lightly. "We'll take things

slow until we know for sure." Even as he spoke, he continued to stroke her lightly, moving his finger in and out of her. "How does this feel?"

"Good," she sighed, relaxing and raising one arm to brush his side.

"And how about this?" He added a second finger to his ministrations, stretching her just a bit more.

"Lovely," she answered, closing her eyes.

"And this?" He shifted to stroke her clitoris again.

She responded with a rush of breath that turned into a moan. She hadn't realized how much she'd craved this intimacy between them until she had it back. It was glorious, and she let herself go to the pleasure of it as Alex patiently stroked her until she was quivering on the edge of release.

"Come for me," he whispered, his voice tense with desire. "Let me feel you come."

Her breath came in shorter and shorter gasps until the coil of pleasure building inside of her burst into waves of throbbing pleasure. It was so good and so pure, and came as such a relief that she could still feel pleasure as she once had, especially when Alex slipped his fingers back inside of her. She squeezed around them, wanting more, wanting all of him.

He must have heard her heart's cry. He shifted atop her once more, nudging her legs apart as he guided himself to her still tender and throbbing entrance. With the gentlest movement possible, he pressed inside of her. It felt so good to take him in, to feel him stretch and invade her, that she sighed aloud.

He paused. "It's not too much, is it?"

She could have laughed. "It's wonderful," she mewled instead. "More."

A deep, hungry sound rumbled up from his chest as he

pushed deeper. He circled a hand around her backside, squeezing and lifting her to meet a second, gentle thrust.

It felt different to join with him in slow, careful strokes. She wasn't sure how, but it went far beyond her body's reaction to being filled by him. His caution quickly drove her mad, and she bore down on him, urging him to move faster, to go deeper. He responded with a gentle increase in speed and intensity, still driving her to distraction. His control was astounding and far beyond her own.

"More," she whispered when her body reached the point where it was ready to shatter with pleasure once more.

He seemed to have reached the limit of his patience as well, and once given permission, his thrusts became less controlled, more urgent. Within minutes, they were rocking together in a powerful rhythm, bodies entwined and sweating, their sounds of pleasure forming the sweetest song Marigold could imagine. She wanted him to enjoy himself to the fullest and moved and sighed with his thrusts to encourage him. At the same time, she felt as though he were waiting for her to climax yet again.

That feeling of working together with him for both of their pleasure was what pushed her over the edge, sending her into another tremor of release, harder and more potent this time. He tensed as she did, and within moments, his love sounds pitched to cries of release. His body was hot and heavy against hers as he spilled his seed into her, and even though part of her mourned that nothing would come of it, the communion between them was magical. Every part of her belonged to him, and him to her.

The deep, heated glow was so overpowering, that as they both floated down from climax, Marigold could hardly move. She didn't want to break away from Alex, didn't want him to disengage himself from her. When he rolled to the side, she clung to him, moving with him, reveling in the feeling of him still inside of her. She wanted to be with him that way forever.

CHAPTER 18

*A*lex hadn't slept so well since returning to Wiltshire. The strain of his falling out with Marigold was gone, and the last bit of fear for her health and well-being had melted away at her sighs of pleasure as they made love. It was more than the feeling that he'd gotten his wife back that sent languid warmth through every part of his body as the two of them lay tangled up in sleep. It was the feeling that he'd gotten his life back. He could conquer the world.

Marigold stirred as she napped with her back pressed against his chest. He hoped she wouldn't wake up, not yet. He loved the sensation of sheltering her naked body with his, of the two of them being lazy together. And his cock was already getting ideas about making love to her again, perhaps in the position they lay in now. But he wasn't in a hurry. They had their whole lives to make love.

He was just falling back to sleep, working out ways to explain that the cottage they hid out in had been Violetta's home without upsetting Marigold, but a distant shout kept him from drifting off.

Marigold drew in a breath, proving that she wasn't as asleep as he'd thought. Her body stretched along his, her soft, round backside rubbing against him in the best possible way, as she twisted to face him. "What's that?" Her voice was groggy and adorable.

"Nothing we need to worry about," he told her, sliding a hand over her stomach and up. He caught her breast and kneaded it.

Marigold hummed with pleasure, wriggling against him and encouraging him to do more. He nudged his knee between her legs and traced his fingers down from her breast to tease between her legs. Her soft gasp and the way she pressed against his hand, taking her pleasure as he stroked her, was so powerfully erotic that he was hard in no time.

"James? James, where are you?"

His arousal hit a bump, and he lifted his head. His pulse sped up, but he shook his head slightly and reminded himself that James was a common name.

"James? James!"

"Is that Ada?" Marigold asked, her body losing its liquid feel.

"Why would Ada be looking for him here?" Alex asked. "He's with Ruby and Miss Goode."

"James!"

The call came from just outside of the cottage. There was no mistaking Ada's voice. Alex barely had time to frown before the maid pressed her hands and face against the window just above the bed, peering in.

She instantly pulled back with a yelp as Marigold gasped in shock. The bedclothes were bunched around Marigold's hips, and no doubt Ada had seen much more of her master and mistress than she'd ever cared to see.

"I'm sorry, sir. I'm so sorry," Ada's muffled voice came from the other side of the window.

Alex would have roared with laughter at their unfortunate discovery if not for the panic that edged Ada's voice.

"Something must be wrong," Marigold said, slipping out of bed and searching for her clothes.

With a sigh, Alex climbed out of bed himself. But the discomfort of his erection was the least of his problems.

"Have you seen James?" Ada called from the cottage's front door, sounding upset. "Is he here?"

"He's not," Marigold called back. The bedroom door stood half open, though she kept well on the side of the room hidden from view as she dressed.

Alex spotted Ada standing in the main room with her back to the bedroom as he pulled on his drawers and trousers. "He's with Ruby and Miss Goode," he told her.

"No, he's not," Ada replied. She was facing determinedly away, but he could tell from the stiffness in her back and the set of her shoulders that she was beside herself with worry. "Ruby went to check on Master James after she finished cleaning up tea, but he wasn't in his bed. Ben never saw him come back into the house. Neither did Mary or Martha."

"He was with Miss Goode," Alex repeated, though the more he thought about it the more alarming that prospect was. Miss Goode wasn't one of their own. He didn't know her from a hole in the wall.

"Did you check at Mr. Turnbridge's school?" Marigold asked, frantically hooking her corset.

"Why would she take him there if he was supposed to be having his nap?" Ada asked.

Alex rushed to put himself together enough to step out

into the main room, his waistcoat and jacket in hand. "Where have you searched?"

Gingerly, Ada turned to face him. When she saw he was mostly dressed, one kind of embarrassment left her face to be replaced by a far more worrying fear. "We've checked all over the house, inside and out, sir. He wasn't in any of the gardens. Ruby is beside herself. She thinks she should have kept a closer eye on the lad."

Alex wasn't about to upset Ada even more by agreeing with that statement. "Has anyone called on Rev. Fallon and his wife? James might have wandered down to their house."

Ada nodded. "Ben was on his way to check there. I thought I'd come here, seeing as it was his mother's house."

"What?" Marigold emerged from the bedroom at that moment, her eyes round with concern.

Dread nipped at Alex's insides, but Marigold seemed more concerned about James than whose bed they had just made love in.

"This was Violetta's cottage," Alex admitted. "No one's lived here for years, but I have the staff clean it quarterly." There wasn't time for more. He turned back to Ada. "James hasn't been here. But he does have a habit of wandering off. He was at the train station when we arrived in July."

"We should go to Clara and Arthur first," Marigold said, marching for the door. If she was angry with him for failing to mention the cottage belonged to Violetta, it didn't show. Her only outward emotion was deep, motherly concern.

"Head back up to the house to see if they've found him there," Alex instructed Ada as he followed Marigold to the door. "Then send someone to Mr. Turnbridge's school."

"Yes, sir." Ada curtsied, then bolted along the river path toward Winterberry Park.

Alex paused only long enough to close and lock the

cottage, then to hide the key. "Are you angry with me for not telling you whose house this was?" he asked as he and Marigold rushed down the path toward Lanhill. His hand twitched to grab hers, but he held back.

"You did tell me," she answered, her expression all business. "You said that you owned the cottage. It's irrelevant who once lived there."

The burst of relief Alex felt at her words was quickly swallowed by an even greater fear. James was missing. And while he was the sort to wander off on an adventure, the fact that Miss Goode was very likely involved didn't sit well with him. Even if she were as innocent as a saint, the distant cry of a train whistle brought to mind a thousand dangers a toddler of James's age could find himself in. He tried not to think of his son crushed beneath a train or drown in the river or worse.

"We'll find him," Marigold said, grasping his hand as they reached a set of stone stairs leading from the valley of the river up to one of the larger streets that lead into the village. "It's only a matter of time."

But when they reached the vicarage, Alex's hopes were dashed.

"I heard James is missing," Arthur greeted them before they could even set foot in the vicarage's garden. He was putting on his coat, looking as though he were ready to join the hunt.

"He's not here?" Alex's chest squeezed. A few months ago, he wouldn't have given a second thought to a child, trusting in others to watch out for him. Now, however, he felt as though a part of himself were missing.

Arthur shook his head. "Your footman, Ben, was here not five minutes ago asking if we'd seen him."

"Did they find him?" Clara came rushing out of the

house, an infant in each arm. Her face was drawn with worry, and her cheeks were pink. "Is he home?"

"No," Marigold answered. "We were hoping he was here."

"Oh dear." Clara's voice shook, and her eyes were round. "We have to find him. He could be anywhere."

"Who was the last person to see him?" Arthur asked, stepping forward as if to take charge of the situation.

That show of strength inspired Alex to keep a cool head himself. "Miss Goode took him for a run around the house to get him to settle down for his nap."

"Miss Goode?" Arthur blinked. "Who's that?"

"Mr. Turnbridge's new assistant," Marigold answered.

Both Arthur and Clara looked confused.

"She came up to the house two weeks ago with the children when they performed for us," Alex explained. "Apparently, she just came from London to help at the school."

"I haven't heard of her." Arthur shook his head. "Although I know Timothy has been desperate for help."

Anxiety crawled down Alex's spine. It seemed to be reflected in the uneasy way Marigold glanced to him. All they really knew about Miss Goode was what Ruby had told them. He thought back to the day of the concert, wracking his brain to remember whether he'd seen Mr. Turnbridge speaking to Miss Goode directly. He hadn't chased the woman off or questioned her presence, but he'd had his hands full.

"Has Ruby said anything more about Miss Goode to you?" he asked Marigold.

She shook her head and shrugged. "Only that they'd become fast friends, and that they were from the same neighborhood in Limehouse."

It didn't seem right all of a sudden. "We need to go to

the school." He took Marigold's hand and started off down the path that led deeper into town.

"I'll come with you," Arthur said, nodding to his wife.

The three of them marched swiftly across the tiny village of Lanhill to the unassuming schoolhouse bordering a field on the other side. Children ran through the yard, screaming and playing, which may have indicated some sort of recess, or perhaps simply Mr. Turnbridge's inability to discipline his students. The only supervision for the younger students were a trio of distracted older girls who were making eyes at a young man with a sweat-soaked shirt unloading crates from a wagon across the street.

Mr. Turnbridge himself was inside, attempting to explain what looked like algebraic equations to a group of older boys while a small pack of younger students practiced drawing numbers on slates.

"Heavens, this is a surprise," he said, glancing up as though he'd been caught handing out candy and fire-crackers to the children instead of teaching them.

"Turnbridge." Alex nodded as he marched up the aisle between school desks to the man. "Have you seen James and Miss Goode?"

Mr. Turnbridge blinked and shook his head. "No. Should I have?"

Marigold squeezed Alex's hand harder.

"James has gone missing," Arthur explained while Alex sent Marigold what he hoped was a reassuring look. "Your Miss Goode was the last person he was seen with."

"*My* Miss Goode?" Mr. Turnbridge blinked.

Alex's heart sank. Suddenly, being crushed by a train or drown in the river seemed like a small problem.

"You remember, sir," one of the older boys piped up.

"The pretty lass who helped out at Winterberry Park that time."

In an instant, Mr. Turnbridge looked as alarmed as Alex felt. "I don't know who she was," he said, putting his chalk aside and cutting through the boys to stand closer to Alex. "I didn't think to question, since she seemed so willing to help out. I needed the help. But that was the first and only time I saw her." He paused, glancing to Marigold as she drew in a breath and clapped a hand to her chest. "Honestly, sir, I thought she was a new maid at Winterberry Park."

"She wasn't." Alex's voice had gone cold and hard. He didn't truly blame the schoolmaster, but too many mistakes had been made.

"We need to find out if anyone saw her," Arthur said. "I can ask around town to see who she had interactions with."

"I'll help," Mr. Turnbridge said. "I can send the children home for the day. It's almost time anyhow."

"Want me to dismiss 'em, sir?" the boy who had spoken up earlier said.

"Yes, please, Ned."

"You heard Sir," Ned spoke up to the children left in the room. "Get yerselves gone!"

Alex, Marigold, Arthur, and Mr. Turnbridge headed out of the school house in an avalanche of rushing boys. The chaos of the schoolyard as Ned repeated his announcement did nothing to soothe Alex's fraying nerves. There was no way to deny that something far more sinister than James simply wandering off was at hand.

"The train station," Marigold suggested as they made their way back to the street. She'd gone pale, and her voice was wispy and uncertain. "We should check the train station. That's where he'd wandered on the day I met him."

Alex nodded, taking her hand and starting off in that direction.

"I'll check down by the dairy, just in case," Mr. Turnbridge said. "He also likes to visit the cows."

"And I'll start asking around to see who knows anything about Miss Goode," Arthur said.

"Miss Goode," Alex muttered as he and Marigold turned onto Station Street. "I'm beginning to wonder if that name wasn't designed to lull us into complacency."

"Don't say it," Marigold whispered, squeezing his hand tight. "I can't bear to think about the possibility that...."

She didn't finish her sentence. She didn't have to. Alex had a terrible feeling that they were thinking the same thing.

By the time they reached the station, the only activity they found was a few people wandering the garden as they waited for the evening train and the porters putting away a few pieces of baggage from the last train.

"James?" Marigold called out, heading straight to the spot where they'd first found him. "James?"

"James?" Alex added his call to hers, but the suspicion that it wouldn't do any good already had him in its grip.

Mr. Bolton, the stationmaster, popped his head out through one of the stationhouse's windows. Alex spotted him right away and let go of Marigold's hand to march over to him.

"Bolton, have you seen James?" he asked.

"No," Mr. Bolton answered, frowning and scratching his head. "But I thought I heard him out here earlier."

"You did?" Hope surged in Alex's chest.

Marigold rushed to join him, just as full of hope, but Mr. Bolton's expression wasn't at all reassuring.

"It was strange," he said.

"What was?"

Mr. Bolton gestured for them to walk around to the archway that separated the street from the train platform. Even the tiny delay was maddening, but Alex took Marigold's hand and rushed to meet Mr. Bolton as he came out of his office.

"There was a strange fuss earlier," Mr. Bolton began immediately. "I thought I heard James, so I came out to take a look. He hasn't wandered down to say hello in every so long. I didn't see the lad anywhere, but before I got a really good look, a stack of luggage was upset on the platform."

"Luggage?" Marigold blinked.

Mr. Bolton rubbed his neck, looking uneasy. "We have spills now and then. That much wasn't unusual. What was strange was how long it took to set things to right. This bloke waiting for the train kept trying to help, but he was a clumsy sort. The whole thing took me and both my porters to set to rights. By the time we were done, I felt as though I'd been spun around, turned upside down, and shaken out. The bloke disappeared an instant later."

"That's not so strange, is it?" Marigold asked, false hope bright in her eyes.

Mr. Bolton winced. "The strange bit was that I could have sworn I heard James's voice on the train after that."

Panic gripped Alex so suddenly that the edges of his vision went black. The pieces were falling together too perfectly. James wasn't just missing, he'd been kidnapped. Alex was almost certain of it.

"Was there a woman in the vicinity of the train station earlier?" he demanded of Mr. Bolton, perhaps a little too forcefully. "Brown hair, brown eyes, medium height."

Mr. Bolton flinched, flushing. "I'm sorry to say, sir, but

that description could fit a dozen or more women who have passed through the station today."

Alex could have punched his way through a solid brick wall. Miss Goode was unremarkable looking. Perhaps a bit too much so. He could give out her description in as much detail as he wanted and still come up with nothing. Just like the driver who'd run off with his carriage and caused the wreck.

His thoughts were interrupted by a scruffy young boy asking, "Are you Mr. Croydon?"

Alex blinked and twisted toward the lad. In the process, he noticed that Marigold had gone paler still and was shaking. "I'm he," he said.

The boy held out an envelope. "She gave me a sixpence for handing this to you when you came by."

Alex took the envelope, anger and fear roiling in his stomach. Whatever was in the envelope wouldn't be good.

"Open it," Marigold implored him, her voice hoarse.

Alex turned to her, ripping through the envelope's seal. A single page was folded inside. It simply read, "If you want to see your son alive again, put an end to the scandalous rumors immediately."

Dread gaped in Alex's gut. He didn't need to ask who had sent the note or what it was about. It had Turpin's signature all over it. Worse still, Alex's first instinct was to do everything Turpin wanted, just to get his son back.

"He can't get away with this," Marigold said, her voice shaking. Evidently, she didn't need to be told what the letter meant either. Her burst of fury turned quickly to tearful panic. "He didn't even say how or where we could get James back."

"London," Alex growled. "If she took James away by

train, they're headed to London. Turpin has more allies there, more places to hide him."

The horror filling Marigold's eyes was more painful than any wreck or wound. "What do we do?" she asked, clapping a hand to her mouth.

As far as Alex was concerned, there was only one thing to do. He took Marigold's hand and marched out of the train station. "We go back to London."

CHAPTER 19

*I*t shouldn't have come as a surprise to Marigold that her world could be turned upside down in the blink of an eye. For the third time in almost as many months, everything changed in an instant, leaving her with the feeling that she'd been hurled from a catapult into the unknown.

"The next train to London leaves in just over two hours," Mr. Bolton informed them as Alex grabbed Marigold's hand and shot out of the station. "Do you want me to make out a ticket?"

"Make out two," Alex called to him, clearly anxious to get moving. "I'll need Phillips with me."

"Three," Marigold corrected. "I'm coming too."

Alex stopped his rushed steps to pivot to her. "Are you sure you feel well enough?"

Marigold stared at him, her brow furrowed in determination. "He's my son too."

The corner of Alex's mouth twitched, and a momentary spark of joy lit his expression. He wanted her with him, no matter the danger. She would fight for James, fight for them to be a family, as doggedly as he would. "Three," he called to Mr. Bolton, then set off with Marigold as fast as she could run.

Winterberry Park was in an uproar when they returned. Word had somehow gotten back that it was very likely Miss Goode had run off with James. Everyone from Mr. Noakes to Annie, the scullery maid, were beside themselves. And Ruby was inconsolable.

"I didn't know," she sobbed, crumpled up on one of the benches in the front hall. "She seemed like such a nice woman. She was from the same place as me, the same street I was raised on."

Marigold broke away from Alex to rush to Ruby's side. "Have you not had many friends, Ruby?" she asked, gently rubbing the distraught woman's back.

Ruby hid her face in her hands, shaking her head. Marigold hugged her, bitterness and pity warring in her heart. It didn't take much to deduce that Miss Goode had told Ruby everything she'd wanted to hear in order to get close to her, just as she may very well have chosen a false name that would prompt them to trust her. Which meant that whoever Miss Goode was, she was an expert at deceit.

"Phillips."

Marigold and Ruby both looked up as Alex turned to greet Mr. Phillips, who ran in from one of the sitting rooms. His face was splotched red with exertion, which, combined with his auburn hair and the fury in his eyes, made him look as though he were ablaze.

"I've just heard, sir," he said. He sent an unreadable look in Ruby's direction before marching up to Alex. Ruby buried her face in her hands once more, weeping twice as hard. "I was searching down by the Portis's farm. Mabel

Portis said she saw Miss Goode walk past, carrying James, about an hour and a half ago."

Alex nodded, then started for the stairs. "We leave for London at once. Pack what you can in a suitcase." He glanced up the stairs to where Ada was just coming down from the first floor. She stopped, then turned to head back up. "We only need enough for a day or two. Everything else will have to follow after."

"Yes, sir," both Ada and Mr. Phillips said.

"I'll pack my own case, Phillips," Alex went on. "I need you to hurry down to the train station to telegraph Malcolm Campbell. Give him as much information as you can, and tell him we're on our way."

"Yes, sir." Phillips pivoted on the stair, then raced down again. He jumped the last three stairs and shot toward the front door.

Ruby raised her red, tear-stained face from her hands and called, "I'm sorry, Gil."

Mr. Phillips skittered to a clumsy halt and turned to her. He opened his mouth, but nothing came out. His frown darkened, and he pursed his lips before turning and dashing out of the house.

Ruby burst into a fresh veil of tears. "He's never going to speak to me again," she wailed. "He told me I shouldn't be so trusting, that we knew nothing about Miss Goode. I should have believed him. He'll hate me now, and I don't think I can live with that."

Marigold's brow inched up. They didn't have time for romantic drama, but the hint that there was an entire story taking place under her nose that she hadn't guessed at surprised her. She continued to rub Ruby's back, as frustrated with her as she was sympathetic.

"You didn't know," she sighed. "But I suppose trusting people is a sign of a good heart."

"No." Ruby shook her head. "I'm of no use to anyone. You never should have taken me out of the workhouse, ma'am. That's what I deserved." She glanced mournfully at Marigold. "You'll send me back now, won't you?"

Marigold let out a tight breath. "We'll discuss that later. As for now, we all need to concentrate on is getting James back." She stood, starting for the stairs.

"I should come with you, ma'am," Ruby called after her, jumping to her feet. "There's places I know, places where they might take James, places I've been. Surely someone here could mind Faith for me. I...I owe it to you to help."

A terrifying kind of hope surged through Marigold as she paused, waiting for Ruby to catch up to her. "Turpin is behind this." She intended her words to be a question, but there was no doubt in her mind.

Ruby looked equally convinced. "He must be, ma'am, what with you and Mr. Croydon exposing him. And I know how his mind works." She lowered her head as she spoke.

Marigold reached for her hand. "Then you're right. You should come with us."

The race to be ready in time to catch the train kept Marigold far too busy for the next hour to worry about Ruby's part in James's kidnapping, or, blessedly, what might be happening to James. When panic started to overtake her as she helped Alex and Ada pack suitcases, she forced herself to remember that James was of more use to Turpin alive than dead. But with that thought, she couldn't shake images of how frightened and lost her little boy must feel. Her little boy. He'd only just walked into her life, but she would fight for him as fiercely as any mother.

Marigold didn't have a chance to catch her breath until she and Alex were seated side-by-side on the train as it pulled out of Lanhill's station. They'd managed to secure an entire first-class compartment for themselves, allowing Mr. Phillips and Ruby to ride with them rather than buying them second-class tickets.

"Time is of the essence," Alex told Mr. Phillips as all four of them wriggled with impatience. "Turpin will know we're coming after James. Who knows how long he's had to plan for this."

"There's only so many places they could take the boy, sir," Ruby spoke up tentatively. "There's a house in Kensington, one across the river in Vauxhall, one in Spitalfields."

"Unless he's set up more places since you left him," Mr. Phillips cut into her explanation. Ruby snapped her mouth shut and turned away from him, misery twisting her face.

That misery seemed to fill the compartment as the train chugged on. None of them felt much like talking, although if the others were anything like Marigold, their thoughts refused to stay still. The sun set, leaving them in tense, lonely darkness as the hours ticked slowly by in time with the train clattering over the tracks.

At one point, Marigold dozed off, her head lolling against Alex's shoulder. She woke up with a start as the whistle sounded. Outside the compartment, a conductor passing through the train car shouted, "Paddington! London, Paddington, next stop."

Relief spilled through Marigold as she and the others gathered their things and prepared to leave the train. The moment it stopped, Mr. Phillips shot forward, opening the door and stepping down to the night-blackened platform. Alex climbed down next, giving Marigold a hand as she disembarked. Mr. Phillips waited to give Ruby a hand down, rippling with tension. They exchanged a look that was heavy with emotion before both looked away.

"Alex!"

Lord Malcolm Campbell's voice as he greeted them on the platform was the first encouraging thing Marigold had heard in hours. She rushed to Alex's side, ready to greet Lord Malcolm as he marched toward them.

"Malcolm." Alex paused only long enough to shake Lord Malcolm's hand before their entire group headed for the station's exit. "What have you been able to find out?"

Without hesitation, Lord Malcolm said, "Turpin's people are definitely on the move. There was too much coming and going at his townhouse, and at the other houses he owns, for this time of year."

"Did anyone see Miss Goode arrive here with James?" Alex asked.

"We have a few leads," Lord Malcolm answered with a frown. "But a woman traveling with a child isn't unusual enough to stand out."

"Someone must have seen something," Marigold said as they stepped through the station door and into the bustling, London street. Even late at night, the area was full of activity and noise. The rush had always been a comfort to London-born Marigold, but for the first time, it unsettled her.

"We're following several leads," Lord Malcolm told her. He pointed down the street to one of at least a dozen waiting carriages.

Their conversation was interrupted by the bustle of climbing into Lord Malcolm's carriage. There wasn't enough room for Mr. Phillips and Ruby, so Mr. Phillips offered to take Ruby to Croydon House in a hired hack. Their small amount of luggage was sorted out, and after what felt like far too much time passing for Marigold's liking, the carriage pulled out, taking them home.

"We have to move fast," Lord Malcolm began as they rolled along. "There's no telling how deep they could hide James if we don't go after him immediately."

"What if they hurt him?" Marigold asked, her heart fluttering to her throat. "Will they hurt him if we close in too fast?"

Lord Malcolm didn't answer immediately.

"I'm sure they'll keep James out of bodily harm," Alex said, though his words felt more like they were designed to placate her than to be truthful.

Marigold swallowed, clinging to Alex's arm.

"My men are already on the alert," Lord Malcolm went on. "Turpin is being watched in every way. We'll know soon where he's taken James, and once we do, we'll move in."

Lord Malcolm and Alex continued to discuss their plans as the carriage rattled on, but Marigold had a harder and harder time paying attention. All she could do was imagine James, scared and crying. Would he call out for her? Could he possibly understand how desperate she was to save him, and then to hold him and never let go?

By the time they arrived at Croydon House, Marigold was a bundle of frazzled nerves. Alex helped her down from the carriage and took her arm as he led her up the stairs to the front door, which Mr. Poole held open for them. But she wasn't entirely ready for the shock that met her in the front hall.

"My dear, I've been worried sick about you all night." Lady Stanhope stepped out of the front parlor, her arms outstretched to embrace Marigold.

Marigold blinked at the woman, astounded that she, of all people, would be standing in the front hall to greet her under such dire circumstances. But between the confidence in Lady Stanhope's fierce expression and the weariness that clung to every fiber of her being, Marigold was so over-whelmed that she broke away from Alex and rushed into her friend's arms.

The comfort of Lady Stanhope's greeting was cut short a moment later as Lord Malcolm growled, "What the devil are you doing here?"

A surge of tension encompassed Marigold until Lady Stanhope let her go. Marigold stepped to the side as Lady Stanhope stiffened her back and stared at Lord Malcolm. Her eyes narrowed, and a wicked grin played across her lips, making her handsome, angular face shine with challenge.

"Good evening, Malcolm," she said, taking a few, swaying steps toward him.

"You have no business interfering." Lord Malcolm stepped forward to meet her, his eyes narrowed as well.

They came to within a few feet of each other, Lord Malcolm glowering and Lady Stanhope staring down her long nose at him with a grin that grew by the second. The air in the hall crackled, and Marigold felt her temperature rise by several degrees.

"I heard you might need me," Lady Stanhope said at last, when it felt as though the standoff would ignite the house and burn it down.

"I've managed well enough without you so far," Lord Malcolm replied.

"Have you?" One of Lady Stanhope's eyebrows twitched up.

A tense silence followed as the two stared each other down. Marigold glanced past them to Alex. The frustration dripping off of him was obvious. Marigold couldn't blame him. They had more urgent matters to deal with than the friction that obviously existed between Lord Malcolm and Lady Stanhope.

"How do we make contact with your men in the field to discover what they've found out?" Alex stepped in, breaking Lord Malcolm and Lady Stanhope apart.

In an instant, the tension in the room lessened. Lady Stanhope continued to smirk as though she'd won the confrontation. Lord Malcolm frowned at her, then turned to Alex.

"I have runners scheduled to report to me when they learn more," he said.

Alex didn't seem at all appeased. "They should have already reported in. Someone must know something by now."

"As soon as we discover where James is being kept—"

"We already know where James is being kept," Lady Stanhope interrupted, her voice sharp and a tad bored. Both men and Marigold snapped to face her. She shrugged. "As I said, you might need me."

"This is no time for your petty games, Katya." Lord Malcolm marched back to her, but his frightening glower barely made a dent in Lady Stanhope's regal calm.

"Who's playing games?" she asked, batting her eyes as though they were at a parliamentary debate instead of desperate to rescue a helpless three-year-old from a man who wouldn't think twice about killing him. "I had my people out looking the second I heard James was taken."

"You don't have people," Lord Malcolm rumbled.

Lady Stanhope returned his stare with fire in her eyes. "I can assure you, I do. Reliable people. People who know Shayles's operatives on sight and who spot them the moment they arrive by train."

"Shayles?" Marigold pressed a hand to her thundering heart.

"Yes, my dear. I'm afraid Lord Shayles is the mastermind of this whole, dreadful thing. Turpin counts Shayles as a friend. Shayles sees Turpin as his vote in Commons. The Devil is loath to lose his power."

"Your operative saw Miss Goode with James at Paddington?" Alex stepped forward before Lady Stanhope could finish shooting her grin of triumph in Lord Malcolm's direction.

"Yes," she answered, rolling her shoulders and assuming a more business-like mien. "Your Miss Goode is one Amelia Blunt, one of Shayles's toadies. She was followed to a house on Pollard Street in Bethnal Green."

"Then we should go at once," Alex said. He marched to the door, Lord Malcolm following him.

"I wouldn't do that if I were you," Lady Stanhope called after them.

Marigold gaped at her. "Why not? The sooner we recover James, the better."

Lady Stanhope shook her head, resting a hand on Marigold's arm. "They will know that you're coming," she told the men, who had reached the door which Mr. Poole held open. "They will know, and they'll be ready for you. If you take the direct approach, without adequate planning, you'll put yourselves and James at risk."

"Whether they know we're coming or not," Lord Malcolm argued, "they won't have had enough time to plan against a full assault of my men."

"They're present and accounted for and ready to move in?" Lady Stanhope asked.

"Yes."

Lady Stanhope shook her head. "All the more reason to proceed with caution. Shayles and Turpin know your men just as you know theirs. If they've seen them lurking anywhere near their safe houses, they'll already have a plan."

"We can't just sit here and do nothing," Alex hissed.

"No, you can come up with a better plan," Lady Stanhope countered.

Marigold was torn between the two. She wanted more than anything to trust her husband, but to her ears, what Lady Stanhope was saying made sense. All the same, she couldn't bear the thought of James in trouble for a moment longer than he needed to be.

"Every minute we stand here debating is a minute lost," Lord Malcolm said at last. He glanced to Alex, then nodded to the door.

Alex sighed, glancing quickly to Marigold. "I'll find him," he said. "I'll find him and bring him back."

Marigold rushed across the hall to grab his arm. She lifted to her toes to kiss him. "Hurry," she whispered.

He kissed her back, nodded, then rushed out into the night.

CHAPTER 20

*L*ondon in the dark was a menacing place, no matter what Alex's reason for being out. It was well past the hour when decent people were sound asleep, as the hired hack wound its way through one of the more dangerous sections of town. Phillips and Ruby had arrived at the house as Alex and Malcolm rushed out, and with a little persuading in the form of a gold sovereign, the hack's driver had been convinced to take them and Phillips on to Bethnal Green.

"Speed is of the essence," Malcolm explained, his Scottish accent more pronounced than usual. "If Turpin and Shayles have noticed my men keeping an eye on them, they might very well be ready."

Alex grinned in spite of the seriousness of the situation. "Don't tell me you agree with Katya."

Malcolm made a bitter scoffing noise. "Not even if she told me the sky were blue."

The mystery of Malcolm and Katya's tangled relationship kept Alex distracted as they journeyed on through streets teeming with men who kept their faces hidden and women who left very little to the imagination. The sense of time ticking away plagued Alex, and along with it, the sickening sensation that the entire situation was completely his fault. If he had been a better father, if he had put his family before his career, if he hadn't rushed to attack Turpin with the information about Ruby, none of this would have been happening. Turpin wouldn't have lashed out at him, causing the carriage wreck. Marigold would still be carrying his child and capable of carrying more. Lives had been shattered because he let ambition rule him. He wouldn't let James's life be ruined as well.

"Stop here," Malcolm called out to the driver, though they were several blocks from Pollard Street.

The driver dutifully brought the hack to a stop under a flickering, gas streetlight. Malcolm jumped out of the carriage first, Alex and Phillips right behind him.

"Wait here," Malcolm told the driver, handing him another large coin. "We shouldn't be long, but we may need to beat a hasty retreat when we come along."

"Can't pay me enough for this," the driver mumbled under his breath, but he hunkered down into his coat all the same. He set the reins aside and looked ready to wait things out, which was all that mattered.

"This way," Malcolm whispered, gesturing for Alex and Phillips to follow him.

Between the feeble glow of a few streetlights placed far apart and the light of the moon as it flickered in and out of clouds, Bethnal Green left Alex with an unfriendly feeling. Almost all of the windows in the craggy and dilapidated houses around them were dark. The only sounds were the occasional bark of dogs or human coughs that reminded them they weren't alone. A man stepped quickly into the alley between two houses as they rushed down the main street, then turned onto a darker, narrower one.

"Psst."

The signal came from the shadows at the corner of Florida and Pollard Streets. Malcolm abruptly stopped, leaving Alex and Phillips to collide as they tried to stop as well.

"What news?" Malcolm asked the shadow.

A grey-haired, grizzled man, leaned toward them from the corner of a house. "They've got the child there, all right."

Alex's chest tightened painfully, and he stepped up to Malcolm's side.

"He was crying and kicking, so Fulton dosed him with laudanum to shut him up," the man went on.

Rage spread through Alex like a wildfire. "We have to get him out of there."

Malcolm nodded. "Do you know where in the house he's being held?"

The man in the shadows shook his head. "I only saw them take him in and heard Fulton talk about dosing the boy. Don't know where they went once they were in the house."

"It's likely they'd've taken him in as deeply as possible," Malcolm said, his expression darkening. "Do they know we're coming?"

The man in the shadows rolled his shoulders uncomfortably. "Hard to say. They're playing it close to their chests, they are."

"We haven't got a moment to lose," Alex said. "We need to go in, even if we have to break down the doors to do it."

The man in the shadows didn't seem impressed by Alex's bravado. He let out a breath and reached for something in his coat. "If you're planning to storm the castle, you'll need these." He drew out two revolvers, handing one to Alex and one to Malcolm.

Alex swallowed. He hadn't used a weapon since his days in the army, decades ago. He'd believed he was past such uncivilized behavior. It was strange how quickly his instincts returned once he had the cold metal in his hands.

"Hurry," Malcolm said, nodding to the man in the shadows, then walking on. "The longer we wait, the more of a chance they have to guess we're here and what we're up to."

Alex followed him, mouth pressed tightly shut. He'd never been to that part of the city and didn't know where they were going. He was at Malcolm's mercy, and glanced furtively at the houses looming around them. None of them stood out from the others, but all of them had an air of mischief at best, evil at worst.

A few yards down Pollard Street, Malcolm held up his hands, bringing them to a stop. He pointed to the only building on the street that had a light in one of its windows. Then he held up his gun. With a gesture toward the alley beside the house, he set off, silent as a specter.

They slipped around the corner of the house. The scent of sewage and rubbish hit Alex's nostrils, adding to the sense of danger pressing down on him. In spite of his determination to find and rescue his son, no matter what it took, things didn't feel right. The house was too quiet, their progress too easy. He paused to glance over his shoulder at Phillips, who stood out, white as a ghost, even in the dark. Phillips returned his look with one that said they were a bunch of fools to go charging in, but he continued to follow.

When they reached the back of the house, they were joined by three other men. Alex swallowed his initial instinct to shoot as Malcolm gestured to the trio, signaling that they were his men. They evidently knew how to take silent orders as well, and within seconds, their band of rescuers closed in on the kitchen door.

Before they could reach the door, it burst open. Light poured through, enough to blind them, as half a dozen lanterns were uncovered. They blazed throughout the house's cramped back garden, completely stunning Alex. He raised his arm to his face to shield his eyes, his revolver useless in his hand. He didn't think to use it before someone shouted, "Stop where you are!"

The next thing he heard were shots being fired. Before he could get his bearings, pain seared through his arm, then his side. Then the world went black.

THE CLOCK IN THE DOWNSTAIRS HALL AT CROYDON House chimed three in the morning, and Marigold sighed in agony. Time was crawling. Alex and Lord Malcolm should have been back hours ago, as far as she was concerned. She should have gone to bed, but it would have been pointless. Not to mention the fact that Lady Stanhope was still with her. She stood with her elbow propped against the mantel, her face more angular than usual, as it was pinched in thought. Marigold watched her from the sofa across the room, her legs tucked under her. The pensive scene was rounded out by Ruby sitting on the very edge of one of Alex's overstuffed chairs, as though it might burst into flame under her. Ruby's expression of guilt was as powerful as Lady Stanhope's ruminative look.

A thousand questions ricocheted through Marigold's mind. Where exactly had the men gone? Why were they taking so long? Would they have help, or were they on their own? But more than anything, prayers poked their way up through the questions. She prayed for Alex to stay safe. She prayed for James to be returned to her whole. She would sacrifice her entire life for that boy, if only he were returned to her arms.

A clatter at the front door seemed like an answer to her prayers at last, and she leapt to her feet. Lady Stanhope sucked in a breath and turned away from the fireplace. Together, they marched from the parlor into the hall, Ruby jumping up to follow.

But the bustle and throb of energy that shot through the front door wasn't what Marigold hoped for.

"We need to get him upstairs," Lord Malcolm shouted at Mr. Poole.

"Yes, my l—" Mr. Poole's words dropped into stunned silence.

Marigold gasped, a small scream escaping her as she saw what Mr. Poole had. Lord Malcolm and Mr. Phillips carried Alex's limp, bloody form between them through the hall and up the stairs.

"My God, Alex, Alex!" Marigold shouted, tearing up the stairs after him.

Lady Stanhope was hard on her heels. "What happened?"

"It was an ambush," Lord Malcolm growled. "Alex got in the way of a few bullets."

"No!" Marigold yelped, trying to push her way past Mr. Phillips to see if her husband was still alive.

Lady Stanhope held her back as the men rounded the landing and mounted the last of the stairs, heading down the corridor to the master bedroom. "You'll get in the way," she said.

"But Alex," Marigold panted, beside herself. "He'll die."

Lady Stanhope's hand tightened on Marigold's wrist.

"If they're hurrying, then he isn't dead. Which means he lasted all the way from Bethnal Green to here. Which means he has a fair chance of making it through, if we don't get in the way."

"But—"

"Go fetch Dr. Armand Pearson," Lady Stanhope ordered the small cluster of anxious servants that had gathered at the bottom of the stairs, cutting off Marigold's protest. "Don't fetch any doctor other than Dr. Pearson. Do whatever you must to get him here. He lives at—"

"I know where he lives, my lady," Mr. Long, the footman interrupted, shooting straight toward the still-open front door.

Marigold clutched a hand to her chest, sending her prayers with him, then continued up the stairs.

"Ruby, do you know the Pollard Street house?" Lady Stanhope continued to take command of the situation.

"Yes, my lady."

"Then get there as fast as you can and watch to see if they move James. Which they're bloody well likely to do at this point," she added in a grumble.

"Yes, my lady," Ruby said, curtsied, then dashed out into the night as well.

Marigold didn't wait to see if Lady Stanhope gave any more orders. She picked up her skirts and ran along the hall, bursting into the bedroom she shared with Alex. Lord Malcolm and Mr. Phillips had deposited Alex on the bed, bloodying the coverlet as they did.

"How did this happen?" she asked, pushing past Mr. Phillips as he backed away to sit by Alex's side. She started to reach for his hand, but was taken aback by the blood soaking his right sleeve.

"The bullet only grazed his arm and his head," Lord Malcolm said. "It's the one in his side I'm worried about."

"He has a bullet in his side?" Marigold's voice rose to a terrified squeak.

"It's not deep," Lord Malcolm insisted, though he didn't sound certain. "Phillips staunched the bleeding as best he could."

Marigold spared a quick glance over her shoulder to Mr. Phillips, who looked equal parts furious and anxious, and was wearing only his jacket without a shirt underneath. She didn't have time to worry about him, though. She turned back to Alex, taking his hand in spite of the blood.

"Alex, Alex, my darling, can you hear me?" she pleaded with him. "Alex, wake up."

He didn't respond. Blood was still seeping from a wound under his hairline, slowly dampening the pillow beneath his head. The worst of the bleeding in his arm seemed over, although it still oozed. It was Alex's tightly-bound middle that had her shaking.

Gingerly, she lifted the hem of his bloodied shirt to get a closer look. Mr. Phillips had done an admirable job of binding whatever wound lay under what looked like torn pieces of a shirt. He must have used his own shirt to stop the bleeding. A circle of red marred the white cotton all the same. There was no telling how bad the wound beneath it was.

"I'm here, Alex," Marigold said, calmer, even though there was a catch in her voice. "I'm right here with you. I'm not going to leave you."

"I should fetch clean water and bandages, if we have any," Mr. Phillips said. "Dr. Pearson will need them when he arrives."

"You do that," Lord Malcolm said. He stayed where he

was as Mr. Phillips left the room, but after a few minutes, when Marigold didn't even look at him, let alone speak to him, he too left.

It was a strange sort of relief to be alone with Alex, as dire as his condition was. At last, Marigold felt as though she could weep freely and clutch his hand, kissing it the way he'd kissed hers when she lay in bed with a fever, her body broken after the carriage wreck. She prayed that Alex would recover, that they were experiencing all of the sorrow of their lives at once, right at the beginning of their days together, and that the rest of their lives would be blue skies and calm seas.

"I don't know what I would do without you," she whispered, leaning closer to kiss his sweaty, blood-speckled cheek. "I love you, Alex. I do. You can't leave me now."

She bowed her head, afraid to rest it against his chest, but wanting to hug him all the same. Her heart felt as though it was in danger of shattering if Alex was grievously injured. She hadn't realized it was possible to love someone so much. The agony she felt now made the scintillating infatuation she felt in the spring pale into nothingness.

And then he raised his left hand, resting it on her side. Marigold gasped, lifting enough to look at his face. His eyes opened just a crack before closing again, but that was all she needed. Alex was alive, and he was fighting.

She wasn't sure how long it was before another commotion started downstairs. She heard steps coming upstairs, then Dr. Pearson burst through the door, medical bag in hand.

"How is he?" he asked.

Marigold pushed away from Alex and stood. "He's alive." She blinked and swallowed. "Do you treat men as well as women?"

Dr. Pearson sent her a sideways look as he reached Alex's bedside. "We are all trained in the basics before studying our special tracks."

It was all the explanation Marigold felt she was going to get, but it was enough. She stepped back, watching with wide, horrified eyes as Dr. Pearson cut Alex's shirt and Mr. Phillips's makeshift bandage away to assess the damage. He was silent as he worked, leaving Marigold to guess at the extent of Alex's injuries, but the fact that he left the wound in Alex's arm and head in favor of focusing on the bullet in his side was enough to indicate even to Marigold's uneducated eyes where the real problem was.

Mr. Phillips entered the room less than a minute later, his arms filled with linen and a steaming pitcher. "We have some carbolic acid in the scullery, if you don't have enough."

"What I have should be fine," Dr. Pearson answered him. "The bullet isn't lodged deep. Whoever fired this one must have been standing farther away. I should be able to extract it."

Marigold took another step back as Mr. Phillips brought his things to the bedside and climbed around to where he could assist Dr. Pearson. She watched for as long as she could, until Dr. Pearson took what looked like a long, thin pair of tongs from his bag. A flash of ice-cold poured through her, along with unaccountable fear. Her mind grasped futilely at another memory, one she could barely recall of writhing in pain as she lay on her back, Dr. Miller hovering over her. A wave of nausea hit her, and she rushed into the hall.

There wasn't much in the way of fresh air in the hall, but it was enough to steady her stomach and her nerves. She marched a few steps, then leaned her back against the wall to catch her breath.

The sound of raised voices downstairs pulled her out of her attempts to calm herself.

"...never listen to me, even though I'm right," Lady Stanhope shouted.

"You're a bloody fool for thinking you're right all the time," Lord Malcolm answered her.

"I *have* to think I'm right all the time," Lady Stanhope argued on. "Do you know what happens to women if they don't demand what's theirs?"

"Yes, they live happy, peaceful lives!"

"They get plowed under with the rest of the refuse that men like you think they don't need."

Marigold pushed away from the wall, her face burning. As curious as she'd always been about Lady Stanhope and Lord Malcolm's past, a sudden, towering rage filled her. She charged down the stairs and across the hall to the parlor, where they stood face-to-face, toe-to-toe, glowering at each other.

"If you had listened to me," Lady Stanhope continued, "none of us would be in this mess."

"Listening to you was what started this mess in the first place," Lord Malcolm shouted back. "You and your bloody wedding present. You knew as well as I did Alex would run off half-cocked to bring Turpin down on his own. You're always causing trouble, always instigating disasters because you can't stand how dull your life has become."

"How was I to know—"

"Stop!" Marigold shouted, holding up her hands.

Lady Stanhope and Lord Malcolm jumped apart, radiating fury as they turned to Marigold. Marigold balled her hands into fists as she continued to hold her arms up.

"My husband is upstairs fighting for his life," she flung at them. "My son has been kidnapped by notorious men who have already tried to kill us once, and who have caused irreparable damage. I will not stand here listening to some foolish lover's quarrel."

As soon as her speech was finished, she gasped at her own audacity. Lady Stanhope, on the other hand, sent her a quick grin of approval.

"Forgive me, Mrs. Croydon," Lord Malcolm said, darting a vicious sidelong look to Lady Stanhope. "Alex and James are our first priorities."

"Are they?" Marigold lowered her arms at last. Her hands and her gown, the same dusty gown she'd been wearing since dressing at Winterberry Park that morning, what felt like a lifetime away, were dotted with dried blood. "What do you propose to do about them, then?"

Lord Malcolm stepped toward her. "Our first attempt might have failed, but Turpin is bound to contact us with his demands before dawn."

"He has already contacted us with his demands," Marigold said. It took all of her willpower not to shout. She felt as though she'd reached the end of her tether, and there was nothing but anger and determination left in her. "He wants us to put an end to all of the rumors about Ruby and to restore his good name."

"But he hasn't yet said how or when he'll return James," Lord Malcolm added, softening his voice. "There will be more demands to come."

"And he'll move James," Lady Stanhope added. "Now that he is aware we tracked him the first time, he'll move James somewhere he thinks we can't track him."

"Are there such places?" Marigold asked.

Reluctantly, Lady Stanhope nodded. "They're not the sort of places you would want any child."

"Then we have to stop him." Marigold glanced between

Lady Stanhope and Lord Malcolm. "Would I be right to assume that if we wait too long and James is slipped out from under either of your web of spies, we would have no choice but to play along with Turpin and to give him what he wants?"

Lady Stanhope and Lord Malcolm exchanged a look. It was the first look of accord Marigold had seen pass between them, but it wasn't comforting.

Lady Stanhope stepped toward her. "If Turpin's men steal James away to a place we aren't aware of, yes, it would complicate matters. If Lord Shayles is involved, which I am absolutely certain he is, it could present an even greater set of dangers." She paused, pressing her lips together gingerly as if debating sharing something even more horrible. At last, she said in a cryptic rush, "Shayles has no scruples at all and would seek to profit off of whatever assets he thinks he has."

Marigold swallowed, though all moisture had left her throat. She couldn't quite piece together why Lady Stanhope's words frightened and horrified her so much, but she remembered the terrified young woman she'd seen in the window of the Black Strap Club just after her marriage. She didn't want to know why her fear was suddenly doubled, she only wanted to take action.

"What can we do?" she asked, her voice hoarse.

"As soon as we know where James is being held, if they've moved him or if he's still at Bethnal Green, we move in to extract him the same way he was taken from you," Lady Stanhope said.

Marigold blinked and shook her head. "We kidnap him from the kidnappers?"

"We use stealth and cunning instead of announcing ourselves with a full, frontal assault," Lady Stanhope answered, sending a dismissive glance in Lord Malcolm's direction.

"How the devil do you expect to use stealth to best a man who prides himself on being one step ahead of everyone else?" Lord Malcolm growled, narrowing his eyes at Lady Stanhope.

She didn't have a chance to answer. The front door flew open once again, letting in the first rays of dawn, and Ruby with them. The pink-faced maid rushed into the parlor, a hand clasped to her chest. She gulped for air, then announced, "They've loaded him in a carriage and are taking him to the Club."

CHAPTER 21

*M*arigold clasped a hand to her chest, her heart aching with fear. But behind the fear, a new determination was growing.

"We have to go to him," she said, starting across the room to prove her point.

"You can't rush into a confrontation as if we're in a Wild West show," Lady Stanhope said, stopping her.

Marigold whipped around to face her friend and mentor. "What do you suggest we do, then? Let Turpin or Shayles or whoever it is who has my son captive do what they'd like to him?"

Lady Stanhope pursed her lips and let out an impatient breath through her nose. "Of course not. But they far outnumber and out-power us. We cannot hope to rescue James with a direct attack."

"Then what?" Marigold balled her fists, feeling the heat of desperation pulse through her.

A stilted silence followed her words, then Lord Malcolm let out a breath and stepped toward Marigold. "If we act fast, there's a slim chance we might be able to get to the Black Strap Club before James arrives. If we had someone on the inside, someone already in place, it might simply be a matter of waiting until they let their guard down."

"They never let their guard down there," Ruby spoke up from the doorway, where she still stood, pale and rigid. Her eyes had a glassy, terrified look.

A spark of inspiration lit Lord Malcolm's face. "You've lived there." He broke away from Marigold and Lady Stanhope to approach her. "You know your way around the house."

"What are you saying?" Lady Stanhope followed him, glaring at Lord Malcolm as though he were the enemy.

"I'm saying that Ruby should sneak into the house and wait," Lord Malcolm snapped, seemingly irritated that Lady Stanhope would question him.

"Oh, no." Ruby shook her head and backed into the hall.

"You can't send her in there," Lady Stanhope said at the same time, her voice rising. "After what I assume happened to her there? What kind of a cruel tyrant are you?"

"We need someone who can slip in unnoticed, who knows the house, and who has escaped once before," Lord Malcolm raised his voice as well.

"I couldn't," Ruby wept. "Please don't make me go back there."

"It's the best chance we have of ending this swiftly and effectively," Lord Malcolm said, addressing Lady Stanhope without looking at Ruby.

"Malcolm, she's obviously too terrified to even think of it." Lady Stanhope threw out an arm at Ruby, glaring at Lord Malcolm. "It's about time you pulled your head out of your arse and considered the feelings of others above your own machinations for a change."

"I could say the same about you," Lord Malcolm said, taking a step toward her in what appeared to be an attempt to tower over her.

"*I'll* do it," Marigold shouted, if only to stop the whirlwind of tension between the two from spinning out of control.

Lady Stanhope and Lord Malcolm jerked away from each other and faced her. Lord Malcolm blinked, incredulous. Lady Stanhope narrowed her eyes as if considering the plan.

"I'll go," Marigold repeated. "I don't care how dangerous it is. Dress me as a maid, and I can slip into the house."

"You don't know the house's layout," Lord Malcolm argued.

Marigold swallowed, thinking fast. "Bring Ruby some paper and a pencil. She can draw a map of the rooms for me."

Ruby gasped, but the fear in her eyes turned to a frantic sort of agreement. "There's not too many places they'd keep a young boy," she said. "Not in the dungeon, and not in any of the rooms. They'd most likely put him somewhere quieter, out of the way."

Marigold had no wish to know what Ruby meant by "dungeon" or "rooms", but she crossed to Ruby, putting a hand on her arm. "Anything you can remember and draw, anything at all, would be helpful."

"This is madness," Lord Malcolm interrupted. "You can't go into a situation like this, Mrs. Croydon. You have no training, no experience with these sorts of things. It would be like sending a lamb to the slaughter."

"A lamb has already been sent to the slaughter," Lady Stanhope interrupted. "James. And if we don't hurry, everything will become far, far more complicated."

"So you agree with this daft plan, do you?" Lord Malcolm rounded on her.

"No," Lady Stanhope replied, incredulous. "But we don't have any better plans or options." She turned to Marigold. "I have several sets of eyes and ears inside and outside of the Black Strap Club."

"You do?" Ruby blinked, shaking her head. "Where? Who?"

Lady Stanhope let out an impatient breath. "Yes, dear. I do. How do you think you were able to escape in the first place?"

Ruby clapped a hand to her heart. Marigold's brow shot up, and her awe of Lady Stanhope doubled.

"As to who, the fewer people who know the better." She turned back to Marigold. "There isn't time to contact my girls on the inside, but every one of them is smart as a whip, and if they sense what you're there to do, they'll help, I'm sure of it."

Lord Malcolm made a scoffing noise.

"Oh, and the brute force will be waiting outside to bungle everything a second time if you should need help," Lady Stanhope went on, dripping with sarcasm.

Marigold nodded, turning to Ruby. "Do you have a uniform I could borrow?"

"If I don't, I'm sure Mrs. Clifford does."

With Lord Malcolm still grumbling in protest, they jumped into action. Ruby took Marigold downstairs to the servant's hall, where she quickly changed her worn and dusty dress for a simple, ill-fitting maid's uniform.

"It's not the same as the maids at the Club," Ruby said

as she helped Marigold do up the buttons, "but it's black, and that's what counts."

By the time they were done dressing and Ruby had undone Marigold's elaborate hairstyle to braid her hair and fasten it in a bun at the back of her head, Lady Stanhope had called her carriage and driver around to the front door. Ruby had sketched out a map while Marigold dressed and thrust it into her hands.

"Are you ready?" Lady Stanhope asked as she handed Marigold up into the carriage.

"No," Marigold answered truthfully.

"I'm going with you," Lord Malcolm announced as Marigold rushed out the front door into the spreading dawn light.

"And I'm staying here," Lady Stanhope said, sending Lord Malcolm a peevish look. "There are things I can do from afar that I wouldn't be able to do right there at the Club."

Marigold wasn't sure what she meant, but she didn't have time to consider it. The moment she was secure in the carriage with Lord Malcolm, the driver set off.

"This is madness," Lord Malcolm muttered as they rolled along. "If I had time to educate you, show you how to use a weapon, that would be one thing." He shook his head. "You're far too good and innocent for a mission like this."

"I will do anything to rescue my son," Marigold said, staring at him with steely determination.

"He's not—" He snapped his mouth shut and let out a breath through his nose, gaze stony. "Make yourself as small as possible," he told her. "Walk normally, not too fast. Carry yourself as though you're supposed to be there, but keep your face down. It's early, but the other servants will be at work already. They have a steady stream of new servants coming in and out, especially maids, so it might not be as unusual as all that for a new maid to be wandering the halls. But whatever you do, do *not* let Mrs. Black see you."

"Mrs. Black?" Marigold asked, her voice trembling.

"The housekeeper. She'll know you aren't meant to be there."

"But how will I know which one she is?"

"The same way you know in any house, by how she's dressed."

The carriage rolled on, and Lord Malcolm continued to load Marigold down with advice and cautions. By the time they came to a stop at the end of the lane that contained the Black Strap Club's mews, her head was spinning. She hadn't slept in far too long, she hadn't eaten more than a mouthful since her hurried supper before leaving Winterberry Park the day before. Her nerves were frayed, and she knew full well she wasn't thinking clearly enough to do what she needed to do. But she climbed down from the carriage when Lord Malcolm said it was safe.

Marigold hadn't had time to memorize the map Ruby had drawn for her, so as she hurried along the narrow mews toward the Black Strap Club, she took the folded bit of paper from her apron and scanned it. The house that adjoined the Club itself had been built on the same design as a hundred other houses in London, so navigating it wouldn't be the hard part. Finding James without being seen was where things would get tricky. At least she was able to locate which kitchen door belonged to the Club, based on both Ruby's and Lord Malcolm's descriptions.

Anxiety prickled down her back as she approached the back of the house. A wagon waited on the cobblestones just behind the house, its horse still harnessed, hinting that it must have just arrived. There was no guarantee that it was the wagon that had brought James from Bethnal Green, but Marigold chose to think it was. Which meant James was already in the house but not deeply settled yet. She prayed it was true.

Lord Malcolm was right about the servants already being up and hard at work. A maid walked out the kitchen door carrying a bucket of slops, which she disposed of in a trough-like drain. A second maid walked swiftly out of an out-building with a basket of what looked like eggs. Marigold glanced between the kitchen door and the out-building, then dashed into the latter.

The building was some sort of storehouse, with a thick padlock hanging open from the clasp that would normally keep it sealed tight. A woman dressed all in black stood with her back to the door, a clipboard in hand, staring at one of the shelves.

"Only two pounds of butter today," she said without turning to look at Marigold. "Cook has been shamefully lax lately, and I'm not standing for it anymore."

Marigold swallowed her gasp. Between the clipboard, the way the woman spoke, and the ring of keys hanging from her belt, she had to be Mrs. Black. Marigold had run into the one person she needed to stay clear of the moment she set foot on the Club's property. The only thing she could think to do was to silently grab a slab of butter from one of the shelves, then turn and flee the room.

"Send Lotty in for salt," the housekeeper called after her.

Marigold rushed toward the kitchen door, praying Mrs. Black hadn't turned around, or if she had, she had mistaken her for a maid who was supposed to be there. As soon as she darted into the house, she deposited the butter on a counter just inside the kitchen door, picked up a dustpan and brush that sat nearby, and marched deeper into the house. If anyone asked, she could tell them she was off to clean something.

But no one asked. No one seemed to be of a mind to ask anyone else anything. The maids Marigold crossed paths with kept their faces downcast. Every one of them looked miserable and trapped, like threadbare rabbits in a cage who knew they would be supper soon. The hall-boy she met on her way up the servant's stairs was painfully thin and stunted. A deep sense of foreboding shivered down Marigold's spine.

There were fewer servants on the upper floors. As much as she wanted to reach for the map in her apron to orient herself, there wasn't time. She poked her head into as many rooms as she could instead, listening intently for any sign of James.

She searched through the entire house, finding nothing. The dread that had been spreading through her filled her stomach with acid and left her heart beating too fast. The urge to cry was far too powerful. She blamed it on her lack of sleep and the madness of what she was doing, but it didn't help. Nothing helped. She was trapped in the lion's den, the lion's mouth, even, with no sign of James.

The only thing that kept her from giving up was when she stumbled across a door that opened onto a much longer corridor, stretching into the adjacent house. Marigold swallowed hard before stepping into the corridor. While drawing the map, Ruby had mentioned that part of the house was where the women, girls, and young boys who served the Black Strap Club's clients were kept and where they did their business. She hadn't thought there would be any need to travel into that part of the house. She was wrong.

Gathering as much courage as she had left, and gripping the handles of the brush and dustpan as though they were weapons, Marigold moved quickly along the hall. Instinct told her not to open every door in this part of the house, but she listened at each one as best she could. There were sounds everywhere, even though morning had barely broken. Strange sounds that filled her with revulsion and fear.

At one door, she was certain she heard the soft, plaintive cry of a child. She shifted the broom and dustpan to her left hand and turned the door handle with her right, cracking it just enough to see in. The sight that met her was a woman who couldn't have been even Lavinia's age, on her knees on the bed, her hips in the air, her hands tied behind her, some sort of large gag in her mouth, as a swarthy man slammed into her.

Marigold stifled a scream and jerked away, shutting the door as quickly as she could. She couldn't stop the tears from falling then. What kind of a horrible place had they taken James to? She wanted to run as fast as she could, to flee the terrible place, but not without James, not without saving her boy.

She hurried down the hall, trying to listen and not listen at the same time. Exhaustion and horror were turning her brain to mush at the time when she needed to be most on top of things. It didn't help to hear screams and pleas for mercy coming from a room at the end of the hall. Marigold clapped the back of her hand to her mouth and ran up the stairs, desperate to get away.

Fear made her careless, though, and as she shot out into the hall one floor up, she came face to face with two burly men in worker's clothes.

"You're not allowed up here," one of them told her in a rough voice. "Get gone."

Marigold froze to her spot, gaping at the two men, her imagination filling with everything they might do to her.

"Are ye daft, girl? Get!" the rough man said, gesturing for her to go.

"Hang on," the second man said. "I think I know her."

Panic took over, making Marigold dizzy. "No, you don't," she said.

It was a terrible mistake. Her voice and her accent were too refined for any maid. The moment the words were out of her mouth, the men knew she was an imposter.

"That's Croydon's wife," the second man announced, the light of recognition in his eyes.

Somehow, Marigold managed to lift her feet to turn and run, dropping the dustpan and brush as she did, but she was no match for two toughs. She didn't make it three steps before the rough man grabbed her, yanking her off her feet. She screamed, but screams seemed to be a common thing in that house.

"Get her in the room with the brat," the second man said as the rough one dragged her farther down the hall.

Marigold was too stunned to struggle, and when the two men pulled her into a small bedroom, its curtains drawn, she spotted James lying unconscious on the bed.

"James!" she shouted.

James didn't move. His face was pale and his eyes were closed, although he seemed too still for sleep. Marigold broke away from the man holding her, her fear for herself eclipsed by fear for James. The men didn't try to stop her as she rushed to him, grabbing him and hugging him. James didn't wake up, but he didn't have any injuries that she could see.

"What did you do to him?" Marigold demanded.

"Shut him up," the second man answered, rubbing his hands together. "Just like we'll do with you if you're not a good girl."

For a split-second, Marigold remembered what Ruby said about James being given laudanum. That thought vanished as the second man stalked closer to her, licking his lips.

"Shayles wouldn't like it," the rough man warned him.

Marigold wouldn't like it either. She leapt away from the bed, dashing toward the window. The woman she'd seen all those months ago. She'd tried to signal for help. Marigold could do the same. She threw back the curtains, banging on the glass even as she searched for a way to open the window. Someone below, Lord Malcolm or anyone on the street, had to notice her, had to send help.

"Help!" she cried, unable to tell if anyone on the street had seen her. "Help! He—"

A hand closed over her mouth and an arm went around her waist. But rather than simply suffocating and silencing her, the hand held a cloth from which a strange medicinal smell emanated. Panicked, she breathed it in. Within seconds, the world swam away into blackness.

For a moment, Alex thought he was back in the field hospital in Sebastopol. His side ached, and his head and arm stung. He knew battle wounds when he felt them.

But as he opened his eyes, the sunlight pouring through the window illuminated the room where he lay. His bedroom. In London. Everything was exactly as it should be...and yet not.

"You're awake, sir."

285

Phillips jumped up from somewhere nearby, rushing toward him. The young man's face was a mask of worry.

Alex pushed himself to a sitting position, the throbbing and stinging increasing. "What happened?"

"You should rest, sir," Phillips said. "You've been injured."

That much was obvious. Alex winced, but continued to muscle himself to sit with his back against the pillows behind him. Someone had removed his clothes and dressed him in a nightshirt, but they hadn't been as careful with the bed. The coverlet was irreparably stained with dried, dark red spots of blood. Mrs. Clifford would be beside herself. Marigold would be upset as well.

He snapped his head up. "Where's Marigold?"

A moment later, Armand strode into the room. "You're awake?" he asked.

"Evidently," Alex answered. He shifted his position, gingerly testing his side. "I was shot."

"And lucky for you, they nearly missed," Armand said.

"Nearly," Alex snorted.

"The bullet in your side didn't go deep, and it failed to hit anything other than muscle."

"Don't sound so disappointed," Alex teased his friend, grunting and grimacing as he swung his legs over the edge of the bed. "Where's Marigold?"

"Sir, you shouldn't get up," Phillips insisted, reaching out as if he would tuck Alex into bed like a child. "You lost quite a bit of blood."

Alex frowned. He didn't need to be told things he already knew. "Where's Marigold?" he repeated, beginning to have the sense his friends were hiding something from him.

"She and Malcolm went after James," Katya said, stepping into the room as if she'd been hovering just outside the door.

"Katya," Armand scolded her.

Phillips glared in her direction.

"What?" Katya shrugged, her outwardly calm demeanor failing to hide the anxiety Alex could see in her eyes. "He was going to find out soon enough."

Alex pushed himself to stand, grabbing the bedside table to steady himself as his head swam. "Whose idiotic idea was it for Marigold to get involved with this?" he hissed.

"Marigold's," Katya answered. "Malcolm tried to stop her. He wanted to send Ruby into the Club instead, but as I reminded him—"

"What?" Alex roared, cutting her off.

In a move that was as rare as an eclipse, Katya bowed her head, looking guilty and sheepish. "We concluded that the best way to rescue your son was to attempt to extricate him from Turpin and Shayles's grasp before they had a chance to move him somewhere out of our reach. Ruby scouted the house in Bethnal Green and discovered they were taking James to the Black Strap Club, so that is where Marigold and Malcolm went."

Alex raised a hand to his forehead to fight the pain gathering there. "She can't go into a place like that. She doesn't know. It would terrify her."

"She was determined to rescue James," Katya said. "Malcolm is with her. She'll be all right."

"Since when have you had faith in Malcolm Campbell?" Alex growled.

"Since always," Katya answered, staring at him, unflinching. The depth of her faith and her love was unquestionable.

Alex shook his pounding head, moving gingerly away from the bed and toward his wardrobe. "I'm going after her."

"Sir, you can't," Phillips said.

"You haven't even begun to recover from your wounds," Armand said at the same time. He followed Alex, grabbing his arm to stop him.

Alex used Armand's arm to steady himself, picking up his pace. "I'm up, aren't I? If I can walk, I can go after her."

"You're not ready," Armand argued. "You won't be for some time."

"I'm going after her," Alex repeated, determination making him stronger. He would probably pay for it and then some later, but for the time being, nothing would get in his way.

"This is foolishness," Armand continued. "As your physician, I cannot condone any sort of madness that would put you in greater danger."

Alex yanked open the wardrobe door and turned to him. "You specialize in treating women's complaints. I'm not a woman."

"No, but you're acting—"

"Don't you dare equate being a woman with foolishness or weakness," Katya interrupted, voice raised. "Marigold walked into danger to save your son, with nothing other than courage and the love of a mother. She has more strength in her than the lot of you."

Alex's brow shot up. He wasn't about to argue with passion like that. In fact, he agreed with it, which was why he was so desperate to come to Marigold's aid.

"My wife needs me," he told Armand. "I almost lost her once. I'm not about to lose her again."

"Then I'm going with you," Armand sighed, reaching into the wardrobe to pull out suitable clothes for Alex.

"I'm coming too," Phillips seconded.

Alex nodded to him.

"You'll need me along as well," Katya said, heading for the door. "I'll fetch the carriage."

Alex watched her leave, uncertain whether he should applaud the madwoman's bravado or rue the day he first called her a friend. He was lucky she was on his side, that much was certain.

"If I'm only able to sit in the carriage and watch while the two of you go in after Marigold, then so be it," he said. "I'll not leave her in over her head, though."

"All right," Armand said, scrubbing a hand over his face. "We'll do what needs to be done."

Phillips nodded silently, looking as angry about the situation as he did determined to help.

"Good," Alex said. "Then help me get dressed."

CHAPTER 22

*E*verything was dark when Marigold clawed her way out of the groggy sleep she'd fallen into so suddenly. She'd never been dosed with chloroform before and hoped she never would be again. Her father had described the sensation to her after a minor surgery, but he hadn't told her that blindness was an after-effect.

"...can't keep her here," a peevish voice said somewhere nearby. It wasn't either of the men who had attacked her just as she'd found James, although something about the voice held a hint of familiarity.

"Why not? It's the perfect solution. She's pretty, nubile, and I can think of half a dozen men who would pay whatever you asked to fuck the wife of a political nuisance like Croydon."

Marigold would have gasped if the chloroform hadn't left her so hazy. Turpin. Turpin was the one talking now. She would know his voice anywhere, even in the dark.

Although it wasn't dark. She was blindfolded and gagged, and had her hands bound behind her back. Her feet were bound as well, and she lay on her side on something hard.

"It's too dangerous," the voice she didn't recognize argued. "She's too well known, not just as Croydon's wife, but as Percy Bellowes's daughter too."

Turpin grumbled wordlessly before saying, "That jumped-up cockney has his fingers in too many pots. Our fathers were fools not to put a stop to the degenerate classes getting above themselves."

The unrecognized man snorted. "Why Daniel, I had no idea you were such a snob." To Marigold's ears—the only part of her that seemed to be functioning adequately—the unrecognized man sounded as though he were laughing at Turpin.

Turpin didn't seem to catch on. "Quite right I am, if being a snob means I believe God set His creation in a natural order, and it's blasphemy to go against that."

The unrecognized man laughed outright. "Don't tell me you still believe in childish fantasies and fairytales like God."

"Well...I...um...."

"Believe what you want," the unrecognized man went on. "In the meantime, we need to take care of our little problem."

Two sets of footsteps moved closer to where Marigold lay. She kept as still as possible, forcing herself to regulate her breathing, as though she were still asleep. The chloroform had dulled her fear, leaving her with just enough presence of mind to try to figure out the situation she was in.

"We can't leave her here," the unrecognized man repeated. "There's too much activity, too great a chance someone might wander off where they aren't supposed to be and discover her and the boy."

"So what do we do?" Turpin asked. "Kill her? Toss her body down a well? We only need the boy."

Marigold bit down hard on her gag to stop herself from screaming. She couldn't keep as still as she knew she needed to.

Until the unrecognized man snorted in derision. "Really, Daniel. Have you no sense of subtlety? Not to mention the value a man places on his woman."

"But we would make it look as though she was attacked on the way home from an illicit assignation," Turpin argued. "We could humiliate Croydon the way he's humiliated me."

"No." The unrecognized man was clearly out of patience, and Marigold was out of time. "She's awake," he announced.

"What?" Turpin panicked. "She knows who I am. She can't see me. I can't be incriminated in this."

Hasty footsteps followed as Turpin rushed out of the room. The remaining man sighed and leaned closer to Marigold. "Take care with who you throw your lot in with, my dear. You may find yourself saddled with more of a burden than an asset."

Marigold whimpered as something tugged at the back of her head, but it was only the man untying her blindfold. It sagged free, letting rays of late-afternoon light in at the corners of her vision, then was pulled away entirely. Marigold blinked and squinted, trying to work moisture into her mouth in spite of the gag. She was lying on the floor in the same bedroom where she'd been rendered unconscious. James was still limp and pale on the bed across from her. But it was little comfort.

She twisted to look up at the unrecognized man, and her heart sank. Pale blond hair, angular face, icy blue eyes. She would know Lord Shayles anywhere.

"As you see," he said with a thin smile. "I will not run from the room in terror simply because you recognize me. My reputation is the least of my worries as, unlike our timid friend, I do not rely on votes to secure my position in the world."

Marigold started to ask what he wanted from her, but all that came out was a muffled sound.

Lord Shayles laughed. "You had no need to get involved in all this, you know. We would have kept Croydon's little bastard safe while he undid the damage his little ploy caused."

Once again, Marigold made a noise that was unrecognizable as the vow to defeat them that it was intended to be.

Lord Shayles raised one pale eyebrow. "Is that so?" he mocked her as though he'd understood her threat. "Well, next time you see your beloved husband, if you ever see him again, which is up for debate at the moment, you must give him my compliments for marrying such a feisty woman." He sighed. "Turpin is right. You would have made a lovely addition to my menagerie."

Marigold's eyes widened.

A sly grin spread across Lord Shayles's face. "You had guessed that was Turpin earlier, hadn't you, my dear?" He played with her as though her shock were for the revelation of Turpin and not the mention of the horrible things that went on in his house. "It's not important."

He stood from his crouch and brushed his hands as though wiping away filth.

"We have to move you now, and I'm afraid your accommodations won't be nearly as nice as this." He gestured around to the simple room. "Of course, it'll be risky to move you in daylight," he went on. "But who would suspect we'd be daring enough to move such precious cargo without the cover of darkness? You must promise me you'll be very quiet indeed."

Marigold let out a muffled shout, sounding far braver than she felt.

"Oh?" Lord Shayles arched a brow as if he understood her. "You're a very naughty girl who was never taught to keep quiet and do as she was told?" He broke into a smile that sent chills down her back. "I have a staff full of men who are extremely proficient in the art of training women to do as they're told. Guards?" He twisted to the door.

Panic sharper than anything Marigold had ever known shot through her, bringing her near to hysterics. The two men who had attacked her earlier stepped immediately into the room. The leaner of the two wiped a hand over his mouth, staring at Marigold with hungry eyes. "I can train her up good, sir," he said as though he'd been standing within earshot the whole time. He reached for his crotch as he stalked closer to her.

"Not yet," Lord Shayles said, checking the gold pocket watch tucked in his waistcoat. "Only if she turns difficult. And even then," he sent a threatening look to the lean man, "only if I give you permission."

"Y-yes, sir." The lean man stepped back. Seeing the man who terrified her cowed did nothing to lessen Marigold's panic. In fact, it made her fear of Lord Shayles soar.

Lord Shayles let out a pleased sigh and tucked his watch back into his waistcoat. "Well, my dear, it's about time." He turned to the men. "In ten minutes, take them downstairs. The wagon should be prepared by then. I need to make sure that Turpin knows his part before the curtain goes up."

"Yes, sir," the two guards answered in unison.

Lord Shayles marched out of the room as though he were on his way to a garden party. Marigold's guards stood dumbly where they were, the lean one scratching his head and staring at her as though debating whether punishment from Lord Shayles would be worth enduring if he interfered with her.

"Don't," the rough one warned him when he appeared to make up his mind and took a step in Marigold's direction, loosening his trousers as he did. "You'll regret it."

The lean man sniffed, wiped his mouth with the back of his sleeve, and grumbled something Marigold couldn't make out.

They waited for ten minutes before the lean one marched to the bed to scoop James roughly into his arms. The rough one stomped over to pick Marigold up and tossed her over his shoulder as though she were a feather.

Marigold's head spun with the motion. She felt as though she might retch, which would have been horrifying with her gag. All she could do was hold on, force herself to breathe, and keep her eyes on James as much as she could as the guards and Lord Shayles carried her down through the house.

Waiting was torture. It was far worse than the painful throb in Alex's side as he tried to make his body relax in the cramped carriage. He refused to admit it had been a terrible idea to get out of bed so soon after being shot. It wouldn't have mattered if he'd been riddled with bullets. As long as Marigold was in danger, he would ignore any sort of pain of his own to go to her.

Which was why sitting for hours in a carriage fifty yards

down the street from the Black Strap Club was driving him mad.

"There has to be something we can do," he muttered to Katya, who sat on the seat across from him.

Katya's jaw had been clenched for the better part of the hour, the only outward sign that she was running out of patience, just as Alex was. "Malcolm and Armand will let us know when there's anything we can do," she said. "And my operative says Marigold is unconscious but unharmed."

The last thing Alex wanted was to take the word of the spindle-thin young woman with a faded bruise on the side of her face who had walked past the carriage earlier and thrown a wadded-up note through the window, as if tossing away rubbish, but Katya seemed to trust her.

"Why would any woman voluntarily submit to the things that happen in there just for you?" he said, narrowing his eyes at Katya.

"Not for me." Katya's eyes went wide in offence, and she sat straighter. "They do it so they can get others out."

"Who would do that to themselves?" Alex shook his head, knowing his peevishness came from his impatience and pain.

"Your wife, for one," Katya continued to scold him. "And any other woman willing to sacrifice herself if it means sparing another even one moment of unnecessary pain. But I suppose men will never understand the bonds of sisterhood that are formed because of the injustices we face every single day of our lives."

Alex opened his mouth to reply, but all will to fight her fell flat. Instead, he sighed and said, "Why do you think this bill of ours is so important? No woman should have to suffer injustice simply because of her birth."

Katya's expression softened, though she didn't quite smile. She wasn't given a chance to reply, though. A short knock sounded on the carriage door before Malcolm threw it open.

"They've just brought Marigold and James down to the mews and are loading them into a wagon."

That was all the prompting Alex needed. In spite of the pain that jabbed him from every angle and the stiffness of sitting in the carriage, he hurled himself out of the carriage and rushed down the street a step behind Malcolm. The stitches Armand had sewn in Alex's side pulled, forcing him to slow down and let Malcolm rush ahead of him.

They crossed the street in front of the Black Strap Club, then hurried on to the mews entrance. Before they could get close, a wagon rattled out into the street. In spite of the pain tearing at him, Alex picked up his pace.

Alex and Malcolm weren't the only men waiting to take action. Phillips and half a dozen of Malcolm's men jumped out of the spots where they had been waiting, concealed around the corner, from a second hired cab waiting across the street, pretending to be a fishmonger loitering on the corner. The wagon's driver shouted in alarm at the ambush.

"Stop where you are," Malcolm shouted.

The driver yanked the two horses pulling the wagon to a stop, dropped the reins, and reached for something under the seat. Two men standing in the back of the wagon on either side of a canvas-wrapped bundle stood. Each held a gun and instantly started to fire.

Alex flinched to the side, taking cover behind the stone balustrade for a moment. He reached for the pocket of his jacket, cursing when he didn't find the gun Malcolm had given him there. The initial volley of shots had given way to fists and wrestling as Malcolm's men stormed the wagon. Alex saw his chance and burst forward.

The scene was chaos. Several passersby were caught in the conflict and screamed, running away from the fight. Alex dodged one terrified maid, but bumped into a fleeing young man on his way to the wagon. The impact sent blinding pain through him, and he cried out. But there was no time to give in to the blackness that threatened the corners of his vision. Marigold needed him.

He grabbed the side of the wagon as Malcolm dragged the driver to the pavement, punching him square in the face. The two toughs that had stood with their guns had been pulled to the pavement as well, and the canvas-covered bundle writhed as though someone underneath were trying to break free.

"Marigold," Alex called out, struggling to make it to the back of the wagon. Warm wetness trickled down his side, and he was certain that if he peeled back his jacket and waistcoat, there would be blood. But he pushed on, rounding the wagon. "Marigold!"

"I'll save her."

The shout came seemingly out of nowhere, and before Alex could get his bearings, Turpin came flying up to the back of the wagon. Alex was too stunned to do anything but watch as the man who was responsible for so much pain and misery leapt into the back of the carriage and tore away the canvas.

Underneath, Marigold twisted and thrashed to break free of the ropes binding her hands behind her. A thick length of black material gagged her, but the moment she met Alex's eyes, she cried out what he was sure was his name. Curled up against her chest and stomach was the limp, whimpering form of his son.

"James," Alex cried out. He attempted to hoist himself into the wagon, grimacing with pain.

"Stay right there, Croydon, you're wounded," Turpin said, standing with exaggerated regality, holding out a hand to keep Alex where he was. "I have everything in hand."

"Turpin, you bastard," Alex shouted, managing to roll into the back of the wagon, even though his strength was quickly fading. Phillips broke away from the man he'd been fighting to rush to the wagon's side.

A policeman's whistle sounded a moment later, and the noise and commotion of the fight stopped suddenly.

"There they are," another, all-too-familiar voice called out. Shayles. "I told you Turpin wouldn't let them get away."

Through his shock of incredulity, Alex crawled toward Marigold and James. "My darling, are you all right?" He pulled the gag out of Marigold's mouth.

She wailed and struggled to get closer to him. "Alex." Her voice cracked.

"Thank God you were here to stop these hideous kidnappers, Turpin," Shayles said, overly loud, as he and a small handful of policemen raced to the wagon. Three other men in suits, two with small notebooks, joined the fray.

"What?" Malcolm shouted as they made the already crowded street corner a jumble of confusion. "Turpin is the kidnapper, and Shayles is his accomplice."

"How dare you affront me so, Lord Malcolm," Turpin called down on the scene. Alex glanced up, sickened by the way Turpin stood as though he were Wellington defeating Napoleon. "I saw Mrs. Croydon ambushed by these black-guards and rushed to help her as fast as I could."

"No," Alex said, pushing himself to his knees. "You're behind this, you merciless bastard."

"Mr. Croydon, is it true that your wife and son were kidnapped from Paddington Station when they arrived this morning to join you in town?" one of the men with a notebook asked.

"No." Alex gaped at the man.

"Is it true you received threats from the same man who has been blackmailing Mr. Turpin all summer?" the second man demanded.

"Back away, gentlemen," Turpin interrupted before Alex could deny the story and tell them the real villain was standing right before them. "Mr. Croydon is injured. He was shot in the fray and would have died if I had not protected him."

"Bollocks," Malcolm shouted. "He's the kidnapper. He's the criminal."

In spite of Malcolm's vehemence and the furious look Alex threw at Turpin, the policemen were either too busy gathering up the driver and two toughs or too confused by the conflicting claims to do more than stand there and gape. Malcolm shot looks to some of his men, who fled the scene.

Armand finally left whatever perch he'd been watching the conflict from to rush toward the wagon. "Stand aside, I'm a doctor," he called.

"Tend to Marigold and James first," Alex ordered him, but he was already faint from loss of blood and utter bafflement.

"I had gone to Paddington Station myself to meet my wife," Turpin said, stepping over Alex without a second look and hopping down from the wagon to speak to the three men, who, Alex realized with a sickening lurch, must have been reporters. "I followed them all the way across London before seeking the help of Lord Shayles to apprehend them and rescue Mrs. Croydon."

"You're a true hero, Mr. Turpin," one of the reporters said.

"No, no he isn't." Malcolm tried to elbow his way through the reporters to Turpin, bloodied fist raised. "He's a liar and a criminal."

One of the stunned policemen seemed to come to his senses and grabbed Malcolm's arm, holding him back.

Alex didn't see more of the confrontation before Armand grabbed his shoulders and forced him to lie down in the wagon. "You've broken your stitches," Armand said. "Hold still or you'll lose too much blood and we'll be worse off than before."

"But Turpin," Alex panted. "The bastard."

"Probably staged this whole thing," Armand growled.

"He didn't," Marigold gasped, scooting closer to him. She'd freed her hands while Alex watched the horrific scene unfold around them, and gathered James into her arms. "Lord Shayles planned it. He said as much before we were brought down."

"I'll kill him," Alex growled, although it came out as more of a weak pant than anything that would strike fear into Shayles's heart. "I'll tear him limb from limb."

"...which is why the rumors that have plagued me all summer have been so frustrating," Turpin was in the middle of saying to the reporters. "Women are precious to me. They should be nurtured and protected at all costs, by their husbands, fathers, and brothers. It astounds me that a man like Mr. Croydon, who claims to champion the rights of women in Parliament would, in fact, be so heartless as to let his own wife travel alone with a small child, leaving both of them vulnerable to exactly the sort of horror they befell today. What would have happened if I had not been on hand to stop these vicious kidnappers?"

"Liar!" Alex tried to lift himself so that he could stop the wildly false story from going any further. Only a bastard like Turpin would use kidnapping and attempted murder as a chance to further his political aims. His arms shook, though, and he fell back against the wagon bed.

"We need to get you out of here and to a proper hospital," Armand said, glaring as though he was ready to throttle both Turpin and Alex.

"We'll help," one of the reporters said, looking into the back of the wagon. He flinched and turned white at the sight of Alex's blood-soaked shirt.

Alex had no choice but to let himself be inched to the back of the wagon, where a pair of men were waiting to receive him.

"I won't leave you," Marigold said as Armand helped her to stand, taking James from her to examine him. "I don't care what that blackguard Turpin says happened here. We have James. We're safe."

Alex had never heard words so bittersweet. Hot with fury, he shot a glare at Turpin's back, but his gaze settled on Shayles, watching the whole scene from the far side. His arms were crossed, and he grinned as though watching an old Punch and Judy show. One he'd written, directed, and pulled the puppet's strings for. He met Alex's eyes and laughed.

Alex's hatred for Shayles and Turpin burned an acid hole through his gut. But there was nothing he could do about it, and the hatred paled compared to the joy and relief at having Marigold and James back. "Go home," he said. "Go home at once and stay there. As long as I know the two of you are safe, I can endure anything."

"I'll see that she gets there, sir," Phillips said, joining the men who were helping everyone down from the wagon.

"No," Marigold said. "I won't leave you." She turned to Phillips. "Take James home if you must. He's been dosed with laudanum, but he's starting to come to." She faced Alex again. "I'm coming with you. I'm never going to leave your side again."

CHAPTER 23

"Oh, ma'am, I've been so worried!" A frantic Ruby greeted Marigold in the front hall of Croydon House, long after night had fallen.

Marigold was so exhausted, and her nerves so shattered, that she ran into the maid's arms as though she were a sister and not a member of her staff. "I've never been so afraid," she confessed.

Ruby hugged her tightly, but a moment later, burst into a tearful squeal. She broke away from Marigold and ran to the door, where Mr. Phillips was carrying a sleeping James into the house. "He's alive," she wept, pulling James out of Mr. Phillip's arms and holding him as close as if he were her own. "Thank God, he's alive."

James stirred and started to fuss, but as soon as he saw who held him, he flopped his head against Ruby's shoulder and slept on. Genuine, healing sleep, not the stupor induced by laudanum.

At last, Alex entered the house, supported by Armand on one side and Malcolm on the other, Lady Stanhope trailing them.

"I'm not an invalid, you know," Alex told his friends with a frown. "I can manage on my own."

"You are too an invalid," Lord Malcolm argued with him.

A change had come over the gruff, mysterious man. The tension of doing battle with Turpin and Shayles that had creased his face and made his whole body appear tense as the confrontation unfolded had given way to a defeated looseness at the hospital while Alex and James were being treated. Now it had settled into a weary kind of resolve, marked by a hint of a relieved smile that came from being with friends, safe and more or less sound. Or perhaps Marigold was only ascribing to Lord Malcolm the emotions she herself felt.

"I'll take Master James up to bed, ma'am, sir," Ruby announced, sniffling through her tears. "The poor thing has been through so much."

"We've all been through a lot," Alex said. He broke away from Armand and Malcolm to approach Marigold and close his arms around her.

"You should be more careful of your injuries," she scolded him, but sagged into the solid warmth of his body all the same. He was as worn out as she was, hadn't bathed in more than a day, and the scent of the hospital still clung to him, but Marigold couldn't bring herself to pull away. So much could have gone wrong. She could have lost her life or worse, but by the grace of God, she was home again, with James safe, tucked in her husband's arms. That was all that mattered to her.

"My wounds will heal," Alex said, then let out a breath on a tired laugh. "But I will admit, they'd heal much faster in bed."

"Up you go, then," Armand stepped forward, tapping

Alex's shoulder to get him to release Marigold. "Your doctor prescribes sleep."

"You're my friend, not my doctor, Armand," Alex said with a teasing smirk. "But I'll do as you say. I owe you an incredible debt of gratitude."

Armand brushed the sentiment away with a modest gesture. "Just doing my part."

"I'll help you to bed, sir," Mr. Phillips stepped in, as fussy as a mother hen.

Alex exchanged a wide-eyed look with Marigold, as though he'd better do what Mr. Phillips wanted or risk his wrath. Marigold pressed a hand to her mouth to stop herself from laughing.

"I'll be right up," she said as Mr. Phillips bundled Alex up the stairs. She turned to Lady Stanhope. "Will you come back in the morning? I'd like to find a way to properly thank you."

Lady Stanhope shook her head and came forward to take Marigold's hand. "There's no need to thank me for anything. You made it out of that hellhole in one piece and brought James out with you. That's all the thanks I need."

Those words stuck with Marigold as she made her way upstairs, dressed for bed, and joined Alex, who was already mostly asleep by the time she carefully cuddled against him. They'd been beyond foolish to handle the situation the way they had. Both of them should have left finding and rescuing James to professionals, like Lord Malcolm. But what was done was done, and they were safe. It was a miracle of epic proportions.

That thought was the last Marigold had before sleep claimed her. She slept harder than she had in weeks, her body and mind completely worn out. When she awoke, Alex was still in bed beside her, though sitting up and reading a newspaper. The sunlight streaming through the window was more of the afternoon variety than morning.

"Good heavens, what time is it?" she asked, rolling to her side but not quite summoning the will to sit.

Alex lowered his newspaper to stare at the clock on the mantel across the room. "Past noon," he said. But it wasn't the time so much as the bitter scowl on his face that caused Marigold to sit up, instantly awake.

"What's wrong?"

Alex sighed. "I don't suppose there's any point in keeping it from you, even though you'll be calling for blood when you see it." He shifted the newspaper so that she could read as well as she inched to his side.

Marigold hugged his arm as she stared at the open newspaper, wondering what its pages could contain that could possibly upset her that much.

A moment later, she saw it. The headline read, "MP Hero in Rescue of Colleague's Wife."

"What?" she exclaimed, snatching the newspaper and leaning closer to gape at the story.

It began with, "Minister of Parliament, Daniel Turpin blasted away rumors of his scandalous character by rushing to the aid of Mrs. Alexander Croydon yesterday as she was accosted by thieves in the street."

"That isn't even remotely true," Marigold nearly shouted at the newspaper. "Not even a tiny bit."

She scanned the next few sentences of the article, which went on to praise Turpin's heroism and suggest that his actions could finally put an end to the obviously false rumors that had plagued him through the summer. Marigold could only read half of the lies spewed across the page before she pushed the newspaper aside with a disgusted grunt.

"How can anyone believe such tripe?" she demanded.

"I have a terrible suspicion that many people will," Alex growled. "And an even worse suspicion that Shayles planned the entire thing specifically to achieve this outcome."

Marigold stared at him, incredulous. "Do you mean to tell me that our James was kidnapped and we were lured into the trap of rescuing him specifically so that that devil of a lord could orchestrate favorable press for his crony?"

Alex sighed, folding the newspaper and tossing it aside. "The one ray of sunshine in this debacle is that not all of the newspapers agree. A few question the incident. Shayles's scheme might not have worked the way he must have hoped it would. Only an election will tell."

He circled his arm around Marigold and pulling her against his good side. He winced and moved stiffly, but Marigold was grateful to be able to snuggle against him, angry as she was.

"I'm not saying that Shayles wouldn't have hurt James to punish me, if given half the chance," Alex began. "But he's a great deal smarter than the average criminal. And murder is not his forte." He paused, his expression hardening as though he were thinking about what Lord Shayles's forte was.

"I was inside that house," Marigold told him in a hushed voice. She swallowed. "I saw things I wish I hadn't. That's an evil place, and anyone involved with it is an evil man."

Alex hugged her closer. "I wish I could disagree with you."

"Can't anyone do anything about it?" She turned pleading eyes to him.

"Malcolm has been trying for years," Alex said. "Katya as well. Though if you ask me, they could do a lot more if they'd work together to bring Shayles down instead of bickering with each other."

Marigold couldn't have agreed with him more, but she rushed on with, "What about the police? Don't they care what kind of a place that is?"

Alex blew out a breath and rubbed a hand over his face. "Shayles pays them to look the other way. Pays them quite a bit."

"Then the government should do something," Marigold argued.

"My darling, there's nothing we can do." He turned to her, brushing a hand over her heated cheek. "Not until Shayles is caught breaking a law."

"But he is flagrantly defying every law of God and man that I can think of."

"I know, I know, but no one can prove it. Yet." He kissed her forehead. "But we will, my love. We most certainly will."

Marigold huffed, balling her body against Alex's side in frustration. After everything they had been through, the least they could be rewarded with was for bad men to be brought to justice and for good to prevail. But it seemed that they would have to wait a bit longer for their ultimate victory.

"Here," Alex said, reaching for the paper once more. "You might be interested in this as well."

He turned a few pages, then lay the paper flat, pointing to a small article in the middle of one page. Scowling, Marigold read the dry headline, "Political Climate Shifts in Signal of Sea Change".

At first, there was nothing that would have even remotely assuaged her disappointment or given her any faith in the world. It was simply a dry political article rehashing everything the Liberals had tried to do in the last parliamentary session and all the ways they had been defeated by the opposition. But halfway through the article, Marigold's brow inched up.

"An election?" She turned to Alex. "They think there's going to be an election next year?"

Alex hummed, then said, "Read on."

Marigold turned back to the article. A few sentences on, Turpin was mentioned by name. The author of the article was certain Turpin and his cronies would lose their seats, as the world was changing but they refused to change with it.

She finished the article and let out an impatient breath. "This is the least satisfying bit of good news I've heard in a long time," she grumbled.

To her surprise, Alex laughed and hugged her. "It means that, even though Turpin somehow managed to come out of the trouble he caused smelling like a rose, his days are numbered."

Marigold frowned, but Alex's smile was making it hard for her to stay angry. "I still don't feel satisfied."

Alex opened his mouth to reply, but jerked to a stop. A wry grin played across his lips. "Putting aside the fact that I cannot help but reply to that statement by saying as soon as my injuries have fully healed, I will make certain that you are utterly and completely satisfied in every way—" Marigold blushed and filled with heat and anticipation. "— we will have another chance to nab Turpin, and Shayles. I'm certain of it."

The determination in his expression and the promise in his eyes was enough to leave Marigold prickling with restless energy, and anxious for her husband to recover completely from their misadventures as soon as possible.

"We'll continue to fight him, and we'll win," she said.

"We will."

She risked further injury—or worse, fanning flames that he wasn't ready to tackle—by surging toward him and kissing him soundly. Sure enough, Alex pivoted to take her more fully into his arms, returning her kiss with a potency of emotion that left Marigold aching to make love to him.

They were spared the temptation of ignoring injuries and doctor's orders as their bedroom door clicked open. James rushed into the room, leaping onto the bed, as Ruby chased after him.

"No, no, Master James," she scolded, red-faced. "We knock first."

"Mari!" James shouted. "Macky!" The bed bounced and jostled as James crawled across to throw himself into Marigold's arms.

Alex grimaced with pain, but that grimace turned into a smile as soon as James stopped wriggling. Whatever pain he was in, he ignored it to draw his son carefully into his arms, hugging him as though the threat against him were still present.

"Good morning, my darling boy," he said, kissing James's head.

Marigold's heart squeezed in her chest, and she followed Alex's lead, kissing James's head and face. Pure joy filled her heart. As horrific as the last two days had been, they were over. James was there with them, perhaps a little worse for wear, but as happy as they were to be together.

"Macky, we go home now?" James asked, crouching in the snug space between Marigold and Alex.

Alex glanced to Marigold with a smile that felt like the sun shining through clouds at the end of the storm. "I think that sounds like a grand idea."

"Won't you be needed in London?" Marigold asked, running her fingers through James's hair.

Alex shook his head. "Not until Parliament reconvenes this winter. And even if I was needed," he went on, "I need to be with my family right now. At Winterberry Park."

"Really?" Marigold grinned at him, arching a brow.

Alex leaned forward to give her a quick kiss. "It suddenly occurs to me that there are things in this world more important than politics."

Marigold settled into his side, drawing James fully into her arms. "I couldn't agree more."

*C*hristmas in Wiltshire was far more beautiful than Marigold ever could have dreamed of. Winterberry Park was decorated from top to bottom with holly, ivy, silver bells, and the bright red berries that gave the estate its name. A Christmas tree that reached up to the ceiling took up one entire corner of the front drawing room, where Marigold, Alex, James, and their guests were gathered to celebrate the season. Its candles burned cheerfully, something Marigold could enjoy much more easily with two footmen keeping close watch from either side to make sure none of the branches caught fire.

"Surely there must be a safer way to illuminate trees," she said to Alex, hugging his arm as they stood side by side, watching James playing with the new toys Father Christmas had brought him and, miraculously, sharing them with the village children who had been invited for tea that afternoon.

"With all the modern inventions sweeping the land, someone will likely come up with something electric soon," Alex commented.

"I'm sure Mr. Edison over in America will come up with something," Lady Stanhope commented as she joined Marigold and Alex in admiring the tree. "That man is a marvel."

"Perhaps you should invite him for a visit, Mama." Lady Stanhope's son, Lord Rupert Stanhope, grinned at his mother, then turned a conspiratorial grin to Marigold. "Mama does enjoy entertaining famous and fascinating people at my house while I'm away at university."

"What this incorrigible scamp means to say is that the doors of Briarcroft Abbey will always be open to those who can provide scintillating conversation," Lady Stanhope said, smacking her son's arm.

Lord Rupert made a show of rubbing his arm with a pitiful expression, but he couldn't hold it. He was back to grinning at his mother in adoration within seconds. She winked at him with all the pride a mother could manage. Marigold had to raise a hand to her mouth to hide her giggle at the exchange.

Even more so when Bianca and Natalia Stanhope joined their group, and fifteen-year-old Natalia said with a dramatic grimace, "Ugh, Mother, are you being embarrassing again?"

"Of course, my dear," Lady Stanhope told her with a smile. "It's what I do whenever you join me in public." To Marigold, she said, "It's our family tradition, you know. I simply couldn't go anywhere without embarrassing my children to death."

Natalia made an undignified noise and looked away. She was the spitting image of her mother, especially when put out, but Marigold didn't suppose the young woman would want to hear that.

"You should be grateful that Mama dragged you out in

public at all," Rupert said. "Seeing as neither of you two are out as of yet."

"I will be next season," Bianca said. "And I plan to make a sensation."

"I'm certain you will," Marigold told her. Bianca had her mother's dark hair and striking blue eyes, but her features were softer and more feminine. She was on the cusp of being a dazzling woman. Lady Stanhope would have her hands full in no time.

"I'm not sure if I should join this group to improve my Christmas spirits or break it up as a threat to our nation," Lord Malcolm said as he approached the group. A young woman with strawberry blonde hair who didn't look much older than Bianca or Natalia held his arm, bright spots of pink on her cheeks. She had Lord Malcolm's expressive eyes and nose, but her mouth was wider, and her lips fuller.

Natalia made another undignified sound, twice as loud as the last one, and shook off her sister's arm. She deliberately turned her nose up at Lord Malcolm, then marched off, crossing the room to join Edward and his friends.

"Like mother, like daughter," Lord Malcolm murmured, sending Lady Stanhope a sly look.

"Of course not." Lady Stanhope met his look with a grin Marigold was certain was intended to inflame. Though whether she was inflaming his temper or his sensual side was unclear. It was probably both. "I have learned to be far subtler with my disdain."

"No you haven't," Lord Malcolm grumbled, crossing his arms.

"Papa," the young woman on Lord Malcolm's arm scolded him under her breath. She glanced bashfully toward Lord Rupert. "I beg your pardon."

Lady Stanhope arched an eyebrow at Lord Malcolm,

but kept her lips pressed tightly shut. She darted a glance to her children, giving Marigold the impression that if they hadn't been standing there, the fireworks display would have continued. She had the feeling that enough family drama was on display in front of her to make the stages of the West End jealous.

"Lord Malcolm," she said, unable to keep the grin from her face as she performed her duties as hostess and brokered peace. "Is this the daughter I've heard so much about?"

Lord Malcolm sent Lady Stanhope one last look before smiling at his daughter and presenting her to Marigold. "It is indeed. May I present Lady Cecelia Campbell. Cece, this is Mrs. Croydon."

"I've heard ever so much about you," the young woman said, bobbing a shy curtsy.

It was a complete shock for Marigold to discover that a man of Lord Malcolm's forcefulness had a daughter who was obviously shy. Then again, perhaps having so much energy around all the time in the form of a parent had left her with little to say. All the same, Marigold held out her hand. "It is a pleasure to meet you. Welcome to our home."

"It's a shame that we couldn't have the whole gang here for the holidays," Lord Malcolm went on.

"What gang?" Lord Rupert asked.

"I'm sure he means the group of us who were chased out of England with pitchforks and torches to go fight in the Crimean when we were your age," Alex answered.

"Oh, Mama's friends?" Lord Rupert asked.

"Don't let Natalia hear you call them that," Bianca laughed under her breath.

"They all were, they all *are* my friends," Lady Stanhope. She smirked at Lord Malcolm. "Most of them, at any rate."

Marigold had to stifle another laugh. Poor Lady Campbell looked embarrassed, but Lord Rupert sent her a reassuring smile. So reassuring, in fact, that Marigold was tempted to laugh harder. She wondered if Lady Stanhope and Lord Malcolm were aware of the attraction between their children.

"Peter won't leave Mariah's side while she's expecting," Alex said with far more seriousness than anyone else was displaying. "And Basil is, of course, still missing."

"And devil take him," Lord Malcolm grumbled, suddenly gruff.

"Who is Basil?" Marigold asked. "And why should the devil take him."

"Basil is Lord Basil Waltham," Alex explained.

Marigold's brow shot up. "Oh! *That* Basil. The Missing Earl?"

"One and the same," Lord Malcolm grumbled. "It's all well and good for him to go gallivanting off to wherever he is when things in London are politics as usual, but not with the upcoming election."

"Do you really think there will be an election, Lord Campbell?" Bianca asked, the only one in the group who wasn't in a position to call him by a more informal means of address.

"Yes," Lord Malcolm answered.

"Most certainly," Alex seconded.

"Is it because of the bill your side has been proposing to increase the rights of women?" Lord Rupert asked. "Which I most fully support, by the way," he was quick to add while looking at Lady Cecelia.

Lady Stanhope's grin widened, and she sent Lord Malcolm the barest flicker of an eyebrow, as if saying not only that she was aware of the connection between Lord Rupert and Lady Cecelia, but she approved and dared Lord Malcolm to do anything about it.

"It's not just that," Alex answered with the briefest roll of his eyes. "The Liberals back a great deal of reforms, not the least of which is the extension of the franchise to a wider swath of middle and working-class men."

"The changes are inevitable," Lord Malcolm continued. "But it's going to take an election to make them. Everyone knows which way the wind is blowing."

"Which is why it really would be useful for Basil to come out of whatever hole he's hiding in," Alex added.

"Why?" Lady Bianca asked with a slight shrug of her shoulders. "He's been missing for two years, hasn't he?"

"Before he got into that ridiculous business with Miss Grey—" Alex began.

"Lady Royston," Lord Malcolm corrected.

Alex nodded. "Before all that, he was one of our chief spokesmen in the House of Lords. He may not hold an elected office, but he is highly respected, particularly amongst the more liberal-leaning upper classes, and his influence could make the difference between another Disraeli government and the change we desperately need."

"So it would be in everyone's best interest, particularly his own, if he ended whatever game he's playing and resumed his position in society," Lady Stanhope finished.

"But where is he?" Marigold asked with a baffled shrug.

There was a moment of perplexed silence before Lady Stanhope said, "Nobody knows. He didn't just slink off to the country to sulk, he genuinely disappeared."

"Did he leave the country?" Lord Rupert asked.

"If he did, there would be records of his travel," Lord Malcolm said.

"Unless he crept away under an assumed name or smuggled himself out in the dead of night," Lady Bianca said.

"He sounds like a fascinating man," Marigold said.

"He's a bookish stick in the mud," Lord Malcolm told her with a wry laugh. "When we were in the Crimea, he spent more time trying to learn Turkish than drilling or planning strategy."

"As I understand it, those skills saved your lives," Lady Stanhope challenged him.

"Theophilus Gunn saved our lives," Malcolm told her.

"Who is Theophilus Gunn?" Marigold asked.

Both Alex and Lord Malcolm laughed. "He's a story all of his own, my dear," Alex said. "But the short version is that he's an American who served as valet to our friend, Lord Stephen Leonard."

"God rest his soul," Lord Malcolm added. He and Alex were solemn and silent for a moment, remembering their friend, before Lord Malcolm went on. "I don't care what embarrassment Basil thinks he's hiding from, enough is enough. I am determined to find him and drag him home by his collar before any election can take place."

"Do you have the slightest hint where he is?" Lady Stanhope asked, crossing her arms.

Lord Malcolm flexed his jaw. "All I know is that he has continued to make withdrawals on his accounts since disappearing, though his solicitor refuses to tell me where the money has been sent or what sort of communication he has had with the bastard."

"Papa!" Lady Cecelia blanched. Lady Bianca too. Lord Rupert looked surprised, but the older people were so used to Lord Malcolm's forcefulness that they barely blinked.

"I wish you well in your search," Marigold said. "Even though it sounds like a difficult one."

"I don't plan to stop until I find him," Lord Malcolm said.

The conversation shifted to far less incendiary topics. Marigold and Alex had other guests to greet, and by the time everyone gathered to go into supper, Marigold's heart felt light.

"If you had told me in August that I would be this happy in December, I wouldn't have believed you," she said, holding tight to Alex's arm and watching as Ruby and Ada gathered James and the village children to take them in to the child's feast waiting for them in one of the other drawing rooms. "It almost doesn't seem right to be so happy when so much is still unresolved."

"There will be time to put whatever is still wrong to rights, my dear," Alex said. Their guests had all gone ahead of them, so he swept her into his arms and planted a kiss squarely on her lips. "Turpin will have his day. Shayles will be brought to justice. Basil will be found. And Malcolm and Katya will stop vexing each other and realize they belong together."

Marigold laughed at the way he added that last item to the list of unresolved problems. "I hope it doesn't take a war to bring those two together."

"Everyone who is supposed to be together ends up in each other's arms in the end," Alex said, kissing her again lightly.

"What a romantic sentiment," she said, smiling up at him.

"Romantic, perhaps, but it is most certainly true. I have proof of that right here in my arms."

He kissed her a third time, and in spite of the guests and the meal waiting for them, Marigold closed her arms around him and kissed him with all the emotion that filled her heart. Their whole marriage was based on heat and impulsivity, after all, and she hoped that it would stay that way always.

§

WHAT HAPPENED TO THE MYSTERIOUS, MISSING LORD Basil Waltham? Don't worry, you'll find out soon enough in *May Mistakes*, the third book of *The Silver Foxes of Westminster* series. It will be released July 20 (which, by the way, is my birthday), but you can preorder now! And since it might just have something to do with the indomitable Miss Elaine Bond of Brynthwaite, Cumbria, you might find clues in *A Wild Adventure*, part of the *West Meets East* series, which is available now. (wink, wink, nudge, nudge)

BUT BEFORE THAT, ARE YOU CURIOUS ABOUT WHAT might have been going on behind the scenes with Mr. Gilbert Phillips and Miss Ruby Murdoch? There's much more to their story than meets the eye, and you can read all about it in *Winterberry Spark*, available April 13th. And what about that hunky schoolteacher, Mr. Timothy Turnbridge? It's possible he might have his eye on Winterberry Park maid, Ada Bell. But someone doesn't want the two of them to be together. Hijinks abound in their story, *Winterberry Fire*, coming April 20th.

BE SURE TO SIGN UP FOR MY NEWSLETTER SO THAT YOU can be alerted when all of these exciting books are released!

Click here for a complete list of other works by Merry Farmer.

ABOUT THE AUTHOR

I hope you have enjoyed *August Sunrise*. If you'd like to be the first to learn about when new books in the series come out and more, please sign up for my newsletter here: http://eepurl.com/cbaVMH And remember, Read it, Review it, Share it! For a complete list of works by Merry Farmer with links, please visit http://wp.me/P5ttjb-14F.

Merry Farmer is an award-winning novelist who lives in suburban Philadelphia with her cats, Torpedo, her grumpy old man, and Justine, her hyperactive new baby. She has been writing since she was ten years old and realized one day that she didn't have to wait for the teacher to assign a creative writing project to write something. It was the best day of her life. She then went on to earn not one but two degrees in History so that she would always have something to write about. Her books have reached the Top 100 at Amazon, iBooks, and Barnes & Noble, and have been named finalists in the prestigious RONE and Rom Com Reader's Crown awards.

ACKNOWLEDGMENTS

I owe a huge debt of gratitude to my awesome beta-readers, Caroline Lee and Jolene Stewart, for their suggestions and advice. And double thanks to Julie Tague, for being a truly excellent editor and assistant!

Click here for a complete list of other works by Merry Farmer.

ALSO BY MERRY FARMER

HISTORICAL ROMANCE

The Noble Hearts Trilogy (Medieval Romance)

Montana Romance (Historical Western Romance – 1890s)

Hot on the Trail (Oregon Trail Romance – 1860s)

The Brides of Paradise Ranch –

Spicy and Sweet Versions (Wyoming Western Historical
Romance – 1870s)

Willow: Bride of Pennsylvania (Part of the American Mail-Order
Brides series)

CONTEMPORARY ROMANCE

Second Chances (contemporary romance)

Nerds of Paradise (contemporary romance)

The Culpepper Cowboys (Contemporary Western - written
in partnership with Kirsten Osbourne)

Heath's Homecoming (Part of The Langley Legacy series)

MORE

New Church Inspiration (Historical Inspirational Romance
– 1880s)

Grace's Moon (Science Fiction)

Made in the USA
Las Vegas, NV
16 May 2024

89960792R00184